D0935033

Safe Harbour

'SHE'S not a child,' Freda's parents insisted, trying to reassure themselves; trying to pretend that the break-up of their marriage wouldn't mean the break-up of their daughter's life.

They were wrong: she was too young to bear such unhappiness, and in her misery and loneliness she clung desperately to Brian, the one person left from her old life.

Freda rebelled; she felt imprisoned and frustrated. And when the plans she had secretly made for the future were shattered, and she found that Brian loved someone else, it seemed impossible that she would ever reach the safe harbour of her dreams.

A story with depth and insight— and a happy ending—that will enhance Anne Hill's reputation and make her many new friends.

By the same author

❧

NO YESTERDAYS
THIS LOVELY THING
FROM THIS DAY FORWARD
THE WHITE DOVE

ANNE HILL

Safe Harbour

The Valentine Romance Club

THE VALENTINE ROMANCE CLUB
178–202 Great Portland Street, London, W.1

This book has been set in Times New Roman type face. It has been printed in Great Britain by The Anchor Press, Ltd., in Tiptree, Essex, on Antique Wove paper and bound by Taylor Garnett Evans & Co., Ltd., in Watford, Herts

1

'YOU won't change your mind, then, Sadie?'

Richard Fennal's quiet voice broke in on the medley of her thoughts, which were already chaotic enough, heaven knew!

'Don't let's start it all again,' she said wearily.

She was tired to death with all the changes of mind she had made within the last few days, the last few weeks and months—even the last few years, thinking back on them.

'It's just that it's going to be hard on Freda, her first day home.'

'Richard, we've worked all that out, discussed it till we're both sick and tired of it. Now let's get it over and done with. After all, she's not a child. She's seventeen, and we've always set this as zero hour, when she leaves school. What's the point of going on? You know as well as I do that it's going to happen, so why lengthen it out?'

Richard looked at his wife, trying to see her dispassionately, trying to see her not as his wife and Freda's mother; not the woman who had shared his home for eighteen years, but as some other woman, just any woman; any woman who was not his wife.

At thirty-seven she was still as lovely, he thought, as when they had married, very much in love, the world their oyster. Her hair, coppery gold, never had to be 'touched up'; her skin was flawless even in the sunshine flooding the room; her figure in scarlet-belted white linen was still like a girl's. If her eyes looked a darker blue than usual, it was because they were shadowed by the restless wakefulness of last night. He had heard her tossing and turning in the next room and seen the thread of light under the door. It would have been worse than useless to open it. They had settled all that long ago.

'Perhaps we've lengthened it out too much already,' he said quietly.

'Was that my fault?' she flung at him.

'No. I knew you wanted to go, even before you told me.'

'You won't change *your* mind, Richard?' she asked in sudden, sharp suspicion.

He laughed shortly, without mirth.

'Haven't you always been able to rely on me?' he asked. 'I assure you that I shall be the perfect model of the erring husband so that you, the deeply wronged wife, can get the remedy provided by our English laws as my just punishment. I shan't let you down. I'm as sick of all this pretence as you are. I'm thinking of the child, though.'

He paused, and as she did not reply, went on, 'Is Erskine meeting you in Italy?'

'Of course not. Isn't the essence of the whole thing the need to keep him out of it?'

'Oh yes, *Paul* must be protected at all costs,' he agreed bitterly. 'Will you be in this evening, by the way?'

'No, I don't feel equal to a farewell banquet. I'm going to the Forwells. You?'

'Oh—club, I expect.'

'You'll be here when Freda arrives, Richard? You promised.'

'Haven't we agreed that I can be relied upon? It's to be hoped that sending Hewet to meet her at Chichester, instead of one of us going, will give her a suspicion that something is wrong. It's bound to be a shock, for all that.'

'She'll get over it,' said Sadie. 'Children soon adapt themselves to different conditions. I may as well go up and change now.'

He let her go without further comment. After all, what was there to say which had not already been said? They had been waiting nearly three years for today, or rather tomorrow.

He went to the club, nominally a yacht club, but not limited to yachtsmen, and spent his usual sort of evening: a few drinks at the bar; a chat here and there; a game or two of snooker; and then home again.

Automatically he glanced up at Sadie's window. The light showed through the delicate pastel colours of the curtains, the soft blues and greys which she liked to have about her. Against them, her own colouring glowed like a jewel.

So she had not stayed out late on that last night she was to spend at Rosemead. Freda had given it its name, but the three of them had made it together. They had waited anxiously for the house to come on the market, had snapped it up, and between them had made it into a place of charm and comfort. Long and low, white-walled and with many windows, it had been extended at both ends to provide for their various activities. Sadie had added a bit to the drawing-room where she and her friends could dance; Richard had put a workshop on the other end, though it was carefully planned not to look like one from the outside; Freda had a playroom which had changed its functions as she progressed from dolls to a gramophone and tape-recorder. Separated from the house by a covered way, was the garage, with living accommodation above it; and as the house itself had grown so had the garden. It lay outspread, gay with flowers, bordered with shrubs, not too far back from the country road to give passers-by a refreshing glimpse of it, and there was no wall or forbidding hedge to block their view. A little stream meandered through it, bordered with clumps of iris and pink and white spiraea; and goldfish lived peacefully in it. A rustic bridge gave access to the gravelled drive before the wide front door, which nearly always stood open, and a more substantial bridge led to the garage. Where the lawn met the road, low banks of flowers were in bloom most of the year.

'Let's make it so that everybody can enjoy our home,' Freda had said, and even if occasionally a passing stranger picked some of the flowers, there were always plenty more.

Plenty of everything for everybody at Rosemead; beauty, hospitality, friendliness, welcome—and, at one time, love and happiness too.

Richard Fennal, as he put his car away and walked into the house, scarcely looked at the summer garden nor smelt its fragrance, though so many hundreds of times he had paused before going in and steeped his senses and his mind in the beauty of his home and given thanks for it.

7

He was thinking of Sadie, his wife, and of Freda, their only child.

He scarcely knew how or when it had started, this gradual weakening of the link which once he and Sadie had believed indestructable. Perhaps he had worked too hard, too absorbedly, building up his business from that of a small country estate agent to the prosperous and far-reaching concern it now was. But, in all honesty, he did not think he was to blame there. Sadie was a volatile thing, needing change, loving excitement, and he had not been able to supply enough.

And then Erskine had come along—Paul Erskine, fashionable London surgeon, dilettante, handsome, amusing, sought after socially as well as professionally. Richard wished he could hate the chap, but he couldn't. The friendship had been between the three of them, the common meeting-ground of the two men being that they liked 'messing about in boats', for Rosemead was in one of the waterside villages of the meandering, unimportant harbour of Tarnby and a natural rendezvous for the keen amateur yachtsmen whose small launches and boats were moored nearby.

Paul's profession made too many demands on his time for him to be able to be at Tarnby often, but Sadie had met him in town, and from these meetings, utterly discreet as befitted a man in Erskine's position, had grown the situation which had now reached its climax. They had agreed, some three years ago now, that this should happen, waiting those three years until Freda should be old enough both to leave school and also, Sadie decided, to accept with the modern view the break-up of her parents' marriage.

Sadie was going to bring an action for divorce against her husband. Richard had agreed that it should be done that way, though the requisite evidence making him appear as the guilty party was to be fabricated. Paul Erskine would have been ruined otherwise, since Sadie was his patient for real and fancied ills. It would not, she argued, affect Richard in any way. They had been out of love too long for it to be a great grief or loss to him. They had kept up the façade of a successful marriage only on Freda's account, so that she might not suffer from any repercussions of a broken home whilst she was still at school.

8

But Sadie, alone in her room on that last night she was to spend in it, was wishing they had not built up so complete a façade.

How would Freda take it? Would the varied interests of her new life, the one she and Richard had planned for her, make up for the break-down of the old one?

But, characteristically, Sadie put the thought from her mind and sat down to write her usual few lines to the man who had waited for her, faithfully if impatiently, for more than three years. Once she was free, they could be married quietly, travel for a little while, and then begin their life together. Nobody thought anything of divorce nowadays, so long as it was conducted quietly and discreetly, and Paul would not appear in it. They would have to be careful for a time, which was why Sadie was going to Italy the next day, leaving Paul Erskine in London and presumably unconcerned.

Freda was fond of Paul and he would make her welcome at such times as it would be convenient to have a grown-up daughter about, and meantime the child (it was difficult to think of her as more than that) would be perfectly happy with Richard's mother, as she always had been. After all, they lived in an enlightened age and no one should be expected to sacrifice a whole life's happiness whilst still—well—young enough for love and romance.

The letter finished, she rose to prepare for bed and looked at herself critically in the mirror. Had she already wasted, for Freda's sake, too much of the precious wine of youth? Would she be able to hold Paul, or was hers the sort of beauty which would not outlast the years? When the gold of her hair had to be touched up, when she had to watch for lines, for sagging muscles, for the first thickening of her slim waist and hips, the first hint that her abundant energy was lessening. . . .

She pushed aside the frightening thought. She would hold Paul. She must hold him. She had not held Richard, but only because she had not wanted to do so. Richard would not have cared if she had begun to slow down, to age, to be less lovely to look at, because he would not have demanded everlasting beauty. Even now, if she crossed the room and opened the other door which had been closed between them for so long, she could have

9

got him back. Love had died for both of them, but she could have got him back for the sake of Freda and their continuing home and the existence which had become humdrum to her, but not to him.

But the door remained shut and when she had faithfully completed the nightly ritual of face creams and oils, the perfumed spray for her hair, she swallowed the sleeping pill which of late had become a necessity, and got into bed. She had no regrets.

Before Richard went to his own room, he pressed the bell which rang in the space above the garage which had been made into comfortable quarters for Hewet, who was chauffeur, gardener, boat crew, and almost personal friend.

Brian Hewet had come to them soon after the end of the war, no more than a boy then and one with a pathetic background. His parents had been killed in an air-raid and it was shock rather than any specific injury which had made it necessary for the seventeen-year-old boy to live an open-air life until the incipient lung weakness had disappeared, as it had now done.

Richard had known the Hewets and had taken the boy under his wing from his great liking for the parents, and for the past thirteen years Brian had lived at Rosemead and had become almost a part of the family. He had been a quiet, studious boy who might have made a career for himself in a variety of capacities and there would have been no thought of his earning his living in the way he was doing had it not been for his broken health.

He had never made a trouble of that, had accepted the conditions with courage, and had indeed made himself almost indispensable to all three of the Fennals.

But Richard, aware of the boy's diverse capabilities, had been insistent on his not having his whole time absorbed by whatever work they found him to do, and it was to give him space and opportunity for developing these varying gifts that he had made the quiet, comfortable rooms over the garage and limited the demands of Sadie, Freda and himself on Brian's time.

And, somewhat unexpectedly, Brian had elected to paint and had had a picture exhibited in the Royal Academy. Richard had intended to buy it, but instead it had been bought by a discriminating American business man, and Brian's future status seemed to be assured.

10

He had laughed to scorn the idea that he might give up his work for the Fennals.

'One swallow doesn't make a summer nor one painting a successful artist,' he had told Richard, who had suggested it. 'I'm happy here. I like the work, specially with *Sprite*, and what sort of a home should I have anywhere else or with anyone else? I'd like to stay with you as long as you'll have me,' and Richard had willingly agreed, although by that time he had known what was going to happen to him and Sadie and that it was going to hurt Brian almost as much as it would hurt Freda.

He had insisted that Sadie should undertake the job of telling Freda, but had accepted that of telling Brian, which was why he had rung his bell that night.

'I hope you hadn't gone to bed,' he said when Brian appeared.

He had developed from a gangling, delicate-looking youth into a tall, well-built young man, his thick dark hair always well brushed, his lean face tanned by sun and sea air, his blue eyes those of a sailor. His inherent love of the sea and ships had found expression in looking after and running *Sprite*, the small auxiliary cruiser which lay in Tarnby harbour and which was one of Freda's special delights. Sadie could rarely be persuaded to join them, so the three of them, the two men and Freda, had spent many companionable hours navigating the creeks of the harbour or, on occasion, the south coast of England or the Isle of Wight.

Life aboard a small cabin-cruiser was too messy and uncomfortable for Sadie, she told them.

'No, I hadn't even begun to think about it, sir,' said Brian, who had managed to achieve a nice discrimination in his attitude to his employer, never presuming on his somewhat indeterminate position.

'Sit down, Brian. Smoke your pipe if you want to. What about a spot?' opening the cupboard in the corner of his workroom which held merely masculine drinks, beer, whisky, the odd bottle of Plymouth gin beloved of sailors. Sadie kept a more comprehensive selection in the cocktail cabinet in her drawing-room.

'Thank you, sir,' said the younger man, taking out pipe and pouch but not sitting down until Richard had done so.

'Cut out the "sir". This is personal and between friends and I'm not going to like it much, and neither, I am afraid, are you.'

11

'Something wrong?' asked Brian, looking at him.

'Yes. Badly so, I'm afraid. The fact is—we're breaking up, Sadie and I,' but his hand did not tremble as he set down the two glasses and he seemed perfectly composed.

'Breaking up? Your marriage, do you mean?' asked Brian, startled. 'You can't mean that?'

'Yes. Yes, I do. It isn't a sudden idea, though I can see that as far as you're concerned, we've been very successful in hiding it. It's been going on for a long time and now—well, she's leaving me. Tomorrow, in fact. It's been my fault, of course'—steadily.

Not even to Brian was he going to give a hint of the truth. He had given his word to Sadie that he would take the blame and that he would safeguard her reputation at the cost of his own and, except for its effect on Freda, he did not really care.

But Brian was not deceived.

'I can't believe that,' he said quietly.

'I'm going to give her grounds for divorce. I'm concerned about you, of course, Brian.'

'And about Freda?' asked the other shortly.

He admired and liked Richard Fennal quite apart from the debt which he felt he would never be able to repay. The short, slightly tubby little man with sparse hair going grey might long have ceased to be a figure of romance to a wife ten years his junior but in Brian Hewet's eyes he had few faults. He had always found Sadie charming, kind, generous, but had never thought her good enough for the man who, by sheer hard work, had provided her with so much that might have brought her contentment.

'Yes,' said Richard now. 'Yes. Freda. Is it too much to ask you to help me over this difficult stile, Brian?'

'Nothing would be too much for you to ask me to do for you, Mr. Fennal, if there's anything that can be done about it.'

'There's not much, is there? It's quite final between Sadie and me. The thing is that Freda has no idea, no idea at all, and she'll be home from school tomorrow and she's got to know. Whether rightly or wrongly, we decided a long time ago that we'd keep up the pretence that everything was as it should be here so that she should not be upset or disturbed during her school life and the growing-up stage, but now that she's leaving school, the in-

12

evitable has got to be faced. My wife's going to stay with friends in Italy for the time being, and I've decided to accept an offer for the business and take a partnership with a man in New York. I couldn't stay on here.'

'And Freda?' persisted Brian, shocked at the impending tragedy for her.

'We've decided that it will be better for her not to be with either of us, for the time being, anyway. There's no question of custody, since she is over sixteen, and we feel that she should be given a chance to readjust herself and to decide what she wants to do about us. We don't feel that she should be swayed or claimed by either of us at this juncture.'

Brian, taken into confidence though he was, felt he had no right to express an opinion and to say that she would feel that she was being thrust out by both of them. He knew her warm and loving heart, her passionate devotion to her parents and all that made up her home, and her vital need to give expression to that devotion. She was so vulnerable. She experienced everything too deeply. He remembered, inconsequently perhaps, her inconsolable grief when one of the cats had been run over and killed and that, though they had other cats, she still mourned him and tended the grave which they had dug for him together.

She could not bear anything to be hurt or frightened or homeless, which was why Rosemead housed a motley collection of animals. How was she going to feel when she herself was one of the lost ones, hurt and frightened and homeless? And the blow was going to be dealt to her by the two she loved best in the world and trusted implicitly.

Though he did not believe Richard Fennal's statement that he was to blame for the break-up of his marriage, for the first time in his life he had hard feelings against him. A wall had gone up between them.

'I can guess how you feel about it,' said Richard, as Brian remained silent. 'There seems no alternative, however. Neither her mother nor I will have a settled home or any suitable environment for her and, as I have said, she must not have a choice thrust upon her. Sadie will be visiting friends and travelling about for a time, and I could not take Freda to the States with me.'

13

'Would that be so impossible?' Brian ventured to ask.

'Quite. For one thing I shall be taking "the evidence" with me,' said Richard Fennal grimly, 'and I suppose that eventually I shall marry her. In the circumstances, you will realize that I could not have Freda about, and so I'm asking you to help. To begin with, I'd like you to meet her tomorrow at Chichester, which may give her some inkling that things are not quite as usual. And after she has been told the facts, I want you to take her down to her grandmother's in Cornwall in *Sprite*. The weather seems set in for a fine spell. You can hug the coast and take as long as you think necessary, keeping my mother advised of your whereabouts. She is, of course, expecting you, and I have told her that you may take a day or two over the trip, according to weather conditions and so on. You might put in somewhere, say at Poole or at Salcombe or both, spend a day or so there if you like. Once you've delivered her safely to Mrs. Fennal, you can lay up *Sprite*, which I shan't need again, and come back yourself by train to settle up your own affairs. I don't know what you will decide to do with yourself, but I take it you will want to go on with your painting and do it in earnest now?'

Brian's faint nod seemed to be sufficient comment, and Richard went on smoothly.

'If you feel that you still need to have some sort of job until you get more established, I have ascertained that the people who are buying this place from me would be glad if you stayed on. They are only going to use it in the summer, so there won't be as much to do for them as you have done for me, and you will be able to keep on your rooms undisturbed during the winter. I haven't committed you at all, but I thought you might find it a temporary solution.'

'Thank you, sir,' said Brian mechanically, reverting to his position as employee now that that wall had grown up between them. 'I should want to think about that.'

'Naturally. I'm sorry to spring this on you so suddenly, Brian, but it was the only thing to do as we wanted to keep Freda ignorant of what was going on as long as possible. Needless to say, I shall see that you are all right as far as money isconcerned, and whether you take on the job with the new people or not, I'd like to give you six months' wages.'

'Thank you, sir,' said Brian again, and rose to go.

He felt numbed by the shock, not for himself but for Freda, though this was going to make havoc of his own life as well. His one thought was, however, 'How can they do this to her?'

.   .   .   .

Though it was long after the lights had gone out in the dormitory, Freda was still awake.

The three girls who shared the room had pushed back the curtains which gave them their small private cubicles and were perched on the window-seat of the big bay window which made this the most coveted room in the school and kept it sacred to senior girls nearing the end of their school life.

Freda, as usual, was doing most of the talking, which had to be in whispers even though discipline was relaxed on the last night of term.

She was small and rounded and at seventeen deplored both facts. She would have loved to be tall and elegantly slim like her mother and had no idea that some day when she had lost what Sadie laughingly called her 'cream-bun' look, she might well be even more attractive than that adored person. Her hair, like her mother's, was coppery gold and had a maddening way of curling up instead of lying in flat, shining waves. Her eyes were sometimes brown, sometimes green, and a light sprinkling of freckles adorned her little nose, infuriating her.

'I'm not going to get married for ages and ages,' she was saying. 'I couldn't bear to leave the parents and darling Rosemead, especially to go far away. I can't think how you can, Una!'

Una Peary looked down at the engagement ring which she was wearing for the first time at school, and smiled. She was only twelve months older than Freda in actual time but immeasurably older in experience and had lived a far more sophisticated life.

'Kenya's not far nowadays,' she said, 'and it doesn't take any time to get to and fro by air.'

In less than a fortnight, she would be flying out to Nairobi with her parents to marry John.

'Well, if anybody ever wants to marry me,' said Freda, 'which is most unlikely, they'll have to live next door to Mummy and

15

Daddy. I couldn't possibly be separated from them. Just fancy! Tomorrow I'm going home and never coming back here.'

'What will you find to do?' asked Una, her thoughts going to all the new and fascinating things her life with John in an unknown country would include.

'Heaps of things, and all of them just wonderful. We're so *united*, Mummy and Daddy and me. We love doing things together. Mummy's not so fond of *Sprite*, but we both love the garden and do that between us, with Brian, of course. Now I shall go about more with Mummy and I think I shall ask to learn typing so that I can help Daddy at his office sometimes. It doesn't really matter what we do because we do nearly everything together. Oh, but I'm happy—happy!' and she did a little whirling dance in her regulation school-pattern pyjamas which tomorrow would be things of the past. She had not decided whether to go in for the new 'shortie' kind or the ultra-feminine, flowing, gossamer things her mother wore.

Maisie, the third one of the trio, got up suddenly.

'I'm going to bed,' she said curtly, and went to the other end of the room and drew the curtains which cut her off from the other two, and Una and Freda exchanged sympathetic glances.

'Poor Maisie,' whispered Una. 'Where's she going this hols? Isn't it rotten not to have a home or proper parents or anything?'

'Awful,' agreed Freda in deep compassion. 'Mustn't they be beastly people, her mother and father? They never even come down for Speech Day.'

'They couldn't very well, I suppose, both being married to somebody else by now. Isn't it disgusting for people to get divorced and have other husbands and wives?'

'Revolting,' agreed Freda with a little shiver. 'Thank heaven it could never happen to us. I wonder if I could bring myself to ask her to spend part of the hols at Rosemead? I don't like her much. None of us do, do we? But just think! She had to spend Easter with old Spilliken because nobody else could have her. Must have been grim! I bet old Spilliken's idea of entertainment was to spout Shakespeare at her. Oh well, I'm going to bed to make tomorrow come sooner.'

Before settling down to sleep, she did what she always did. She

16

looked lovingly at the two photographs side by side in their leather frame.

'Good night, darlings,' she said.

The glass over the pictured faces was always smudgy from kisses.

When she jumped out of the train the next morning without waiting for it to stop at the station, she found Brian Hewet waiting for her.

His heart gave a lurch of pity at sight of the familiar figure in the brown school uniform which she was going to cast off for ever. Her felt hat was stuck at the back of her curly head, one hand grasped her overnight bag with the inevitable brown-paper parcel attached to it, and the other her hockey stick and tennis racket.

She thrust the lot into his outstretched hands.

'Hullo, Brian,' she cried cheerfully. 'Where are they?'

'I've come to meet you instead, Miss Freda,' he said, and for the life of him he could not smile.

She laughed. 'Golly! Am I going to turn into *Miss* Freda now? You'll never keep it up, you know. I suppose it was Mummy's idea? As if you were the chauffeur or something. Why couldn't they come? Have they got people there? My first day home?'—disgustedly, for the first day of the holidays had always been sacred to her and visitors tabu. They went all over the house, looking at anything new in it, and then round the garden, even visiting the rabbits and the hens and the old horse which she had tearfully persuaded her father to buy so that it could spend its few remaining years in peaceful enjoyment of the paddock beyond the garden.

'No, they're alone, but they asked me to meet you,' said Brian stoically. 'Is your luggage in the van?'

'Supposed to be,' she said gaily, and then, with some anxiety, 'Not ill or anything, are they?'

'No, they're quite well. I think I can see your trunk being taken out now,' and he went to the other end of the platform whilst she made her usual search for her ticket and, having found it, stood chatting with the station-master whom she had known all her life.

'It's lovely to be home,' she told him, 'and now I'm home for

17

ever. I've left school and am going to be in dear Tarnby for good. Isn't it wonderful? Oh, Brian, there's a suitcase as well,' as he appeared with a porter and her battered trunk.

'I'll go and look for it, Miss Freda,' he said, and she made a grimace at the appellation and went to the car and got in beside the driving seat.

If he thought he was going to turn her into 'Miss Freda' and act as if he were a real chauffeur or something instead of her friend and boon companion, just because she'd left school, he had another think coming.

She watched him as he came in sight, the suitcase swinging easily from one hand.

He was really very good-looking, she thought, with the recently acquired awareness of members of the other sex. Tall, dark, and if not exactly handsome, at least he had broad shoulders and slim hips, nothing flabby about him. Darling Daddy was short and a bit fat, but he was Daddy and everything a father should be.

As Brian put the case into the back of the car and got in beside her, she gave him her first almost grown-up look. She wondered if he had a girl friend anywhere yet and for some reason felt she would mind that quite a lot. He belonged to them, the Fennals, and she did not want to give up anything that made up her home life.

On the way to Tarnby, six miles away, she chattered to him in her inconsequent fashion, about school and the friends she had left, about home and the ones whose acquaintance she would renew, about the many things she wanted to do now that she was going to have unlimited time for them, and about *Sprite*.

'When shall we be able to take her out?' she asked.

'I'm just going down to give her a check-over now,' he said, depositing the luggage outside for Tims, the odd-job man, to take upstairs.

What a damned shame, he thought, to let her come home to this, without any preparation or warning at all. He felt murderous against Sadie Fennal, who he felt sure was at the bottom of it all.

Freda ran into the house, calling out gaily: 'Mummy! Daddy!

18

I'm home!' But she had to stop in her headlong flight down the hall to receive the ecstatic greeting of the two golden cockers, Simon and Whisky, sitting down on the floor with them and letting them lick her hands and face whilst Mrs. Carter, the cat, waited with more decorum in the background, knowing that her turn would come. The spaniels, father and son, had long pedigrees and the tabby cat no known ancestry at all, but nobody minded, least of all Freda. She was called Mrs. Carter because the carrier had found her, a bedraggled, lost kitten, and, in handing her over to Freda, knowing that she would find a home at Rosemead, he had remarked facetiously that she was 'just like my old woman'.

'Then she must be very beautiful,' Freda had remarked politely, and 'Mrs. Carter' had moved in.

'Oh, my darlings,' she cried now, her arms full of madly quivering golden brown fur, 'and dear, darling Mrs. Carter! I'm home. I'm home, and I'm never going to leave you again!'

Then she saw her father coming out of the dining-room which was the general living-room and struggled out of the mass of dogs and launched herself upon him.

'Dearest darling,' she said, 'do you know it's six whole weeks since we've seen each other? A shame you couldn't come down for the sports because I'm always so desperately proud to own you and Mummy, but it doesn't matter now I'm home. Where is she?'

'Here, dear,' said her mother's voice from the drawing-room, and the girl rushed at her with more hugs and kisses, took off the hated school coat and hat, flung them on the floor and finally dropped into a chair in mock exhaustion, looking laughingly from one to the other.

'Thank goodness there's nobody here,' she said. 'I was afraid there might be when you didn't come to the station. Why didn't you?'

Husband and wife looked at each other. Now that the cruel moment had come, both would have been glad to postpone it, but postponement would only make it worse.

Sadie, pale but determined, did not look at Richard again after that one glance.

He closed the door and in the momentary silence Freda looked from one to the other, sensing something strange in the atmosphere.

'Is anything the matter?' she asked, her voice a little shrill with that nameless apprehension.

'Well—yes, there is something,' said her mother slowly.

She had known that it would be difficult, but it was worse even than she had imagined. It would have been useless to turn her eyes in appeal to Richard. He had laid on her this one thing which she must do without help from him and she knew that he would not diverge from his decision that she was to make the initial disclosure to Freda.

Even now it was not too late, and she knew it. One word from her, one gesture, and it would all be over. She could stay at Rosemead, stay with Richard and with Freda, abandon Paul Erskine and never see him again.

She knew that she was not going to speak the word or make the gesture.

Freda had been quick to take alarm.

'Mummy, you're not ill or anything? Or Daddy?'

Only a few days ago, just before the end of term, one of the girls had been sent for. Her mother had been taken suddenly ill, and had had to undergo an immediate operation from which she had not recovered. It had cast a shadow over the whole school, each girl thinking 'Suppose it had been *my* mother!'

'No. Nothing like that,' said Sadie. 'It's something I'm afraid you're going to mind quite a lot though, dear, just at first. You see—I'm going to Italy, to stay with the Perieras. Do you remember them?'

Heavens, what did it matter whether the child remembered them or not, thought Sadie desperately. How difficult it was, with the wide-set eyes fixed on her with that puzzled look in them.

'Yes, I think I remember them,' said Freda. 'You mean that you're going and Daddy and I are staying here on our own? How long will you be away? When are you going?'

'Quite—quite soon, dear. Actually, I'm going up to London tomorrow—and—and your father has to go away too, to New York, on business. . . .'

Freda could not remember her mother ever having referred to

Daddy as 'your father' before. It sent through her the first thin shaft of premonition.

'Then what am I going to do whilst you're both away?' she asked blankly.

'You're going down to Gran's, darling,' said Sadie, trying to sound bright but failing miserably. 'Hewet's going to take you in *Sprite*. You'll like that, won't you? And you'll be able to have the dogs and Mrs. Carter, though they'll go down by train after you get there.'

'But—but we never take Mrs. Carter to Gran's. She'd be miserable. She always stays with Peaky,' said Freda, the shrillness in her voice intensified by that nameless apprehension.

Something was happening to her, or about to happen, and she didn't want it to. 'Don't let it happen, don't let it,' she was saying inside her, but did not know what she feared.

Mrs. Peak was the daily woman who slept in the house at such times as the Fennals were away, and looked after all the animals.

'Mrs. Peak's leaving, dear,' said Sadie, 'but she's going to look after the dogs and Mrs. Carter till they can be sent to you, and she's going to take the rabbits and the chickens herself, and the people who are coming here say that old Benney can stay in the paddock for the rest of his life.'

'People—coming here?' echoed Freda. 'But how can there be anybody else here? It's ours.'

'We—we're giving up Rosemead. We shan't any of us be living in it any longer,' Sadie forced herself to say.

Thank heaven she was getting through it. Soon it would be over.

'Not living here? Giving up *Rosemead*?' asked Freda, shocked beyond belief. 'But whatever for? It's ours, our home. Where else could we possibly live? Oh!' as the germ of an idea entered her mind. 'If you're going to America on business, Daddy, do you mean for good? That you're giving it up here and starting over there instead? That we're going to *live* there?'—between excitement and dismay.

But Richard would not answer her, merely making a gesture towards his wife and Sadie rushed ahead, unable to bear any more questions or suspense.

'No, it isn't like that either, Freda. I told you that you weren't

21

going to like it, but you've left school now and you're grown up, or just about to be, and we thought, your father and I, that you're old enough to take this in an adult fashion and understand it. Your father is going to America, to start a new business there, but I'm not going with him. I'm going to Italy, first of all, anyway. I shall come back to England, probably in a few months, and look for a new home for myself, but your father will stay in New York. Do you understand?'

'And me? What's going to happen to me?' asked Freda in a small, frightened whisper, the incredible truth beginning to dawn on her.

That couldn't be what her mother meant? It couldn't happen to her, Freda? To somebody like poor Maisie Flower, perhaps; Maisie for whom everybody had been sorry though they rather looked down on her because her parents were divorced and she had no proper home—but not to *her*, not to people like the Fennals!

They couldn't mean that! They couldn't do that to her, not to *her*, Freda?

'You'll be with Gran, darling,' said Sadie, with a brightness so hollow that it sounded brittle, like an egg-shell. 'You know you always love it there.'

Freda did not smile. Her face had gone quite grey, even to her lips, and she was shaking from head to foot.

'You can't mean—for always?' she managed to make her voice say. 'That—I shan't have—a home any more?'

'Darling, I expect that after a time you'll have three, one with Gran and one with your father and one with me, though of course your real home will be with Gran.'

'Do you mean that you and Daddy are not going to live together any more?' Freda forced herself to say.

Sadie nodded. Thank heaven it was nearly over.

'Yes, dear, that's what we mean. You see, married people don't always get on. They find that after all they're not quite right for each other and so they do the best thing they can and try to find some other sort of life, some other kind of happiness. We didn't want to upset your school life or make things difficult for you before you could really understand, but now that you've finished with school and can begin to think about what you want

22

to do with your own life—well, it doesn't matter so much, does it?'

The look on the young face was unbearable. In those few minutes her childhood had gone for ever. The two watching her knew that they had killed something defenceless and young and trusting, something which could never be re-created.

Sadie took an instinctive step towards her and laid a hand on the girl's arm, but Freda shook it off as if it had been some loathsome reptile and shrank away.

'Don't,' she said, and her father spoke for the first time, his voice edged with pity. Was anything that either of them might gain worth what they had already lost?

'Look, Sparrow—' he said, using his pet name for her, but she turned on him the same look of dislike and fear.

'Don't call me that. Don't ever call me that again. Oh—I can't stay here with either of you,' and she ran out of the room on feet that scarcely touched the ground, out at the open french windows and across the lawn and to the garage.

Brian Hewet had just put the car away, and though he had meant to go down to where *Sprite* lay at anchor, he had not been able to bring himself to go. Were they telling her now?

Sadie made as if to follow her, but Richard held her back.

'Better let her go,' he said. 'There's nothing more that *we* can do. Brian's there. He'll know how to handle her. I told him last night.'

'She looked so—so awful. What if she tries to do something to herself?'

'Brian's probably watching for her. Besides, what can she do? There's only the water, and she can swim like a fish. How do you feel about what we've done to her?'

His voice was bitter, his eyes hard.

'It was frightful,' said Sadie in a low voice.

'Didn't you know it would be?'

'You put the blame entirely on me, don't you, Richard?'

'No,' he said wearily. 'I don't at the moment see what I could have done differently, but—no, I don't put it all on you, Sadie. You must have wanted something it isn't possible for me to give, romance, glamour, whatever it is.'

'I wanted to be loved, Richard.'

23

'I did love you, Sadie. I do still.'

Her troubled eyes softened for a moment. She knew that it was true. Richard would never have broken up the marriage nor parted from her, and not only for Freda's sake. But she wanted colour and brilliance and excitement in her life and he had not been able to provide it. Richard made her feel that she was an ordinary, nice woman, wife and mother, ready to settle down to being that for the rest of her life, whereas Paul Erskine made her feel an enchantress, a woman to be desired for herself, glamorous, exotic, filled with a capacity for the passionate expression of something which Richard had never discovered in her. Had she never met Paul Erksine, she might never have known of that hither-to untapped source of emotion and excitement and would never have wanted to leave Richard.

But it was too late, and they both knew it. Her husband could no longer give her what body and mind needed to complete them, and hers was not the abnegating temperament which could deny that completion, even for the sake of the child whom she dearly loved.

'I think you do, Richard. I know you do. That doesn't make it easier, does it?' she said after a long pause in which he waited for her reply.

'You feel that you can't live without this man?'

'I can't, Richard.'

'You'd have to if he died,' said Richard dryly.

'If he died, I should die too. Not perhaps with my body, but with all that make it more than a body. You won't try to keep me from him, even now?'

He made a gesture of weary acceptance.

'No. What would be the use? If, as you say, you are nothing more than a body without him, just an automaton going through the motions of living, what use could you be either to Freda or to me? I wonder whether, after all, I ought to take her with me?'

'How could you? And what would be her reactions at finding herself one of a trio of that sort? With you and Eileen Streeter?'

'You're right, of course. No, we'll let it stand as it is. Have you made all the necessary arrangements? About having her belongings sent down to Cliff Top and so on?'

'Yes. I've done everything, and Brian Hewet is going to see

24

about the animals going down. You don't think we ought to send her rabbits, too?'

His face relaxed in a momentary smile.

'I think my mother might take a rather poor view of that,' he said. 'She's being nice about the cat and the dogs, and in any case we're making havoc of her quiet life, aren't we?'

'She'll like it and so will Freda. They'll soon settle down to it,' said Sadie and he thought how characteristic of her that was. Once she had decided on a course which suited her, everything else was expected to fall into place—and he had to admit that it generally did. In all probability Freda would settle down quite happily in his mother's Cornish home, to which the child had always loved to pay visits, and Mrs. Fennal was just the right person for anyone whose life was upset and troubled and whose affairs were in a turmoil.

Freda had not paused in her headlong flight until she found herself outside the garage without having had any definite intention of going there or anywhere else. Her only thought had been to escape from the two beloved people who had suddenly become strangers.

Now, seeing Brian, the only part of the old familiar life that remained to her, she flung herself at him, white-faced and distraught.

'Brian, don't let me go back there. I don't want ever to see them again. Let me stay here with you. Take me away. Don't make me go back or I shall kill myself.'

With his heart filled with pity for her and anger for the two who had done this to her, he caught and held the stumbling, shaking little form as he had done so many times before when something had frightened or hurt the child who was too sensitive to the troubles of others.

'Steady, dear, steady,' he said soothingly. 'Come on up and let's make ourselves some coffee or something, and Mrs. Peak has sent over some of her little almond cakes. I don't suppose you ate your breakfast, did you? Troubles are always worse on an empty stomach, you know'—stroking her hair, taking the handkerchief tucked in her belt to wipe away the tears which had now come in a flood to bring some measure of relief.

She went with him, stumbling up the stairs which led out of the garage into his rooms. He had a small bedroom, a big studio-living-room with a good north light, and a bathroom. By his own choice, since he was often dirty from his work in garage or garden, he had his meals in the kitchen of Rosemead except on Sundays, when he ate with the family, but he and Freda often made tea in the studio, or experimented with cooking, on the little electric griller in one corner.

Today she sat silent and inert, hunched in a chair, whilst he made coffee for them and put out the gay blue-and-white china they had chosen together years ago. They had done many things together whilst she had been growing from a toddler with her dolls into a girl with schooldays already behind her. He had always been there, her friend and confederate, mending her toys or making them, teaching her to ride a bicycle, to swim and dive, latterly to manage *Sprite*, though she was never allowed to take the boat out alone.

Now she had come to him with something he could not mend—her broken life, her home, her faith in her parents.

'You'll never leave me, Brian, will you?' she asked pathetically when she had roused herself to sip the hot coffee and nibble Mrs. Peak's delectable little cakes. 'You're all I've got now. Do you know about—about *them*?'—with a little shiver.

'Yes, I know,' he said cheerfully. 'These things happen to quite a lot of people, but you and I need not talk about parting yet. I'm going to take you down to Sandy Combe in *Sprite* tomorrow. That'll be fun, won't it?'

She gave him a dreary smile.

'You don't have to talk to me as if I were a child any more,' she said. 'I'm not, you know. Not any more. They—my mother—says I'm adult now. Do you think I am, Brian?'

He put his finger beneath her chin and tilted the small, tear-blotched face up to his and smiled down into it. Actually the answer to her question lay in the fact that he no longer thought of kissing it.

'Say half way between the two,' he said.

She got to her feet suddenly, pushing his hand away.

'If we're going, let's go soon,' she said. 'Can't we go now? This very minute? So that I don't have to see them again?'

'I think we'll have to wait till tomorrow,' he said gently. 'No

26

good running away from things, dear. It's always better to meet them and get through them. I don't suppose it's easy for them, either.'

'Why not? It's what they want, isn't it? They've worked it all out. I don't matter to them any more. Perhaps I never have. Perhaps ever since I was born they've been working up to this and waiting for it. How they must have been laughing at me behind my back! All right, if I've got to see them again, I suppose I must. But I shall never, never let myself love anybody or anything else for the rest of my life!'

2

FREDA was saved from the ordeal of facing her parents at lunch that day by Sadie's own inability to meet the situation, though she knew it was cowardly.

She rang through to the garage on the house telephone.

'Is Freda with you, Hewet?' she asked.

Though she did not treat him exactly as a servant, she had never admitted him to the same terms of intimacy as that which existed between him and Richard.

'Yes, Mrs. Fennal. Do you want her?'

He wondered if the dislike and anger which he felt showed in his tone.

'No, but could you keep her there for lunch? Mr. Fennal has gone to the office and I've got a headache and don't feel that I can face lunch. Mrs. Peak is giving me a tray, and I'll ask her to send something over for Freda if she can have it with you.'

'Of course, Mrs. Fennal. I have to do a few things to *Sprite* and we could have something on board without bothering Mrs. Peak.'

'Thank you. That will be a good idea.'

'Will it be all right if we run round the harbour a bit afterwards, just to see that everything is in trim for tomorrow?'

'Yes, that will help. Get her back before dark, won't you, Hewet? And—look after her, though I know I need not say that.'

'I will look after her, Mrs. Fennal,' said Hewet steadily, and heard her put back the receiver—with relief, he thought.

He had never been so angry in his life. He did not believe in the 'headache' though heaven knew there was sufficient cause for one. Having wrecked their child's whole world, all they wanted now was not to have to look at her amidst the ruins.

He did Sadie an injustice. She was feeling it far more than she had ever supposed she would, and the chief reason for leaving her with Brian was that she felt Freda would be happier with him and away from her during these first difficult hours. It was not entirely cowardice.

She had a tray brought to her bedroom and sat down to write to Richard's mother about the immediate arrangements.

I'm afraid she is taking it rather badly, she wrote to the woman who had always been kind to her, and to whom this broken marriage was a bad blow. *We are so thankful that she is coming to you as you always know what to do and say in any emergency, and she will be happier with you than anywhere else. She loves it at Sandy Combe, and as Brian Hewet has been told to make the journey last over a day or two, she will have had a little time to readjust herself by the time you see her. He will, of course, keep in touch with both you and her father and is completely to be trusted if bad weather should blow up or anything like that. He would know what to do and of course he has known Freda almost all her life.*

She paused and then finished the letter abruptly. Her mother-in-law belonged to an older school of thought and of morals to whom marriage, once entered into, is binding and irrevocable. It was, Sadie knew, impossible for her to understand the various and conflicting elements that had to be fused together to make a modern-world marriage 'work'. To women of Mrs. Fennal's mind and day, it was all quite simple and straightforward. You married a man, you bore him children, you looked after the home and family; and he worked for you all and you grew old together until death separated you.

How was it possible even to try to make her understand what a man like Paul Erskine could do to one's life? Or how much more life demanded than what had satisfied Richard's mother? That the care of a home with all modern appliances, and of one child away at boarding-school, could not fill either one's time or one's thirst for life's experiences?

Mrs. Fennal had agreed to give Freda a home for an unspecified period when Rosemead was to be sold and Richard and Sadie went their separate ways, but Sadie doubted if she realized that this was the actual end of the marriage, that the house on the edge of the Cornish cliff was now to be the only home her grand-daughter had.

It was almost as difficult to write to Paul, who had decreed that they must not meet again yet though at this moment Sadie wanted him desperately. It was one thing to be prepared to give up husband, child and home whilst it was still in the future and Paul's arms about her, but it was quite another when she was actually facing it, Richard's cold, enigmatical acceptance of it, Freda's stunned shock, Paul's presence, even his voice over the telephone, denied her.

She did not want Paul to know how much this was costing her. He was proud and possessive, ruthless where decisions had to be made, strong with the strength of the unimaginative. He would have no patience with this gradual breaking-down, one by one, of the adhesions which she had not known until then bound her to the life she was leaving. He would have been quite capable of saying to her, 'Well, my dear, if it matters all that much to you to leave them, let's cut it out,' and she couldn't cut it out; she couldn't.

She finished the letter to him in a storm of tears which must not be allowed to fall on the paper, sealed it and posted it in the letter-box fastened to a post at the entrance to the garden. Then she went in to see Mrs. Peak about the food that was to be put ready for the final loading of *Sprite* the next day.

There was really no need for her to see about this herself. Mrs.

Peak knew even better than she did what sort of food Freda liked and which of them could most easily be dealt with in the little galley of the boat, but Sadie added some half-bottles of light wine. Freda had never shared the wine when it was served at table, having lemonade instead. Sadie thought it might help her with the realization that she was now considered grown up.

When Freda found the bottles the next day, she made no comment to Brian but dumped them overboard.

He did not say anything. How stupidly unperceptive of Sadie Fennal to think that a broken life can be mended with a bottle of wine!

But that moment had not arrived yet, and whilst Sadie was selecting the bottles, Freda was at least superficially happy sharing a picnic lunch with Brian, seated bare-armed and barefooted on the little deck, the sun and wind and salt spray on her face.

She had always loved *Sprite* and life aboard her, and when they had finished their meal and she had washed up and put everything as Brian had always insisted it should be kept, there was plenty to do in preparation for the next day's journey. They anchored off shore and piled the sails into the tender and rowed ashore to spread them out on a dry, sunny patch of grass to examine them for possible deterioration or damage, since they were rarely used. Satisfied, they folded them expertly again, took them back to *Sprite* and stowed them. Then there were ropes, fenders and spare gear to be checked, the slides in which the charts were kept to be inspected, information about the regulations and dues of various ports to be memorized.

Sprite was a trim little craft and well found. The main cabin was also the saloon, with two well-sprung bunks providing seats in the daytime at either side of the folding table, and since Sadie had chosen the furnishing of it, it was as dainty and charming as it was practical, the floor carpeted in grey, the covers and hangings in flowered blue. Freda's own small cabin opened from one end of it, whilst at the other side of the cockpit were the galley, the shower-room and quarters for the crew, that is to say for Brian.

They never used one another's names on board. Richard was the Owner, or sometimes the Master, Brian the Skipper, and

Freda either the Mate or the Cook, according to circumstances. Sadie, if she could ever be persuaded to go with them, was the Passenger.

When there was nothing else at all to do, and Brian was bringing round the tender to row them ashore, Freda hung back.

'Can't I sleep on board tonight?' she asked. 'I shall be quite all right.'

He gave her an encouraging smile.

'Sure you'll be all right. Why shouldn't you be? But there are bad patches in everybody's life and we get through them, so don't try to dodge this one. Go back, show them a cheerful face, talk as if nothing had happened and that we were just going down to Sandy Combe tomorrow on a visit. Then go to bed and to sleep and after that it will be tomorrow.'

She leaned against him. Her head reached just to his shoulder. He remembered when she had been knee-high.

'You've never been—just cast adrift by your parents,' she said shakily. 'You don't know what it's like not to be wanted any more.'

'Haven't I? My mother and father were killed, you know, and I had no home at all nor anyone belonging to me, certainly not a devoted grandmother just longing to have me.'

He rarely spoke of himself and had no use for self-pity, considering that he had been very lucky once that bad patch was over, but this seemed to be an occasion when he might point out what he had lost.

'I know. Forgive me, Brian. You've been wonderful,' giving him a look from eyes which he was beginning to realize were beautiful.

'Rubbish,' he said. 'Just ornary. Come on, shipmate. Who's for the shore? Hop in, you there, and leggo forrard. Look lively!'

After he had watched her go draggingly into the house, he thought about women, a thing he seldom did.

There had never been a woman seriously in his life, and he was twenty-nine. First there had been his doubtful health, making him feel that he was unacceptable to girls even as a casual escort. Then he had come to Rosemead and all his energies had been fully employed by the variety of his work for the Fennals and, of recent years, by his painting. He had had no thought or desire

31

for love and marriage. Now, with the ruin before his very eyes of the marriage which he had thought the one perfect one, he was thankful that no woman had ever had the chance to wreck his life.

Afraid that Richard Fennal might do as he often did, ask him to spend the evening in the house with them, he rang up later.

'If you don't want the car tonight, sir, I'd like to run into Chichester to pick up the old accumulator they've been repairing. We might need it.'

'Yes, all right. Do that, Brian, and thanks.'

'Thank you, sir. Good night. Er—we'll be getting off early to-morrow. Everything's aboard and ready, so I thought we might go out on the early tide.'

'Yes, I should do that if you can. Keep in touch, and when you've made Sandy Combe, better hang about there a bit till we can contact each other again.'

'Very good, sir.'

He thought that Richard wanted to say something more and waited with the receiver at his ear, but after a few seconds he heard it being hung up and he replaced his own.

He wondered if this was the end of his association, for all practical purposes, with Richard Fennal, and whether he would ever see him again. It was a painful thought. The long years of affectionate friendship between the two, and Brian's deep gratitude, could not be wiped out all in a moment by any flaw whatever which had been revealed in the man in a matter which did not concern him. His anger was for Freda, and against Sadie rather than Richard.

But the drive back to Tarnby, much later because he had had to wait in Chichester, reacted soothingly on his anxious mind and ruffled temper. It was a moonless night, black and still, and he liked driving in the dark, especially the big, smooth-running car which he knew so well. The sound of its engine seemed scarcely to touch the edge of the silence. He slowed for a scurrying rabbit caught in the beam of the head-lamps, but otherwise seemed to have the world to himself.

Then, from some distance in front of him, a waving light made him slow down again and finally stop. Someone was signalling with a torch. In the headlights he could see that it was a woman,

32

and tucked into the side of the road behind her was a small car showing no lights.

He pulled in behind it and got out.

'Anything wrong?' he asked.

'Oh yes, lots. The lights have gone wrong and it won't go and it isn't mine.'

She sounded young and worried, but she laughed a little.

'Whoever it belongs to, it's not much good if it won't go, is it?' he asked, and they both laughed.

He got into the little sports car and tried the controls, opened the bonnet and did a few things knowledgeably to the engine, but there was no response. He tried to explain to her what was probably wrong, but she shook her head ruefully.

'It's all Greek to me,' she said. 'I'm all right when the things go, but when they won't, somebody else has got to do something about it, and of course it would happen in the middle of the night!'

Meriel felt a bit annoyed. She could easily have come by train and would have thought nothing of the two-mile walk to the caravan in which she was staying, but Agnes had been insistent upon her taking the car, and now the thing had broken down.

Brian laughed. 'It isn't exactly the middle of the night,' he said. 'It's not much past ten, though it's dark for a summer night. I'm afraid there's only one thing to do. I see you've got a tow-rope in the boot, so probably this has happened before. I can hitch you on and tow you back to Chichester to a garage. Can you manage to steer? I'll drive slowly.'

'But you were going the other way,' she objected half-heartedly.

'That doesn't matter. My time's my own,' and he turned the big car round and fixed the tow rope.

'I've never done this,' she said, getting into the little car. 'I'm a bit scared.'

'You need not be. Just keep her straight, and if anything happens, or if I'm going too fast or anything, pip the horn. That seems to work at least.'

It was not difficult, she found, even when they had to go round the ancient monument in the centre of the town, and when he had pulled up at the garage he had just left and explained the position, he could have his first real look at the girl he had rescued.

She was probably about his own age, he thought, though she had sounded younger. Her small figure was sturdily built, her fair hair was hatless and her eyes were much the same colour as her brown jersey suit. A nice face, he thought with merely casual interest, not pretty but attractive in an open-air way, flushed a little from the concentration needed for the towing business, with very little make-up.

'I can't thank you enough,' she said, and he liked the way she spoke and the frank look in her eyes. There was nothing coy or oncoming about her. If she was sizing him up, she did not appear to be doing so.

'The only thing I appear to have done is to land you up in a strange town—if it is a strange one to you?'

'I know it a bit, and I shall be able to get a bus if they can't make the car go,' she said cheerfully.

Not a girl to make trouble of trouble, he thought, whilst she was thinking that he looked as nice as he had sounded, and obviously well off judging by the big Humber. Not that that mattered to her; she was no manhunter and usually preferred them as poor as she was herself.

'Come and have a drink or a coffee or something whilst they see if they can get the car on the road for you, anyway,' he said.

Something about her, a look of independence, made him hesitate about suggesting that she finished her journey in the Humber, or at least that he took her to a convenient point.

'There won't be any shops open now,' she said doubtfully, 'and I'm not much of a "pubber".'

'If you don't mind it, there's a little place just along here where we can get a very good cup of tea, a "good pull-up for car-men" sort of place. Do you mind?'

'Not a bit,' she said, and thought what an unexpected ending this was to an evening spent with Agnes Witty! Agnes believed that all men were wolves, especially those with expensive cars; though poor Agnes was never likely to be in any danger from their claws or their fangs. The loan of the car had been designed to save her from the perils of a two-mile walk along a familiar country road, but here she was, getting into a car with a completely strange young man and setting off for an unknown

34

destination, and a 'good pull-up for car-men' which might not even exist!

Still, here she was and here he was, and in a few minutes there, too, was the wayside café and the protective company of night lorry-drivers eating thick sandwiches and drinking hot, strong tea out of chipped cups.

Her rescuer evinced no particular interest in her when he had brought their own cups of tea and, unreasonably, she found herself a little piqued by it. She might be a fat old lady with a moustache for all he seemed to notice her! Then she smiled to herself and at herself. After all, even at the best of times she was no film star. Her face was just a face and her vital statistics all wrong, and nobody dressed up for living in a caravan. Still, even if he did have a Humber and she only a borrowed and broken-down sports car, he might show some slight flicker of interest in her!

When they had said all there was to say about the dark night and the threat of rain, about the state of the roads and the sort of drivers one met on them and the disadvantage to Chichester traffic of having that ancient monument in the centre of the town, somehow the conversation turned on his somewhat incongruous appearance in a blue fisherman's jersey and sea-stained slacks.

'I didn't think I should be called upon to rescue a damsel in distress,' he said laughingly, 'or I might have made myself rather more respectable. I've been messing about with boats all the afternoon and as I'm going off on a fairly long cruise round the south coast tomorrow and went to have a last look at the stores before I turn in, I didn't bother to change. Do you like boats?'

'I know even less about them than I do about cars,' she admitted with a laugh, so he then told her about boats, filling in until it was time to go back to the garage.

She would have been surprised to know that she need not have felt chagrined at his lack of observation. She was just the sort of girl he liked—as much as he liked any girl, that was. She was natural and frank and unassuming and she had done almost nothing to make herself look other than she was meant to look. She had not tried to make her fair hair golden—its rather tumbled state could not be anything but natural—and if her mouth wore lipstick, it was not blatant, nor did she do what he always hated to see a woman do: take out things from her handbag and make herself up.

Her hands were small, capable and ringless, the nails well shaped but unvarnished and the only article of possible adornment she wore, apart from the brown jersey suit, was a watch on a plain black ribbon strap.

The car was ready for her, and she was glad that he did not make the mistake of offering to pay the bill.

'I really don't know how to thank you for coming to the rescue as you did,' she said, when she was at the wheel again; and he gave her his friendly grin, said that it was nothing at all, and watched her drive away.

Yes, nice, she thought. Uninterested in her, of course, but definitely nice. He had not even tried to find out her name nor where she lived, and had not offered such information about himself. Lots of men, expecially young men with big Humbers and a boat, would have tried to improve on the chance meeting by suggesting another which would not be chance, and the last thing she wanted in the world just now was to get involved with a man, any man, anywhere.

She was still sore about Frank.

Until a month ago they had been engaged and she, at any rate, had been in love. Now they were no longer engaged and she had assured herself too many times that she was no longer in love and never would be so again.

Perhaps she was well out of it, if he could treat her like that, showing himself to be a man on whom she could place no reliance. Suppose they had been married before she found out?

What she had found out was unforgivable. When he had asked Meriel to marry him, he had been engaged for two years to another girl who had been preparing for their home all that time, spending her earnings on buying things they would need and even ordering, with his knowledge, her wedding dress!

It was the girl herself who had discovered the existence of Meriel and had made the long journey from the north of England to see her, had produced the proofs—the engagement ring, the letters from Frank—of what she told her.

Meriel had been hot with anger, but also ashamed and degraded by knowing to what type of man she had given her wholehearted love. It had not been difficult to give him up, instantly, without question, to the girl who was claiming him, a semi-illiterate girl who still wanted him and was determined to have him and had come meaning to fight for him.

There had been no need for her to fight. Meriel dropped him like a hot coal, handed him back his ring when he came in a frenzy to see her, listened unmoved and disdainful to his protestation that she and she only was the girl he loved and wanted to marry; and in the end he had had to leave her.

That, she told herself, was the end of Frank; the end of love.

But it had not been, in her inmost heart. She had lived in a rosy dream of happiness for those months and found it hard to accept the fact that it had gone, that it had never really existed except in her imagination.

Her personal environment had not made it any easier for her to accept the loss of her happiness, either. She had been an unwanted baby in a family already too large, and when her mother died from this final child-bearing, two spinster aunts had offered her a home and brought her up, but they were old now, and living on very small pensions from a fund into which they had paid during all the years in which they had kept a small private school. It had given them up rather than the other way round, and the best thing Meriel had been able to do for them, with their regretful agreement, had been to leave them and earn her own living. There had been no work for her in the village where they lived, but she had found a post in London which had enabled her both to keep herself and to contribute something towards the comfort of the two frail old sisters.

But just now she had not even the consolation of work with which to occupy her mind.

She was secretary, confidential clerk, occasional hostess and general factotum to an elderly geologist of some standing, but he had left England for six months to join an expedition on which she could not go, and he was paying her a retaining fee which left her free to take other work whilst he was away. Since Frank had talked of an early marriage and she had not had a holiday for a long time, she had not immediately looked for other work, and when her engagement ended so suddenly, she was at a loose end. Even if she had not felt that a visit to her aunts would have imposed a burden on them, she could not have faced their gentle enquiries nor their shocked reaction to her replies about Frank, so she had accepted a friend's invitation to share a fortnight's caravan holiday with her. Her visit to London that day had been to fetch something from the flat she shared with a girl who was kind, generous with an income left her by her father, but boring to Meriel's more volatile temperament.

She meant to find herself a temporary job at the end of the caravan holiday and, when her employer returned, saw herself settling down firmly to an unregretting spinsterhood. She could not imagine herself caring for any man again, and felt that she could never trust one.

Thinking, as she drove away from Chichester, of the man with whom she had spent the last two hours, she laughed in derision at the thought that he was 'rather nice'. He was probably like all the rest of them, not to be trusted an inch. However, it was extremely unlikely that they would ever meet again, and in all probability he had a wife and family somewhere. Not that that mattered to her!

Brian did not think of her for even as long as she thought of him.

His mind was fully occupied with the position at Rosemead and both its immediate and its farther-reaching effect on him. He would probably take on the job with the people who were buying the place, for the time being anyway, since he could not hope to live yet, if ever, on the sale of his pictures. He had no inflated ideas about himself. Since his picture had been accepted for the Royal Academy and had actually been bought by someone, he could take it that it had some merit, but it seemed that nowadays only the portrait painters, and the best of them at that, could hope to make a living by painting. He would go on painting because he must, but he could not look on it as his bread and butter.

However, his first job was to rescue Freda, in so far as he could, and see her safely over the first step towards finding herself again by putting her into her grandmother's kind hands. The poor kid, he thought, had probably cried herself to sleep by now.

But he was wrong.

After the first wild outburst of tears, she shed no more. She had relapsed into stony silence, her eyes averted from her parents, her

38

lips compressed, her response to their attempts to make conversation with her so aloof that it bordered on rudeness, and at last her mother spoke sharply, her own nerves on edge.

'It seems that I made a mistake in thinking you are no longer a child, Freda. At your age, or at any age, tantrums are most unbecoming. Never speak to me in that tone again.'

Freda gave her a cool glance. 'I shan't have an opportunity, shall I?' she asked. 'Besides, I didn't want to speak to you at all. You forced me to,' and she rose from the table and went upstairs to her room.

Sadie looked helplessly at Richard.

'She's got to get over it,' he said heavily, 'and nothing we can say now will make things any better. She's sore and bewildered at the moment.'

But later on Sadie went up the stairs and turned the handle of Freda's door. The door was locked, and when she called the girl's name softly, there was no response, but at least there was no sound of weeping. She felt she could not have borne that.

She went into her own room, a cold feeling at her heart. This had been planned for years, but she knew now that in the passionate expectation of her own happiness and the breaking of a bond of marriage which had become intolerable, she had not sufficiently reckoned with Freda nor the girl's reaction. Accustomed as she was to the lax attitude of her friends and associates towards marriage and divorce, it had not occurred to her that it would mean so much to Freda. After all, she had made it clear to the child that they did not intend to part from her irrevocably, that she would be able to come to either of them, even make her home with one or the other later on if she liked. And she was devoted to Richard's mother, and Cliff Top was almost a second home to her. Why then make such a tragedy out of it?

She did not know about Maisie Flower and the way in which she had always been regarded by her schoolfellows. Maisie's divorced parents and the lack of any stability in her background had made a lasting impression on Freda's developing mind. Maisie had always been an object of pity and, though her position was in no way her own fault, of faint contempt.

Urged by her disturbing thoughts to the necessity of filling her mind with what she hoped to gain by Freda's loss, Sadie opened a drawer and took out a recent studio portrait of Paul Erskine and studied it; the handsome face with the keen eyes which could be tender when they looked at her, the mouth that was both clever and sensual; the look of power and of dominance.

For one wild moment, because of Freda, she had been tempted to give it all up; to ask Richard to condone her betrayal of him; to make the best of things as they were.

Then she put the photograph back, her lovely face hardening. Was it fair that she should be asked to pay all her life for the mistake she had made in marrying Richard when she was too young to realize that a girl's first romance was not really love at all? In a few years Freda herself would marry and by that time, unless she seized it now, there would be nothing left for Sadie. She would irrevocably have lost Paul and would be drifting to the twilight of middle age and the loss of her beauty, with nothing to look forward to but old age with Richard.

The next morning, when she went downstairs in one of her trailing housecoats, Freda had already had her breakfast and gone to the garage, leaving Tims to take down to the landing-stage the small case she had packed. Her trunk and her other personal belongings and treasures, were to be sent down to her grandmother's after she had herself arrived, and the girl had packed them the night before, saying that she preferred to do it herself.

Sadie went up to her room to find that, though the trunk had been packed, all the new clothes which she had bought her were still in drawers and wardrobe. Freda had packed only her old clothes and even some of her hated school uniform. And (this hurt badly) the leather frame with its cherished photographs which had gone backwards and forwards to school with her each term now lay discarded on the dressing-table.

Though Richard had made up his mind that he would let Freda go without seeing her again, he had not found it possible to do so and he, like Sadie, had come downstairs in his dressing-gown. Brian had caught sight of them both when he returned to the kitchen for something, but he could not bring himself to let them know he was there and had gone back to where Freda waited for him, silent and repressed.

40

At his insistence, she went back to the house to say good-bye to her parents, since he said that he would not start until she had done so and they would miss the early tide.

She faced them stonily.

'Good-bye,' she said.

'Darling, you haven't packed any of your lovely new clothes,' was all that Sadie could think of to say. 'I'll send them down to you.'

'I don't want them, thank you,' said Freda curtly.

'Freda, don't be childish. Of course you'll want them. Gran won't expect you to go about looking like a tramp, or in your school uniform.'

'I dare say she will buy me anything she wants me to have.'

'Nonsense,' said Sadie, beginning to feel irritable. 'Naturally we don't expect or want your grandmother to buy your clothes any more than we expect her to keep you. Your father has made proper arrangements for you, and I shall see to your clothes.'

'Take this, dear,' put in Richard, laying some Treasury notes down on the table beside her. 'I don't expect you've got much of your end-of-term money left, have you? You'll need something to spend, and I'll make an arrangement with Gran for something regular.'

Freda looked at the notes without touching them.

'If I need money, I suppose I can work for it like other people,' she said, and walked out of the room whilst the two who had done this thing to her watched her go and could find nothing to say to each other.

Brian looked up from his final checking of the stores before loading them on to the hand-cart to take down to the boat.

'Well? Did you do it?' he asked, with a cheerful smile.

'Oh yes, I did it. I said good-bye,' she told him grimly.

'And I bet you made a really charming job of it, with a face like that!'

For a moment she let herself relax into a half-smile.

'I was pretty beastly,' she admitted.

'That must have been most becoming! Here, catch hold of the other end of this box. Not like that, fathead. Put your fingers under the bottom of it and heave.'

Gradually, by treating her as he had always done and ignoring the new turn her life had taken, he restored things at least superficially to normal, and by the time they had taken everything out to *Sprite*, he making the trips to and fro in the dinghy whilst she remained on board to stow away, she was outwardly her cheerful, busy self. When they finally cast off, he saw that she did not even look back to see if her parents had come down to the landing-stage to watch them go, as actually they had done.

'Not going to leave that rope uncoiled, are you?' Brian called out to her disgustedly. 'Coil it properly and then stow that petrol can.'

'Aye, aye, sir,' she said cheerfully, and scrambled into the stern to obey the orders.

He did not have to invent jobs with which to keep her busy since there was plenty for two people to do when navigating the narrow, winding channel to the open sea. Even with Brian's experience and the many marker buoys, it was easy to go aground with the tide running strongly out, but once they were outside the harbour, there was nothing to do but keep on course, and Freda curled up on the deck and presently he saw, to his relief, that she had fallen asleep. She looked pathetically young and childlike still, he thought, though her face in repose bore signs of the pain and grief she had suffered. She would never be all child again. She had already started on the journey towards womanhood, and he thought compassionately of what would probably lie before her, with her capacity for loving and giving her heart away.

When she woke, he gave her the wheel for a time but she soon tired of the inaction and went below to prepare a meal for them, though she scarcely touched it when she had done so, and he reversed his decision not to speak to her again of recent events.

'You know, kiddie,' he said gently, 'you've got to snap out of this. I can see that you're dwelling on it, but you can get over it if you try. The world hasn't come to an end, you know.'

'Mine has.'

'Rubbish. You've got a lot more than most people, a good home to go to (and you know you love being at Sandy Combe), no need to worry about money, and your grandmother counting the hours till you get there.'

'It isn't the same. Gran's isn't my home. I haven't got one. I wish . . .'

42

'Yes?' prompting her.

'I wish you were going to stay, Brian. I don't really belong to Gran, not the way I belong to you. You're part of my life, my real life. Can't you stay with me?' wistfully.

'I couldn't do that, dear, though I shall be there for a little while. I've only been employed by your father and there wouldn't be a job for me at Sandy Combe. I've got to have a job, you know.'

'You could paint.'

'That wouldn't earn me a living,' he laughed. 'I'll have to look on that as a hobby, I'm afraid, and get a real job of work to do.'

'What will you do, Brian? Where will you be?'

It was touching to see how she was clinging to him and he hated having to cast her adrift, as he knew he must do where he was concerned.

'For the time being I am going back to Rosemead but I expect my rooms will soon be wanted and I shall have to find somewhere else to live. That will depend on what I find to do, of course.'

'You could find a job in Cornwall.'

'Well, of course, it's wonderful country for a painter, but that can't be my first consideration. Anyway, your job is to settle down and try to put all this behind you. You can, you know, if you put your mind to it. Is that all you're going to eat? Not even a banana?'

'I don't want anything else,' she said listlessly, and began to scrape the plates overboard and stack them for washing up.

With a following wind and a calm sea, they made good headway, and the weather remained clear and unbroken. Brian telephoned to old Mrs. Fennal from Poole, and again from Salcombe, and on the third day of their voyage they decided to put into Falmouth rather than meet too late in the day the rougher conditions which could usually be expected in rounding Land's End. Sandy Combe lay on the north Cornish coast.

By the time the harbour formalities were completed and *Sprite* made fast and snug for the night, and petrol and freshwater supplies replenished, it was late enough to turn in. They proposed to make an early start the next morning.

'Are you going to bed now?' Freda asked Brian rather forlornly.

'Quite soon,' he said, 'but I shall be in the saloon for a little while going over the charts again for tomorrow.'

But a long time after she had gone to bed in her own cabin, the sound of a strangled sob told him that she was still awake and that her happiness and sense of security were dying hard.

'Not asleep yet, dear?' he asked gently through the closed door.

'No, I can't sleep,' she said drearily. 'Please come and talk to me for a little while.'

Unthinkingly he opened the door and sat beside her on the narrow bed, but it gave him a queer jolt of something like alarm when she seized his hand and held it against her wet cheek. It was no longer the gesture of a child seeking comfort, but he could not at once take it away.

'I'm going to hate it still more when you leave me as well,' she said. 'Oh, Brian, I do love you so!'

His discomfort increased. It was an expression she had used many times before, for she was affectionate and demonstrative and he had been her refuge and defence in many of her childhood's troubles.

But there was something different about this, and when he found her lips touching his hand, he drew it gently away. She was no longer the little girl, the small sister.

He tucked her arms in firmly and drew the blanket up to her chin.

'We've got to be up at crack o' dawn, Mr. Mate,' he said briskly. 'I'm tired enough to sleep and so are you, so no more tears and no more of this being so sorry for yourself. Orders is orders. Understand?'

'All right, Skipper,' she promised chokily, and he left her and closed the door firmly.

He would not invite anything like that again, he told himself as he went into his own quarters.

3

NEXT day Brian decided that he had made too much of the little episode.

The child had felt lonely and bereft, had always been given to demonstrative expression of her emotions and he had been the only available outlet. Mrs. Carter or the dogs would have done just as well.

It was fortunate, he thought, that the promise of rougher weather round the Lizard was fulfilled, for it gave them both plenty to do and both were good enough sailors to enjoy the buffeting of the waves and the battle to keep the little boat on course. They had to shout to each other against the wind, and laughed and sang the sea-shanties which had been her nursery rhymes. He was thankful to see her at least temporarily happy and forgetful of everything but the fun and enjoyment of the moment, and though they had several tricky little experiences, she showed no fear. What a glorious pal she was going to be some day to some lucky man!

There were no idle moments for her on deck today. *Sprite* was sturdily built for sea-going, but she was small and the big waves could toss her like a cockle-shell, drenching them whenever they had to leave the shelter of the cockpit. Brian, confident of her ability to ride much rougher seas than this, kept her on course whilst Freda made everything shipshape in the cabins and went to and from the galley, bringing him food and hot drinks and helping him to spot the various indications on the chart. She had no time to think of anything but carrying out his orders and keeping herself warm and reasonably dry. She was the best possible companion at such a time, knowing what to do and how to do it, a cheerful little figure in her blue sweater which matched his own, and old slacks, her hair bound tightly in a scarf under a sou'-wester. It was a pity that this would end so quickly, but once they had rounded Land's End, they would be in calmer waters.

45

'Not frightened, are you?' he asked superfluously, as a giant wave swept over the bows and for a moment shut them in behind a wall of water.

'No, I love it! Isn't it grand?' she yelled back, and he laughed and wished she could always be as carefree as this.

It took them most of the day to fight their way round into the calmer waters, and with Sandy Combe and the little sheltered natural harbour only an hour ahead, she grew quieter and sat hunched up on deck, staring, he knew, into the future which she did not want to meet.

'Better get busy,' he called to her when he was turning inland to make the entrance to the tiny harbour. 'Everything shipshape below?'

'Aye, aye, Skipper,' she said at once, and he gave her a rewarding smile.

The fishing boats were going out, and they had to steer a careful course amongst them. Some of the fishermen, recognizing *Sprite*, waved to them and they returned the greeting, and then he ran on into the harbour and tied up at the quay. *Sprite* would not be able to remain there, since permanent mooring was reserved for the fishing boats and presently she would have to be taken further along the coast, but this was the nearest spot for Sandy Combe and a climb over the rocks and up a steep path would take them to where Cliff Top was perched on the very edge of the little promontory.

Old Mrs. Fennal would not expect Brian Hewet to do more than deliver her grandchild to her safely. In her view, he was merely her son's employee, his chauffeur and handyman, and she always treated him as such. She felt that Richard made a mistake in treating him as a friend, almost a member of the family, for she retained the ways of an age that had gone for ever. To her an employee was a servant and, as such, should be kept in what she regarded as his 'place'. Brian knew this and did not resent it, but he felt that at this moment it might distress and hurt Freda to see him relegated to that place.

There were always men lounging about near the sleepy little quay, and it was easy to find one of them willing to carry her suitcase and small personal belongings up the cliff path.

'Aren't you coming up with me?' she asked at once.

46

'I've got a lot to do, kiddie, if I'm to get *Sprite* properly berthed before dark, as she can't stay where she is.'

'Brian, do you really *have* to go back to Tarnby?' she pleaded, the look of strain coming back into her face.

'Afraid so, dear,' he said firmly. 'I can't do anything for you here and I shall be needed there.'

Her face hardened.

'Oh, of course, if *they* need you,' she said bitterly.

'They pay me,' he told her with a determined smile. 'Good-bye, kiddie.'

'Don't call me that,' she snapped, and he knew that in her hurt she was turning on anyone or anything with the natural instinct of any young, half-grown animal to hit back. 'I'm not a child any more.'

'Sorry, Miss Freda'—with another grin.

'And not that either, as if you were a servant.' Then she changed. 'Brian, I shall see you again, shan't I? I couldn't bear it if I lost you as well.'

He was warned again, uncomfortable, but what could he do about it?

'Of course you'll see me again. For one thing I've been asked to bring down the dogs and the cat.'

'Please bring them soon,' she said in a small voice that shook, and she turned and left him, trudging up the rocky path in the cliff face behind the man who was carrying her luggage.

Mrs. Fennal was at the gate to meet her, a small, compact figure which she had contentedly allowed to thicken with the years, her face lined and sunburnt, white hair and very blue eyes contrasting with it. She opened her arms in welcome, but Freda came into them sedately enough, submitted to the loving embrace rather than responded to it and turned her head to catch the last glimpse of Brian still discernible as he made his way back to the quay.

Cliff Top had been the coastguard station before changing conditions had made it necessary to build a new one further along the rocky headland, and it had been turned into a delightful and unusual home. It was long and low and white-painted, most of its living accommodation at ground level, spread out into an L-shape, but at the point nearest to the sea, the lookout tower broke the

47

line of the low roof, and this had always been Freda's room. From the railed balcony which ran round its four sides, one could get a wide view of sea and countryside, and inside everything that a loving imagination could do had been done to make it practical and charming for a young girl.

Round the garden, a patch of land too exposed to the winds and sea mists to make much of, a high wall of the grey, local stone had been built as some protection for the hardy, low-growing flowers and the vegetable patch, but Freda's room was high above it and she loved the feeling of being suspended in space which her balconied tower gave her.

But now she entered the house on dragging feet.

She had always loved being at Sandy Combe, loved her tower room in Cliff Top, loved this white-haired woman whose only grandchild she was, but now she was seeing it all differently.

'This isn't just coming to stay at Gran's any more,' she told herself. 'I'm going to be here for always. They're going to send all my things down here, even Simon and Whisky and Mrs. Carter, as if it was going to be my home. But it isn't! I haven't got a home any more!' and her eyes filled with the tears of self-pity which Brian had derided.

If Mrs. Fennal saw them, she did not say so.

She had been appalled by the position between her son and his wife. She thought they were behaving disgracefully and had told them so in a long, violently expressed letter which had had no effect at all, since they still asked her to have Freda and made no suggestion about its being a temporary arrangement. She was always pleased when the child came to her and loved having her, and in any other circumstances—say the death of one or both of Freda's parents—would have welcomed the chance of having her for good, but this was a different thing. This was a casting-off of a child who, it seemed, had become a burden to them.

She had told them so in no uncertain terms.

Whatever selfish ends you are both serving, you will get no lasting satisfaction out of abandoning the child for whom you are responsible. Of course I will have her. Who else has she got, poor child? And I shall try to make her happy and not to turn her against you for what you are doing to her, but the best thing I can do for her now is not even to mention your names to her—a cruel and abomin-able thing.

So she was not going to start by any attempt to console Freda by talking about it or them.

'Now, my dear,' she said briskly as they went into the long, cool passage from which the ground-floor rooms opened, and at the end of which was the spiral stairway that led up to the tower, 'there's no need for you to change out of those things unless you want to. Hannah will go up with you and show you where we've put the things that have already come down for you, and then we'll have some tea,' and she nodded in friendly dismissal of the girl who must not be treated as a visitor but taken at once into the small circle of the home.

Hannah was even more a survival of past days than was Mrs. Fennal. She had started as a little maid-of-all-work before Richard was born, and she had remained ever since, progressing through the various degrees of servitude until, still in black dress and white apron and starched, frilled cap, she had become the general factotum. With a girl from the village coming in three mornings a week for 'the rough', she did almost everything that had to be done in the orderly little household. Stout and grey-haired, she 'knew her place' just as well as her employer did, and had no wish to alter it. She would no more have thought of not appear-ing in what she regarded as the proper uniform for the time of day than she would have appeared in a bikini. In the morning she wore starched print, a large white apron and a plain cap, and in the afternoon she wore black, with muslin apron and frilled cap. She was the envy of all Mrs. Fennal's friends, but she would never have been tempted away by any offer of higher wages or a title superior to that of 'Mrs. Fennal's maid'.

Mrs. Fennal had told her as much as she had considered it necessary and advisable to say, that unfortunately a little trouble has arisen between 'Mr. Richard' and young Mrs. Fennal, and that Miss Freda was coming for a long visit. Hannah adored Mr. Richard, did not think much of young Mrs. Fennal and shared her mistress's deep affection for their child, and she would not have dreamed of asking any questions.

She followed Freda upstairs, noting with pity the new, forlorn

49

look in her eyes, and began to unpack the suitcase whilst the girl went out on the balcony, winning the final battle against her tears.

'I'll take all these down and see to them, Miss Freda,' said Hannah in her comfortable way. Whatever it might be, Hannah always 'saw to it'.

The case had been packed without regard to the state of the contents, but Hannah did not tut-tut about the creased garments as she might have done on another occasion.

'I expect you'll want to put on a nice frock this evening, Miss Freda,' she said. Though she could dress as informally as she liked all day, Mrs. Fennal always expected her to change into something pretty for their simple evening meal. 'How about this yellow one? I'll iron it by then.'

'Oh—anything,' said Freda, and waited until Hannah had gone, the crumpled clothes over her arm, before she went back into the room.

Against her determined lack of interest in anything, she could not help noticing what had been done lovingly for her comfort.

Some time ago a large cupboard opening out of the tower room had been made into a rather Spartan washroom for Freda's use. Now it had been enlarged and made into a delightful bathroom, with a blue bath and basin, blue and white tiled walls and grey rubber-covered floor. A window had been let into the wall, and between gay plastic curtains with blue ships on them she could look over the broad expanse of sea.

There had been additions to the bedroom, too. The narrow child's bed had been replaced by a full-sized one with a pink eiderdown over a satin cover, and instead of the shelf that had held her picture books and small treasures, there was a bookcase with a writing desk. A lamp with a pretty flowered shade stood on a small table by the bed and suggested that the ban on reading in bed had been lifted. The floor was softly carpeted to tone with cherry-coloured curtains at the long windows leading to the balcony and two folding chairs, covered in striped canvas, were further evidence of her grandmother's loving thought for her. They could be carried out on the balcony and, if left there, would not be damaged by getting wet.

She noted all these things with set lips. She didn't want any of them, she told herself. She didn't want to be forced to feel that

50

this was henceforth to be her home. She resented the need to be grateful for what was being done for her. Did anyone think she could be bought by material things? By a blue bath and a pink eiderdown?

When she had washed in the new bathroom with its fluffy blue towels, and tidied her hair, she went out on the balcony again. Down in the garden her grandmother was busy with trowel and watering-can, catching the remains of the light; also, Freda knew, showing her where she was to be found so that she could, if she wanted to, go and talk to her.

Definitely she didn't want to. She didn't want to talk to anybody or be talked to, to be told that she would get over this, that she still had more in life than many thousands of other girls had —to be told, in effect, to be a good little girl and play with her toys.

But presently she went down. At least she would not be accused of sulking.

'What shall I do, Gran?' she asked without interest.

'Would you do some watering, my dear?' asked her grandmother pleasantly, and the girl took the can unsmilingly and when she had finished that job, went on with the weeding which always needed to be done.

'Don't bother with that tonight,' said Mrs. Fennal. 'Plenty of time tomorrow. I was thinking that perhaps you would like to have part of the garden for yourself now. I got old William to dig part of it up for you. Over here'—leading the way—'it gets the sun and also shelter from the wind.'

Freda knew that it was one of the best spots in the garden, where there was always a defeating struggle against the elements on the windswept headland.

'Isn't this where you had your carnations, Gran?' asked Freda, unwilling to accept gratuitous kindnesses from anyone in her state of hurt withdrawal from the world and her determination not to be healed.

'Yes, but they don't do really well anywhere in this garden, so I decided to give them up and forget how much I like them. You will find plenty of less fussy things to grow here, and when it's time to have the perennials up and divide them, in the autumn, you can have as many as you want. The new catalogues have come, too, so we can go through them together. You don't know how much I am going to enjoy having someone to share my interest in the garden instead of having old William's constant grumbling and discouragement. You know what he is about telling me that none of the things I like will grow here!'

Freda looked at the freshly dug patch without interest.

'I don't think I care much about having a garden of my own, Gran, thank you,' she said.

'Very well, child. All I want is to make you happy here, you know.'

'Thank you, Gran,' said Freda politely. 'I shall be quite happy.'

Mrs. Fennal picked off some dead roses and put them into the trug, pursing her lips, frowning a little. She had guessed that it might be difficult but had expected to have the girl in her arms in floods of tears. This quiet, self-possessed girl who treated her as her hostess was a stranger.

They went into the house, Freda remembering to wipe her shoes meticulously on the mat when she had stood aside to allow the older woman to go in first.

It was the same for the rest of the day, Freda punctiliously polite, expressing superficial interest in whatever was said without adding anything to the conversation herself, and after the simple evening meal they sat down to their customary game of cribbage until Mrs. Fennal, exasperated but having nothing specific of which she could complain, put the cards away and suggested an early night.

'I expect you are tired, my dear, after your journey, and after your cramped quarters on the boat.'

'It was quite all right, thank you, Gran,' but the mention of the boat had brought back painfully the thought of Brian and her longing to be with him, though she had not tried as yet to define that longing nor to bring to a point her feelings about him.

'I'm glad of that,' said Mrs. Fennal, determinedly kind, though she was getting more and more worried about the girl. 'You know, dear, I do so much want you to settle down happily here, to feel that this is your home, and if there is anything you particularly want, or would like to do, tell me and I'll try to get it for you. You don't know how much it means to me to have you here.'

For the first time Freda showed a gleam of interest.

'There's only one thing, Gran,' she said. 'Would it be possible for us to have Brian here?'

'Brian?' asked Mrs. Fennal, startled. Then, 'Oh—you mean Hewet, your father's man?'

'Yes,' said Freda, though she disliked that way of referring to him. 'You see, he won't have a job any more and he'll have to have one, and . . .'

At the surprised, almost affronted look on her grandmother's face, her voice tailed away.

'I am sorry, my dear, but that wouldn't really be possible, would it? There is no way in which I could employ him. I don't keep a car, as you know, and William gives me all the help I need in the garden, or in sawing the wood or bringing in coal and so on. I am sure Hewet will be able to find work, however. There is plenty for young men to do in England in these days, even if he cannot find work as a chauffeur. Your father will give him a good reference, I am sure, so you need not feel concerned about his losing his employment.'

'There's *Sprite*,' said Freda with a gulp, though she knew it was hopeless.

'The boat? Oh no, my dear, that's quite out of the question. I am too old for that sort of thing, and I have never cared to be on the sea, as you know. You will not have any use for the boat here, and your father will hardly want to pay a man just for that, and it will probably be sold in any case. I am sorry, dear, but I am afraid that is one of the things you will have to put out of your mind.'

'Very well, Gran,' said Freda, tight-lipped. 'May I go up to bed now?'

'Yes, dear, of course, and in the morning everything will look brighter. Good night, dear child.'

The girl accepted without response the affectionate kiss, and Mrs. Fennal let her go with a sigh.

Alone in her room, Freda curled her lips contemptuously.

'Anything she wanted,' Gran had said, and then refused the only thing she did want.

She opened the flap of the new bookcase-bureau. Inside were pigeon-holes filled with thoughtful care, paper and envelopes, stamps, little note-pads, paper clips and drawing-pins and a roll of Sellotape—everything her grandmother could think of to make the contents complete.

She looked round the room with more observant eyes and noted the changes that had been made in it, the bedside lamp, the comfortable chair with a low, adjustable table beside it, the new electric fire replacing the old, unusable grate.

Through the open doorway was the charming little bathroom which was all her own.

It must all have been planned and carried out weeks ago, possibly months, even before the Easter holidays and her return to school for her last term.

They had known, all of them, and had kept it from her, left her in her fool's paradise, gone on pretending that everything was all right, that her parents still loved and wanted her and that she had a home—and all the time they had been planning this.

She fought against another burst of tears and sat down to write to Brian, the only part of the old life still belonging to her, the only one who had not been a party to this and had been forced out of his home and his environment just as she had.

Darling Brian, she wrote in her still school-girlish hand,

> *I hate it here and I know I am going to be miserable. Gran's kind, of course, but she doesn't understand how I feel. She's old for one thing, and she's his mother so of course she's on his side. People who don't mean what they say when they get married, shouldn't have any children, should they? If ever I get married, it will be for ever and ever.*
>
> *What I am really writing is to say please take me away from here. I haven't got anybody but you, but this was the only place they had to leave me in. So please, Brian, take me away. As you say you will have to get a job, I can look after you, as you'll want some-one anyway. What I would really like to do is to go away with you on* Sprite *and just live on her somewhere and as we shouldn't need much, no rent to pay or anything, perhaps you could earn it by painting and not have to do anything else, but I know we can't do that because Gran says he is going to sell her. Sell* Sprite *! So you*

54

see, Brian, I have nothing left but you, and please come at once and take me away as I cannot stay here or anywhere that I'm not really wanted.

Your unhappy Freda.

She sent the letter to him at Rosemead, not knowing what else to do, and he read and re-read it with a half-smile for its immaturity of thought and phrasing, and a tug at his heart for its tragic sincerity. Poor little waif, lost between the childhood not yet ended and the womanhood not yet begun, what could he or anyone do for her? He knew that, in the circumstances, she could not be in better hands than the kind and loving ones of her grandmother, and he could not for a moment, of course, consider her appeal to him to take her away.

He was alone by this time at Rosemead, but by the same post there came a letter from Mr. Derring, who was buying the property, asking him to go to see him in London to discuss the arrangement proposed between them.

When the interview had ended, he found himself near the Royal Academy and, with a grin at himself for doing so, he went in to have another look at his picture.

It was a small one and, as befitted its relative unimportance, was hung inconspicuously and only one person was standing looking at it.

He came quietly behind her, careful not to disturb her if she were (as he hoped) admiring it, but she became aware of him and turned, and they looked at each other in pleased surprise.

She was the girl he had rescued when her car broke down!

'Well—you!' said Meriel Dain.

Instead of wearing the jersey suit, she was dressed for town in a trim black suit with crisp white blouse beneath it and a perky little feather hat, but he recognized her at once.

'What are you doing here, of all places?' he asked. 'Just obliged to waste a bit of time or actually looking at the pictures?'

'A bit of both, though I quite often come here. I'm afraid that as far as modern art is concerned, and those ghastly statues with eyes in the middle of their stomachs, I'm completely uneducated. Do you understand them?'

'No, but I try to. They're trying to express themselves, what makes them tick, what makes this crazy world tick. . . .'

She made a grimace. He found something unexpectedly attractive in the way her nose wrinkled and her mouth, wide and generous-lipped, turned up crookedly at the corners, but his mind did not register it at the time.

'Well,' she said, 'if that odd collection of boxes, circles and streaks of lightning called "Composition" is what makes that artist tick, what a horror he must be to live with! Now that little thing up there'—indicating his own picture—'would be possible to live with. It gives me a feeling of peace. I can understand trees and water. I wonder who did it?'

Standing on tiptoe and craning her head forward, she tried to decipher the tiny signature in the corner, and he read it for her.

'Robert Barlin.'

'Well, Robert Barlin, whoever you are,' she said, 'you're the sort of quiet, peaceful, *ordinary* man I could live with. I shouldn't have to keep wondering what made you tick.'

He smiled.

He had signed his very first picture with that name, prompted by the memory he had of his parents, the father whom he had disliked and feared, the mother whom he had adored. If his name went down to posterity, which at that time he had not dared to believe it might, he wanted it to be her name rather than his father's. She had been Roberta Barlin before her marriage.

He was debating whether to reveal himself to her or not when a member of the committee came to speak to him.

'Oh, Mr. Barlin,' he said, 'I've got somebody who wants to meet you, unless . . . ?' suddenly realizing that the two might be together.

Meriel gave Brian a mischievous glance. 'Please don't let me stop you, *Mr. Barlin*,' she said.

'Will you wait?'

She nodded and turned to look at another picture.

He came back to her after some minutes. He looked boyishly embarrassed.

'Sorry,' he said. 'I apologize.'

'What for? For being Robert Barlin, or because somebody

gave you away? Were you going to tell me before I made another *gaffe*?'

'I don't know, but what you said about me and my painting wasn't a *gaffe*, or was it? I expect I should have told you, but I didn't want to sound cocky or let you know how really delighted and amazed I am at having something of mine here.'

She liked the simplicity and candour, which she knew was no false modesty.

'Delighted, yea, but why amazed? Even an ignoramus like me can see why they picked it out.'

'You wouldn't if you saw some of the things they refuse, but a lot of people say it's not really a distinction to be selected, and that the best get turned down.'

'Don't be too modest and rob me of my thrill in knowing a real, live, royal academician, if that's the right word!'

She saw that he did not know what to say to that. He looked at his watch instead.

'Have you finished here?' he asked. 'Are you in a hurry, or what about tea or something?'

She laughed.

'You seem instinctively to associate me with a need for refreshment,' she said, 'but I'm not in any hurry and I should like it. I've got to meet a friend in about three quarters of an hour.'

'Let's go, then, and I don't expect we'll have to come down to a good pull-up for car-men in the middle of Piccadilly.'

He did not know London well but hailed a taxi and had a quick consultation with the driver, who took them to a bright little place where there were flowers and subdued music and small tables not too closely crowded together. It looked expensive, he thought, but this was an occasion. He didn't quite know why, but it was.

'Clever of you to leave it to the taxi-man,' she said approvingly. 'I never know where to go in London and I always seem to end up in some place where I have to get a tray and go in a long queue by a counter and come out at the other end with the last things in the world I really want to eat.'

'I do that too,' he said, 'but it was a sudden inspiration to ask the taxi-driver as they must know all kinds of places. I saw him take one quick look at you and size up exactly what we wanted.

57

Pretty girl, nice suit, silly little hat? Then soft music and flowers and not too many people. And here we are. Always put your trust in a London taxi-driver—or nearly always, though I admit that I once got let down by one. I had to take an uncle out to a late meal, old boy with a bald head who'd led a blameless life with his female counterpart for years, took the plate round in church on Sundays and all that. I was about twenty at the time and felt I was very big and man-about-town in hailing a taxi, which I sincerely hoped my uncle was going to pay for. I told the driver to take us to the sort of place he thought we should like, and we landed up at one of those places with a dance floor about the size of a postage stamp and a cabaret, very cabaret if you know what I mean!'

'I can guess,' she chuckled. 'Clothes stamp-size as well?'

'And how! I was appalled and was wondering how on earth I was going to get the old boy out, and also get him to pay, when I realized that he was thoroughly enjoying himself! I bet he never told my aunt, though!'

'Did he pay?'

'He did, and never turned his last remaining hair at the size of the bill. What are you going to have, by the way? Don't tell me you're on a diet because I'm going to have waffles with maple syrup and oozings of butter.'

'I'll have the same, then,' she said.

'Tell me what you're doing in London, if it isn't a rude question,' he said when he had given the order.

'It isn't, and it hasn't a rude answer. I'm having a sort of extended holiday on half-pay. I work for a geologist; see to his letters; transcribe his notes into something which I hope other geologists will understand—though I don't often do so myself; see that he keeps his appointments and remembers in due course to go home; run errands for him; make lashings of tea and so on. At present he's gone to the ends of the earth with other learned people (that doesn't include me, as you see) and he's paying me a retainer, though he will probably have forgotten all about me by the time he comes back, and the bank will go on paying me my retainer for the rest of his life without his ever being aware of my existence. I don't have to ask what you do with yourself because now I know. It must be wonderful to be creative.'

'But I'm not, you know. Painting pictures of my sort is not creative. The moderns class us with photographers.'

She argued that point, gaily, and somehow from it their talk ranged the world, though neither of them knew how they had travelled from painting pictures to climbing Everest and the easiest way to eat spaghetti, and she made a little exclamation when she realized how the time had slipped away.

'I'll have to treat myself to a taxi,' she said, and when he had found one and put her into it, he was suddenly shy again and tongue-tied and could not summon up the courage to ask where she was going or if he could go in the taxi with her.

'Am I going to see you again?' he managed to ask when the door was shut on her and the driver anxious to get away.

At once she seemed to freeze. All the misery she had suffered at the hands of Frank swept over her. She knew that, if she let herself do so, she could be interested in this man of whom she knew so little. It was too quick, too foolish.

Oh, not again, she told herself, feeling that she had gone slightly mad and had better get back to sanity at once.

'One never knows,' she told him lightly, and leaned forward to give the driver an address which he did not hear, and the next moment she was swept away from him.

Her last words came back to him from the open window of the cab.

'Good-bye, and—thank you for the waffles—Robert!'

And he, like a fool, had never even asked her her name.

'One never knows,' she had said about the chance of their meeting again, but of course one did. An opportunity like that, the chance meeting which Fate might deliberately have arranged for him, was not at all likely to be offered him again.

But it was a dismal thought that she, at any rate, had not wanted it to be offered again, or she would not have dried up like that, frozen like that, at his suggestion. Why? What had he done or said, or not done or said?

Though he was twenty-nine, he was singularly unused to the company of girls of his own age. For years his early delicacy had given him a sense of inferiority so that he had avoided the company of people who could do things that were beyond his strength, and only gradually and recently had he realized that he was now completely strong and fit.

He could not know that the look in his eyes, his anxious, slightly nervous smile, had done something so unexpected to Meriel that she had drawn back from him in fright. The ghost of Frank Lean had touched her and seemed to leer at her in derision, to laugh at her because she had been happy, for this short time, forgetting him. If she ever really forgot, she told herself fiercely that she would deserve all she would get. That was not the sort of lesson one should have to learn twice in a life-time.

Brian decided not to answer Freda's letter. She might already be regretting that she had written it, poor kid. The best thing he could do for her was to let her think he had forgotten it.

He had no idea that she was watching for a reply from him every day, hanging about until Tom, the postman, had either come trudging up with the letters or might be presumed not to have any for Cliff Top that day. She felt sick with disappointment as the days went by. She had been so sure that he would come to her, or that at least he would write at once and tell her when he was coming. Meantime she made no effort, except by outward uninterested acquiescence in anything she was asked to do, to adapt herself to the new circumstances. She was just waiting for him to rescue her.

Had he known it, by not writing he had set himself more deeply in her mind and heart until the thought of him and the longing for him had become the only thing that mattered to her.

Silent and aloof, not to be reached by her grandmother's anxious kindness, she lived within herself. She went over in her mind all that she and Brian had done together, especially during the two days of their close companionship in *Sprite*. She added imagination to memory, exaggerated small incidents into important ones and, without realizing it, was seeing herself as something between the captive princess of the scarcely outgrown fairy-tales and a deeply wronged and tragic woman, with Brian the rescuer and the only hope of both.

Her grandmother, who deplored for the girl's sake the position into which her son and his wife had thrust their only child, apparently content to abandon her to the care of others, did whatever her mind could devise for Freda's happiness without doing what she felt would be the worst thing possible for her by showing her open sympathy. The girl was already too deeply sunk in the self-pity which does no one any good.

Mrs. Fennal was comfortably off without being in any sense wealthy, and though she did not keep a car, having little use for one for herself, she hired one on several occasions so that they could go shopping in one or other of the larger towns, or to the theatre or the cinema, though she herself did not really care for either and was quite content to live her quiet, retired life at Cliff Top. Her chief interest was her garden, and she read a great deal, listened to selected programmes on the radio, and played mild bridge with a few elderly women-friends.

She did not try to make a young girl conform to this life, though it meant an upheaval for herself, and it was the more exasperating to her that Freda made so little effort to find satisfaction in any of the things available.

Sadie had sent down all the new clothes the girl had left behind, but they hung unworn in the wardrobe or lay in neat piles in the drawers whilst Freda went about in her old sweaters and slacks, changing in the evening into the few dresses she had brought with her. Mrs. Fennal, understanding how she felt about the beautiful clothes her mother had bought her in an attempt to soften the blow of abandoning her, did not suggest that they should be worn just yet but, instead, bought others for her when they went on their shopping expeditions and Freda wore these dutifully rather than with any pleasure, taking no interest in her appearance.

Mrs. Fennal tried other tactics.

'Freda dear, your hair! It's so pretty, but not when it's hanging over your shoulders and into your eyes like that! Can't you do something about it?' she said, but the only result was that the coppery hair in which she had formerly taken a good deal of pride was scragged back and tied with any odd bit of ribbon, or even a rubber band, into the pony-tail which Mrs. Fennal disliked even more.

But, baffled and irritated, she felt that there was little about which she could justifiably complain. Freda was always polite, obedient, considerate. She had the good manners in which she had been drilled by her mother and at school, as being an essential part of the equipment of anyone in contact with others. She did not sit if her grandmother or any other woman older than herself was standing, she waited on visitors, carried cushions, footstools, small tables, as soon as they appeared to be needed, and made polite conversation with guests who came to the house.

But to Mrs. Fennal, accustomed as she had been to the bright, lively girl who had paid such happy visits to her in the past, Freda seemed dead—an automaton whose actions, words and occasional grave smiles might have been produced by pulling the strings that made her work; and whenever she could, she slipped away to her own room and spent many hours alone there without giving any evidence of how she occupied the time.

Both her parents wrote to her, Sadie from Italy, Richard from New York, long, chatty letters filled with such of their daily doings as they thought would interest her but with nothing of their more intimate and personal life. Freda opened the letters, skimmed them through and handed them to her grandmother to read.

'I don't want them back,' she would say without comment on their contents, and though Mrs. Fennal knew that the letters were rarely answered, she could not bring herself to insist on this being done.

She herself wrote both to her son and to his wife, but found it difficult, for what could she say about Freda? That she was well, was doing this and that, had been taken here and there, but what else? Certainly not that she was happy and was adjusting herself to her changed life.

She felt that no useful purpose could be served by trying to say again to them what she had said many times before they broke up their marriage. It was too late now, anyway. Nothing she could say would mend things or give Freda back her home, her parents or her lost security.

Sadie, in an occasional short letter to her, did not mention Paul Erskine, about whom Mrs. Fennal knew nothing. Whatever she might have suspected about the reason for the breakdown of the marriage, she had not been told the truth. To her, as to the world in general, the fault was Richard's, and in his own letters he referred once or twice to Eileen Streeter as being with him, though his mother did not believe that this woman, an attractive widow whom she had once met, was actually living with him or had been the real cause of the trouble between him and Sadie. With nothing to go on, and no justification for the belief, she felt that the blame rested on her daughter-in-law rather than on Richard.

She felt intense bitterness towards Sadie, not only because of what was happening to her son and her grand-daughter, but because of the proposed divorce itself. She belonged to the generation and the type to whom the very thought of divorce is hateful, and she had never imagined that its sordidness could touch her own family.

She had no idea how, day after day, Freda was watching for the letter which did not come nor the feelings which she was encouraging in her mind towards Brian until the day came, longer delayed than had been at first intended, when he was coming down with the dogs and the cat. From the moment when Mrs. Fennal received the expected telegram from Brian to say when he would arrive, Freda was a being so changed that her grandmother was uncomfortable and even alarmed. Could all this be ascribed only to the fact that she was to have her pets? It seemed out of all proportion and could only mean that the girl was still clinging tenaciously to her old home and had loosened none of the tendrils that kept her bound to it.

Long before Brian was due, she had changed into one of the frocks which her grandmother had bought for her but which she had not yet worn. It was in a shade of green most becoming to her hair, which was neatly done and had been brushed into shining waves. The saleswoman had been clever in finding just the right style of frock for her. It was beautifully designed for a teen-ager just turning into a woman and was neither too school-girlish nor too sophisticated. Her legs, usually bare, were in fine nylons, and she wore the first grown-up shoes in which her grandmother had seen her, slender and high-heeled. They had been amongst the things which Sadie had bought for her, and though she put them on with some distaste for that very reason, she had decided to do so. Flat sandals, or her old brogues, would have been quite wrong with the dainty green frock.

Mrs. Fennal looked at her with mingled relief at this evidence of a return to life, and that vague alarm as to its cause.

'My dear, you look very nice,' she said approvingly. 'I think you need a little brooch or something, and I have the very thing,' and she produced from her box of treasures a beautiful little clip in filigree silver with a green stone.

Freda thanked her politely but without enthusiasm and went into the garden to bring in fresh flowers and arrange them in the vases. This was one of the small tasks which had been given into her charge, and as a rule she performed it efficiently but without much interest. Now, however, she was taking a good deal of trouble over the selection and arrangements of the flowers, the position of the vases and bowls, the general appearance of the charming, many-windowed room, and again Mrs. Fennal felt that vague alarm. All this for two dogs and a cat?

But it was not until Brian appeared, driving a car hired from the village, that this alarm took definite shape, and then it was something so unexpected as to be a shock.

When the car pulled up at the gate, the girl was out of the house and down the path in a rush of glad welcome, but it was not the dogs and the cat who received it first, but Brian Hewet himself! Before he could let the dogs out of the back of the car or lift down the basket in which Mrs. Carter was protesting loudly, both her hands were in his, her face flushed and eager and lifted to his almost, thought Mrs. Fennal in alarm and disgust, as if she expected him to kiss her!

He did not do so, though a few months ago, a few weeks possibly, he might have done so. As a child, she had often kissed him just as, in the exuberance of her welcome when she came home from school, she had flung her arms round Mrs. Peak and even kissed old Tims' weather-beaten face.

He held her hands for a moment, laughed and released them and turned to open the car door and let the spaniels rush out at her and overwhelm her with their delirious welcome. As soon as they had got over their first transports, she was holding the basket and talking to the still imprisoned Mrs. Carter, but surrendered it to Brian so that, coming up the path with the dogs leaping about her, she could hang on his arm with unmistakable affection.

His slight embarrassment was obvious as they came nearer to the spot at which Mrs. Fennal awaited them disapprovingly.

'I am afraid I am a little late, Mrs. Fennal,' he said in his

64

pleasant way, neither subservient nor familiar. 'The train was held up further along the line, and the car I had ordered had been taken away again and I had to go to the garage to fetch it.'

'It is not important,' said Mrs. Fennal frostily. 'Actually Yeo's van would have been coming along shortly and he would have brought you.'

She was thinking, in her autocratic way, that if Hannah or William had needed a lift from the village, they would have considered the van quite good enough for them. It would never have occurred to them to hire a car, even if either could have driven one. But Richard had always made too much of this young man and given him ideas beyond what she considered his station in life.

'You had better take the animals up to your room for the moment, Freda,' she said, for this had been arranged between them as a temporary guard against any of them immediately getting lost. 'You can give the dogs some water on the balcony and take some milk up for the cat. If you go round to the kitchen, Hewet, my maid will give you some tea.'

'But, Gran——' began Freda in protest, and was silenced by a look from Brian which did not escape Mrs. Fennal's keen eyes. She was remembering the girl's impassioned plea to her to employ this young man herself.

'Thank you, Mrs. Fennal,' said Brian. 'I managed to let Mrs. Carter out of her basket for a few minutes in the garden at the garage, Miss Freda.'

'*Miss* Freda!' echoed the girl. 'Don't be ridiculous, Brian. *Miss* Freda, as if you were a servant!'

He made no reply, did not even smile in her direction, but walked towards the back of the house, dignified and at ease.

'Hewet was quite right in addressing you like that, Freda,' said Mrs. Fennal. 'Times have changed, but not to the extent of your father's chauffeur using your Christian name as your friends do.

'He isn't just a chauffeur, Gran. He's always been like one of the family and he *is* one of my friends, my best friend.'

'Don't talk nonsense, my dear,' said her grandmother, at least outwardly unruffled. 'He is not and never can be a personal friend, and if your father allowed him liberties, these would cease in any case with his employment. You are old enough now to appreciate suitable values.'

Freda caught back the retort that sprang to her tongue and went into the house with the cat-basket and the dogs.

When Hannah brought in the tea-tray with the two cups on it, Mrs. Fennal asked her to tell Freda that it was ready.

'If you have given Hewet his tea, Hannah, he may go,' she added. 'There is no need for him to stay, and he will be able to get the late train back to London.'

'I think he is staying, madam,' said Hannah.

'Staying? Staying where? You don't mean here, Hannah?' asked her mistress, outraged at the thought.

'No, madam, though Miss Freda came down to the kitchen to ask him to,' said Hannah, equally shocked. 'He told her that he has taken a room at the Bull. Something to do with the boat, it was.'

'Oh. Oh, very well. Ask Miss Freda to come down to tea, Hannah.'

When the girl appeared, she still had that look of having come back to life, her cheeks flushed, her eyes bright, though her conversation was of the comfort and protection of the animals, especially with regard to the cat. The spaniels had been to Cliff Top before, but not Mrs. Carter.

But her grandmother felt that it was not just having her three pets again which had affected this startling change. It could only be Brian Hewet.

How could Sadie possibly have allowed such a situation to develop, if it had? And to send Freda off like that, shut up in a small boat alone with him! Certainly the man himself had behaved with the utmost decorum, had not shown any sign of presumption in front of her, but who could say what really had gone on between them? The sooner he left Sandy Combe, the better for all concerned.

But Freda showed no sign of wanting to see him again, not even when she heard the car starting up, but played happily with the wildly excited dogs until bed-time, her only request being that she might be allowed to have Mrs. Carter in her room for this first night.

66

The request was granted at once, though Mrs. Fennal was aware that the cat would almost certainly spend a comfortable night on the pink eiderdown instead of in the basket, and Freda went up to bed, having seen the dogs comfortably settled in the wash-house, which was warm and dry and to which they were accustomed. Mrs. Carter's furry bulk was hugged in her arms, purring loudly.

What Mrs. Fennal did not know was that, as soon as she had gone to her own room at one end of the long ground-floor passage, and Hannah's heavy tread had gone to the other end, Freda crept noiselessly downstairs and let herself out at the back door, careful not to let the dogs hear her.

The village of Sandy Combe was a mile and a half by road, but as it lay at the foot of the cliff, it was only a short distance by that path and it took Freda, bounding down on swift feet now in their familiar sandals, less than ten minutes to reach the door of the Bull, its doors and windows wide open and blazing with light, jovial voices and laughter in deep, soft Cornish tones coming from the bar.

Though she knew most of the men who might be in there, she did not feel that she could go openly into the bar, but she knew the place well and went round to the back and slipped in through a door which led into the seldom used private bar parlour.

It was empty, and she stole across the room to peer cautiously through the crack formed by the half-open door between it and the bar itself.

She saw Brian at once. He was standing with a pewter pot in his hand, talking to some of the fishermen who had not yet gone out in their boats, and she gave the little, low-pitched whistle with which she had so often announced her arrival in the Rosemead garage.

He turned at once, saw her and came to her, closing the door behind him.

'Freda, you shouldn't be here,' he said. 'Does your grandmother know?'

'Of course not, silly, but I had to see you. You must have known I would come. Wasn't that why you told me you were staying here?'

'That wasn't at all the idea, but I saw Hannah's shocked face when you invited me to stay in the house and hastened to assure her that I was not going to do anything of the kind.'

'Why wouldn't you stay there? There's plenty of room.'

'My dear child, to your grandmother I'm a servant, your father's chauffeur! However, since you're here, there's not much I can do about it but get you back there before anyone else sees you. She and that old dragon, Hannah, would wring my neck if they knew you were here!'

Freda giggled, not at all disturbed now that she was actually with him, and they slipped out and made their way down to the water's edge by a route which avoided the front of the house.

'I'm not going back this very minute,' she announced, and sat down on the low coping and he joined her reluctantly.

He was relieved to find her nearer to normal than her wild letter had suggested, the more so because of an offer which he had received and wanted to accept but had hesitated to do so because it would keep her in contact with him. If she were really the hysterical girl her letter had suggested, then the sooner he was out of her reach the better.

He told her of the offer.

A man who had done business with Richard Fennal, a Mr. Preecy, had come to see him at Rosemead and put up a proposition to him.

'I understand that you'll be leaving here,' he said, 'and I happen to know that you've always looked after the Fennals' boat, *Sprite*, and that you have taken her to Cornwall and are going to lay her up at Penn Tor. Mr. Fennal told me this the last time I saw him.'

'Yes, that's so,' said Brian, wondering where all this was leading.

'As a matter of fact, I know Penn Tor well. Actually I've got a little cottage there, and a boat, a small cabin cruiser, the *Sally May*. Perhaps you know her?'

'I can't say that I do, Mr. Preecy.'

'I don't use her much and I might charter her, but I want to keep her in some sort of trim and have someone there, over the winter anyway, who knows about boats and could give her an overhaul and also run her for me if I felt like using her. I'm getting a bit past it myself but I still like tootling about in her with a skipper. When Mr. Fennal told me you would be leaving him, I wondered if it would be of any interest to you for a few months. You could have my cottage there and I'd throw it in in addition to what I could pay you, which wouldn't be much, but there would not be much to do for it. I gather you are not entirely dependent on a job and like to paint, and if you took this on, you'd be completely free when I'm not using the boat, with plenty of time to yourself. How do you feel about it? I don't think I'll want to use *Sally May* or the cottage much and both of them would be practically at your own disposal so long as you kept a room for me at the cottage.'

Brian had not been pressed to make any immediate decision and he was committed to remain at Rosemead for some weeks, and it had been left open for the time being.

Penn Tor was the small town, little more than a fishing village, where *Sprite* was laid up. It was some miles by the road along the top of the cliffs, but within walking distance along the rocks from Sandy Combe at low tide, and it was its near proximity to the place where Freda was living which had made Brian hesitate after receiving her letter, though it was a job which might have been expressly made for him. He would have somewhere to live and enough to live on modestly without being fully occupied in earning that money, and it would be a great delight to him to be able to paint in Cornwall.

To his intense relief, Freda's reactions to the offer of the job made him able to believe that her letter had been nothing but the wild outpourings of a child who at the time had been lonely and shocked by grief. Now, except for her foolish act in coming to find him at the Bull, she was showing nothing of that but seemed to have returned to their previous relationship, which was more that of small sister to older brother than anything else. She was probably, he thought, regretful of having sent him the letter and anxious for him to forget it, which he was only too ready to do.

Actually her present attitude and complete control of herself and the situation were the measure of her growing up. She had realized, by his failure to answer her letter, that he was not prepared for any alteration in their relative positions, and already she had developed the feminine intuition which warned her against too complete a revelation of herself. To that extent he was right in believing that she regretted writing to him as she had done.

'You'd like that sort of job, wouldn't you?' she asked him now.

'I would, very much. It would just suit me, as I should have time to paint and also to mess about with the boats. I should be able to keep an eye on *Sprite* as well.'

'It would be nice for me to have you so near,' she said composedly. 'If my father is going to keep *Sprite*, you would be able to teach me to handle her by myself, perhaps next year.'

He was glad to hear the suggestion that she had accepted Cliff Top as a permanent home.

'You wouldn't be able to do that in the sort of weather we had round the Lizard on the way down here,' he said with a grin, and she laughed in her old, merry fashion.

'I'm not likely to want to do that,' she said, and then rose to her feet. 'I suppose I ought to be going back before they miss me,' she added.

Her tone conveyed no hint of the elation she felt at the prospect of his coming to Penn Tor to live. She was not going to repeat the mistake of that letter.

'I'll walk up the path with you, unless you'd like me to borrow a car and run you back?'

'They'd hear that,' she laughed. 'Let's go back by the path,' and she set off blithely, chattering to him in the old, friendly fashion as they went.

'I hope you'll decide to take the job,' she said when the moment of parting came.

'I probably shall,' he said.

'You'll let me know if you do? And when you're coming?'

'Yes, I'll let you know,' he promised. 'Good night.'

'Good night—and no more of that silly *Miss Freda* business!'

He made a grimace. 'I may have to in front of your grandmother.'

Freda laughed. 'Not between ourselves, though. Good night, Brian, and thank you for coming.'

He waited till she had gone in at the gate in the wall and then made his way back. Thank heaven things had returned to normal

70

between them, and that she had by now been able to accept her new life and be happy in it.

He wrote the next day to accept Mr. Preecy's offer.

4

It was October before Brian actually got down to Penn Tor and took possession of the cottage.

For one thing Mr. Derring had wanted him to stay on for a further few weeks at Rosemead, and also Richard Fennal had still some things he wanted to settle with him and had written to him to ask him to keep himself available until he could fly back to England for a few days.

When the two met, there was inevitably some feeling of restraint between them and Brian was glad to be able to tell him of Mr. Preecy's offer of a job which he had accepted, so that his former employer need have no feeling of further responsibility towards him.

'If you're not going to be too fully occupied, Brian, and would give an eye to *Sprite* for me over the winter, I should be greatly obliged,' he said.

'I was going to offer to do that, Mr. Fennal. I can have her up and scrape her and paint her with that new anti-fouling stuff and get her into the water again, which suits her better than being laid up dry. It seems that I'm going to have plenty of time and I can always get what extra help I need down there in the winter.'

'I should be most grateful. As a matter of fact, though I did at one time intend to get rid of her, I've changed my mind and am going to make her over to Freda. It will please her to be the Owner, though of course she wouldn't be able to manage her by herself; and next season, if you're not available, you may be

71

able to find someone. I'd rather it were you, of course, but I wouldn't interfere with your plans and couldn't give you a real job.'

'I should be only too glad, Mr. Fennal, to do anything I can for you,' said Brian, unable to keep the stiffness out of his tone.

'I know you will, and I appreciate it. I shall be glad for other reasons than *Sprite* to know that you are down there and will be able to see Freda and to let me know, if you will, how she is and whether she is happy, as I am sure she will be once she has settled down. My mother writes, but of course she disapproves of me strongly,' with a wry smile, 'and sometimes I feel that she would be glad if the child forgot her mother and me altogether.'

'She's not likely to do that. She's a very faithful person.'

'I know. That's part of the trouble. Well, keep your eye on her as well as on *Sprite*. See her as often as you can, won't you?'

'I'm afraid Mrs. Fennal does not approve of me either,' said Brian with as wry a smile. 'I have to keep my place.'

'I know. She's a different generation, of course, and keeps people in separate little boxes out of which they must not presume to wander! Still, no doubt you can manage to keep in contact with Freda whether my mother is aware of it or not.'

Brian did not fancy any surreptitious association with Freda nor could he see himself calling at Cliff Top to enquire after her, but he would have to await developments, and when the final details about overhauling *Sprite* and transferring the ownership to Freda had been worked out between them, the two men separated, each wondering when, if ever, they would meet again.

Richard had been puzzled, even a little disconcerted, by the fact that Sadie had not yet taken any steps towards the divorce. He wanted to get it over and have the whole distasteful business behind him, but on the other hand, the longer it was delayed, the further he was from the time when he would be obliged to marry Eileen Strecter.

They had known each other for years. There had in fact been a light association between them before either of them had married, but it had never ripened into an actual romance and it was completely shattered when Richard met Sadie and fell head-long in love with her. He had had no idea that this had been a blow to Eileen until years afterwards, until, in fact, she became aware that the Fennal marriage was going wrong, though this was discernible only by small indications scarcely noticed by the general world of their friends.

Then, some six months previous to the actual break-up, Richard surprised himself by confiding in Eileen Streeter, by this time a childless widow scratching a precarious living as she could, selling to magazines snippets of gossip, odd cookery recipes, advice on a variety of subjects from how to cure a smoky chimney to how to get, or to keep, or to get rid of a husband. He scarcely knew how, from that confidence, there had developed a situation in which she was to become 'the woman in the case'; but he had unintentionally let her see how repelled he was by the necessity for finding such a woman; all the sordid little details of hotel bills, an accommodating chambermaid and the rest of it.

'Better take me with you when you go to America,' she said jokingly, but he soon realized that it was not meant to be only a joke.

'I would go, you know, Dick,' she said. She was the only one who ever called him that. 'You'd have no obligation towards me except to give me a holiday and a good time. No strings attached.'

'I couldn't accept that from you, Eileen.'

'Why not? I've got nobody in the world belonging to me, no family to be shocked, no children—and incidentally, no money and no fun. We used to have fun together. Remember? I hoped in those days that it was going to be more than fun. You never knew that, did you? My dear, I was head over heels in love with you. I took my poor old Vic as the next best thing, but I never had any real fun with him. I'd still like to, before I die, and with you, Dick. Don't look so flabbergasted! I'm not just a wild, wild woman and if you've got to lose your virtue, wouldn't you rather lose it with someone like me than a by-the-hour Popsie?'

His agreement had not been quick or easy, but she was bright and amusing, good company and, by her own showing, amoral rather than immoral.

'I don't want to marry again,' she told him. 'I never have wanted to and now, in the sere and yellow of forty-eight, I'm not likely to have the chance. I'm sick and tired of scratching along on twopence a week, of never going anywhere or having any

73

fun. I don't want to marry you, Dick, and I don't want you or any man to keep me. All I'm asking is a bit of fun before I die; a holiday; perhaps the pretence that I'm having a romance.'

She had talked him into it, but after he had taken her with him to the States, making it obvious to anyone who cared to observe them that they were on familiar terms with each other, and had established her in a small apartment in New York, he had come to the conclusion that he would feel in honour bound to ask her to marry him when the divorce had gone through. Whatever she might have said about that, he knew that she would marry him if he asked her to do so. She was not as hard-boiled or casual as she had made herself out to be, and she was genuinely in love with him, though she made no claims on him and declared herself willing to part from him as soon as she had served her purpose.

So it suited him, though he called himself a skunk for it, that Sadie was so unaccountably delaying her action against him. She had written to him once or twice, just the chatty letters any friend might write, but they did not refer in any way to Paul Erskine or the future. They might, he thought, be any ordinary, long-married couple merely taking a holiday apart; two people no longer in love with each other but who had reached a stage of mutual tolerance and unemotional friendship.

He had considered the possibility of going to Italy to see her whilst he was in Europe, but decided against it and, leaving Brian Hewet, returned to New York. As a parting gift, he had prevailed on the young man to accept the car which he had left in England.

'If it's too big for you, why not sell it and buy yourself something smaller? I don't want it and should like you to have it.'

Brian accepted it after some demur, and was able to replace it by a good second-hand two-seater which had a boot big enough to hold all his painting materials. It would be cheap to run and would enable him to get about and find the sort of scenery he wanted to paint. With this, and the cottage at Penn Tor and the small salary which he was to receive from Mr. Preecy, he felt that the lines of his life had been cast in very pleasant places and left him little to wish for.

He need not have been concerned as to how he was going to meet Richard Fennal's request to him to keep in touch with

Freda, for the day after he arrived in Penn Tor, she appeared as he was inspecting the now hauled-up *Sprite*.

'How on earth did you get here?' he asked. 'Who brought you?' wiping his hands down his overalls.

She laughed.

'Easy,' she said, 'and nobody had to bring me, as you put it. I walked over the rocks,' and he remembered then that at low tide this was possible. When the tide was in, the only route was by the road, a distance of some six miles.

'Do they know where you are?' he asked, not too well pleased.

'Gran and Hannah? No. I told them I was going down to bathe in the cove and I asked for some sandwiches so that I need not go in for lunch. I've done that before. They can't see down into the cove. Gran won't start to have fits for hours yet, and I can be back by then.'

'Doesn't she think it's too cold for you to be bathing now?'

'She doesn't say so, and I've always bathed until right into the winter.'

'How do you propose to get back when the tide's come in?'

'What a lot of questions! Aren't you pleased to see me?'

'Of course, but—how *do* you propose to get back?'

'I thought that you could take me, or I can hire a taxi and get out before I get to the house. Don't be stuffy, Brian! You don't *look* glad to see me.'

'Mrs. Fennal would not be at all pleased to know that you're paying a social call on your father's ex-chauffeur,' but his eyes twinkled and they both laughed and he changed the subject by commenting on the condition of *Sprite*'s hull and what must be done to her.

'I can help you with that, anyway,' she said, and soon was happily employed with the initial and exploratory scraping.

What more was there for him to say? It was, after all, her own boat though she did not know it yet, and he could not see anything very wrong in their doing together a job which they had done before with her parents' complete approval. And, so occupied again, she lost her assumption of being grown up and was the familiar small sister again. Presently they sat on the quayside and shared their lunch, hers dainty sandwiches and small cakes, his slabs of bread and butter and cold sausages.

It was afterwards that the trouble started, when it was high time for her to be thinking of getting back and he would now have to take her in his car.

'Let's not go for another five minutes,' she said.

'Why not?'

'I want to talk to you.'

'And what have you been doing all this time?' he asked with an uncomfortable premonition. 'Come along. Here's the car. Nice, isn't it? Hop in, and we can talk going along. Can't it wait, whatever it is?'

'No. No, it can't,' she said, but was silent then until they had gone a little distance along the road.

Then she burst out suddenly, 'Did you get my letter?'

'You mean—oh—er . . .'

'I only wrote one. You never answered it. Why didn't you, Brian?'

'Well . . . you were upset, miserable, feeling that the bottom had dropped out of your world. I thought it was best to give you time to recover a bit.'

'You didn't think I meant it, did you? But I did. I still mean it. I hate it at Cliff Top and I don't want to go on staying there.'

He pulled up at the side of the quiet road. This would have to be met, and not with a mind which should be fully occupied in driving safely.

Her face was tense and set, the young look had gone from it again and her hands were twisting in each other in her lap. He had no idea how to meet such a situation and during their happy companionship of the past hour he had let himself believe that all that was over.

'I can't believe you mean that, my dear child,' he said.

'I do mean it. I'm not happy anywhere away from you, and I'm not a child any longer. I was until this happened, but I've grown up. You know I have, Brian.'

His heart ached with pity for her, because of the half-truth of what she said and because he knew how hardly things went when one was in between the years as she was. Perhaps if he were ten years older himself, he would have known better what to say.

76

'In some ways you have,' he said gently, 'but, you know, if you were really grown up, you wouldn't be able to say such sweet things to me.'

'I have to. You wouldn't say them to me if I didn't start it, would you? You're trying to make me think of you as Gran does, as somebody *inferior*! That's too silly. We belong to each other. We haven't either of us got anybody else, have we? Don't treat me as if I were a child, Brian, the way Gran treats me, and Hannah. They keep finding things for me to do, as if I still needed toys and occupation.'

'Perhaps you do,' he said, the teasing, indulgent note back in his voice because he did not know how else to treat her. 'Perhaps you've left school too soon, after all.'

That touched off the temper that went with her red hair and could flare up in a moment.

'Don't say things like that to me! Don't think them! You know they're not true,' she stormed. 'If I hadn't grown up before, I grew up all right when I found out about my parents and the sort of life they've been leading, all lies and deceit and beastliness. I'm entitled to make my own life now, not just to be pushed off as it suits them, and I've quite made up my mind what I want to do. I want to be with you, Brian. Please take me away. Take me with you *now*,' the storm of temper subsiding as the pleading note returned to her voice and her vivid little face.

He was seriously concerned. Though the whole situation pointed to her immaturity, there was an underlying suggestion that if she had not actually passed the border-line into the adult state, she was poised on the brink of it ready for him, or some other man, to take her over it. What if it had been some other man? It might be, if he were not wise with her. He wished desperately that he knew how to handle this, that there was some woman in her life, young enough to understand her, wise enough to guide and hold her. He realized how inadequate for any such purpose were the two elderly women to whom she had been entrusted at such a crucial stage in her life.

'I'd love to have you with me, dear,' he said at last, 'but you know it isn't possible. I know that you're not a child any longer, and that's why we must both of us look at this from a grown-up point of view. You know that I couldn't take you to live with me, don't you? For one thing, I couldn't even look after you. I can only just afford to look after myself——'

'I know,' she broke in. 'I've thought about all that, and I shouldn't be a burden or expense to you at all. I get thirty shillings a week for myself. It's sent to me by my father's bank every Friday, and it wouldn't cost more than that to feed me, would it? And you've got the cottage and I can look after it and after you. You know I can cook, and I'd soon learn what I don't know. Brian, please let me! Please have me!'

He hated to refuse her. She was so passionately in earnest and he realized that the grown-upness was, after all, only on the surface. Thank God she was not seeing anything morally wrong in this, nor imagining in the least the construction which other people would put on such an association. In her mind, it was completely innocent.

For her own sake, he had to open her eyes.

He laid his hands gently on the ones twisted together in her lap.

'Look, dear,' he said, 'you must realize why it wouldn't be possible, quite apart from the practical side of it, and of course I'd love to have you living with me as my little sister. But other people wouldn't look at it like that. I'm a lot older than you are, but not really so very old,' with a smile which found no answering one, 'and you're a very attractive girl and not a child any more. It wouldn't do, would it?'

'I've thought of that too,' she said, and though she coloured a little, she did not look confused. 'We could be married. That would make it all right.'

'On the other hand, it would make it all wrong, dear,' he said. 'I'm much too old for you, and you're much too young to think of marrying anyone for years, and when you do begin to think about it, it'll be someone of your own free choice, not just me because I'm the only one who can at this moment rescue you!' with another of those smiles which he was finding so difficult.

'You are my own free choice and it isn't just because you're the only one,' she said, but her face was changing, her mouth trembling, her eyes becoming tragic. 'I love you. I love you very much, Brian darling.'

'And I love you, my pet, but not like that, any more than you do really. Look how foolish it would be if we got married just

78

because you're not very happy as you are and want to have a different home. Sensible people don't get married just because of that.'

'Are you refusing me, Brian?' she asked tragically.

'It doesn't sound very kind, put that way, does it?' he asked, still managing to smile.

'But you mean it just the same. You don't want to marry me, do you?'

'Neither of us really wants to, dear. Marriage is too serious, and it's for ever,' speaking the words before he realized their import to her.

'Are you telling *me* that?' she asked scornfully. 'People don't have to stay married if they don't want to, and if you found afterwards that you didn't want to stay married to me, we could get a divorce and——'

'Look, sweet, let's not go into that,' he said cheerfully. 'Nobody gets married with divorce already in view! You certainly wouldn't want to and neither would I. When either of us gets married, it will be for keeps.'

'It would be for keeps with me if you married me, Brian. There just couldn't be anybody else for me, ever. Oh, Brian, darling, *darling*, couldn't you love me just a little more? Just enough to marry me and try? I—I worship you. It isn't just a crush or anything like that.'

The schoolgirl expression bruised his heart, which was so tender for her. It showed him how young she still was, how unaware in spite of having been shown so much too early how ugly life could be, and by the very people who should have protected her from such knowledge and put an ideal before her.

'What can I say that I've not already said, Freda?' he asked, still gently but letting her feel the inflexibility beneath. 'I know you're fond of me, and I am of you, but it isn't the sort of thing people marry for. I hate to say this to you, but unless you promise me that you will put all this out of your mind, go back to your grandmother's and try to make a life for yourself there, I shall have to go away so that we shan't see each other again. That wouldn't be very fair to me, would it?'

'You mean you'd give up your job here, and the cottage and everything?'

'Well, it would mean that, wouldn't it?' he asked inexorably.

She nodded at last and looked away from him and drew her hands, which he had still been holding, from his.

'All right,' she said in a dull voice. 'I understand. You don't want me. Nobody does really. We'd better go now. You can put me down at the cliff corner so that they'll think I've come up from the cove. I can wet my suit and hang it out.'

He hated to have her involved in such little deceptions. She had always been frank and truthful. This was part of what her parents had done to her.

He drove on without comment though, and when he stopped the car again, she picked up the dry bundle of towel and swim-suit and, just before she hopped out, gave his cheek a swift little peck.

'Good-bye, Brian,' she said, a catch in her voice. 'I do love you, you know, even if you say I mustn't tell you so again,' and she was gone, running across the heath to the cliff path.

Mrs. Fennal was watching for her return but could not have seen the car.

'Had a nice swim, darling?' she asked, giving the girl an affectionate kiss which she did not return. She had discovered that she did not like kissing now, though she had always been lovingly demonstrative.

'Yes, thank you, Gran,' she said politely.

'Isn't it rather too cold now? Won't you have to give it up until after the winter?'

'No, not yet. It wasn't a bit cold.'

'Well, give your wet things to Hannah and come and have tea.'

'I'll hang them out in a minute,' said Freda, ran upstairs, made the suit and the towel wet, tidied herself and went to hang the things on the line at the back of the house.

Mrs. Fennal smiled at Hannah, who was bringing in the loaded teatray, no longer the small teapot and wafers of bread-and-butter which had formerly sufficed for that meal.'

'I think perhaps she's settling down,' she said comfortably.

Freda had no compunction about the small deception. After what life had done to her, all the lies she had been told and the tricks which she felt her parents had played on her, she felt justified in getting what she could out of life by any means.

She realized that she had been unwise in revealing herself so completely to Brian, and premature in asking him to marry her, but she had no intention of giving him up. When he had had time to let it sink in, when she had had an opportunity of showing him what a sensible idea it really was and that she was quite well able to be somebody's wife, he would change his mind.

But beyond everything, she must not let him go away. She would let him think she had accepted his decision that they could never be more than friends. She did not know that she would need her parents' consent to marry before she was twenty-one, but even if she had known, she would have dismissed the idea that they might refuse. They had deliberately lost the right to decide on her future or dictate to her. She did not belong to them any longer in her own mind.

When she had left him, Brian decided not to do any more work on the boat that day. He had his painting kit in the car and there was just enough light, the soft light of the autumn day reluctant to end, which he wanted for a picture he had already started on.

He drove to the spot, the position on which his easel had stood having been carefully marked, set it up and was soon lost in happy concentration on the work.

It was the sort of scene he loved to paint, a tiny stream in a hollow of the Cornish moorland, rough grass, the tawny browns and greens of the autumn bracken and the purple of the heather stretching beyond it, one tree bent by the wind overhanging it, the water running, leisurely still, between grey boulders.

But when the light, which had lingered so long and lovingly, began to fade at last and he could not work, his mind went back inevitably to Freda and the difficulties, the embarrassment, of the situation she had forced on him. How on earth was he to cope with it? He knew that if he did the right thing, he would go away and not see her again, but it was too hard a decision to make. Living in Cornwall, with the cottage, a job which gave him just enough to live on with care, and plenty of time to paint—when would such a heaven-born opportunity come again, and was he to sacrifice it all because of the idiocy of a love-sick schoolgirl?

He rather baulked at the words in which he had clothed his thoughts, for he was really fond of Freda and hated to know that she was unhappy, but there was no reason why he should not speak the truth within his own mind. She *was* love-sick and a schoolgirl and the whole idea she had propounded to him was idiocy. If ever he were going to want someone sharing this little cottage with him, someone to go home to, someone living his life with and for him, it wouldn't be Freda Fennal or anyone at all like her.

Without realizing it, he was forming a picture in his mind which, at first entirely fanciful, gradually began to turn into a real flesh-and-blood girl, the girl he still called in his thoughts, unromantically, 'the girl I towed'.

It occurred to him that she was very much like this scene he had been painting and in the contemplation of which he had been so content, had felt so rested after the tempestuous scene with Freda.

There was about her that same quietness and serenity, and yet he sensed without any reason for so doing that beneath the serenity there could be turmoil, and under the quietness a tornado.

On this calm evening, nothing stirred. The little stream ran with no more than a slow murmur, the leaves on the tree bent above it were still, the heather and the bracken might have been put there by his brush; but tomorrow, or the next day, the water might rush and bubble over the stones, the purple and brown and green smoothness be broken by driving wind, the little tree bend and sway and shed its leaves though it would not break. It had weathered too many storms. But on another day, or by the spring or the summer, all would be calm again as if nothing had happened to disturb its peace.

But, good Lord, why on earth was he thinking in such comparative terms of this girl? He did not even know her name!

He packed up his belongings, deriding himself in smiling contempt, and drove back to his cottage and, in complete satisfaction with life, set the kettle to boil on the oil-range in the kitchen, lit a fire in the little living-room into which the front door opened directly, and set about the preparations for his unpretentious evening meal.

The next day broke in a heavy mist which turned to rain, and it was not possible either to paint or to do any more work on the boat, so Brian, deciding that it would be a good opportunity of doing one or two jobs which he had promised Mr. Preecy to do in the cottage, got down to them when he had had his breakfast and put everything methodically away. At least, he thought, Freda could not make an excuse to her grandmother of going down to the cove to swim on a day like this!

She soon showed him, however, that she was not to be frustrated in her purpose by a mere accident of weather, and whilst he was standing on a plank set across the kitchen, whitewashing the ceiling, she walked in at the back door.

'Look out!' he cried. 'You nearly had me over, pail and all!'

She laughed. 'How was I to know you were up there?' she asked. 'What are you doing?'

'Feeding the canary,' he said. 'What do I look as if I'm doing?'

'That must be good fun,' she said. 'Is there another brush? I'd like to have a slosh.'

He had looked down at her. Now he descended gingerly to the floor.

In an old frock and her school mackintosh, with a scarf tied round her head and her face wet with rain, she looked the familiar Freda, her eyes clear, her voice young with enthusiasm again, and he drew a breath of relief. She did not look as if she had come prepared to take up from where they had left off the day before.

'How did *you* get here?' he asked. 'You couldn't have come over the rocks on a day like this? Or pretended to be going for a swim.'

'No, but it's all right. I got a lift in Joe Perry's van. He comes in most days. He brings stuff from his farm to that place just past the church, a sort of hospital or something. I can see him from my look-out so I went to the cross-roads and thumbed a lift. He says he'll bring me over any day except Wednesdays and Sundays, and you can always take me back, can't you?'

'I see you've got it all worked out, but how about Mrs. Fennal? What had she got to say about it when you told her? I suppose you did tell her?'

'Oh, I fixed all that,' she said calmly, taking off her mackintosh and hanging it behind the door. 'She thinks I've gone to see Ruth Collen. You know about her? The vicar's daughter, the invalid one who can't walk. I shall pop in to see her every time, of course, but I shan't have to stay more than a few minutes and

83

Gran thinks it's so sweet of me,' with a chuckle which brought a frown to Brian's face.

'You mean you've told a pack of lies?' he asked.

'Oh well, not really lies as I do intend to go and see Ruth. Look, I've got a book Gran gave me for her and I've got to bring some others back, so it will look quite all right, and Gran says that if I can't come back with Joe Perry, she'll pay for me to hire a car from the garage.'

'I thought you'd got your own money.'

'Oh yes, but if Gran is willing to pay, I need not use that when I'm going on an errand of mercy!' with an impish grin.

'But you proposed that I should take you back. How are you going to explain that when she offers you the money? Or do I get a taxi fare?'

'Silly, as if I should insult you by offering it! Oh no, I shall take it just the same. After all, why shouldn't she give me the money? It saves her having to come and see Ruth, she or Hannah.'

'You haven't come to see Ruth. Or have you?'

She giggled. 'Of course not. I've come to be with you.'

'Without her knowledge but at her expense?'

'Oh, Brian, don't be so *fusty*! As if it matters! And it doesn't cost her anything to have me. She gets paid for that. Come on. Let's get on with the whitewashing. What can I do?'

He saw that they would only get involved in more futile argument, ending possibly in a scene, and since she was here and there was nothing to be done about it at the moment, he might as well accept it. It was the deception she was practising which irked him, the easy lies which, whatever she might say, were lies. She was changing into something very different from the frank, uninhibited girl she had been.

Still, so long as she remained the comrade and helper of the old days, they could be at ease together, and he found her an old pyjama suit to put on, gave her a brush and set her to whitewashing the walls.

She was a good worker, as she had always been, neat and thorough over any job she had to do, and soon they were on the old, easy terms again, laughing and talking, squabbling amicably over the one pail of whitewash, giving each other a surreptitious

84

dab from their brushes now and then until they were almost as white as the ceiling and walls.

He had to remind her, as they shared a picnic lunch, of the visit to Ruth Collen. She had brought sandwiches with her so that she was not expected back until the afternoon.

'Oh, pest! I suppose I shall have to go,' she said, 'though I'd much rather stay here with you.'

'Well, you can't. And we've finished all you can help me with here, anyway. Get yourself cleaned up, there's a good girl, and nip off. Can you telephone from the vicarage for a car to take you back?'

'Can't you, Brian? Take me back, I mean?' she asked wistfully.

'No, I can't. I'm not going to clean up and get the car out just for that,' he said decidedly. 'Besides, if you're going to ask Mrs. Fennal for the money for it, it must be spent honestly.'

She made a grimace. 'I oughtn't to have told you that, ought I?'

'You jolly well should never even have thought of it,' he said, and she laughed.

'Where can I wash?' she asked. 'The sink's all messy.'

'Take a jug of water and go up into my bedroom. There's a bathroom of sorts up there, but no basin in it, and no hot water. Take some out of the kettle. I live in a primitive style here.'

'I like it,' said Freda serenely, but he hustled her off before she could go further into that.

She was upstairs for some time, and when he went up to his bedroom later, he found that she had remade the bed, which he had done hastily in order to start the whitewashing, and tidied away the things he had left about. She had even moved the dressing-table into a better light, and though it was an improvement, he was sorry she had done it. She was, he feared, seeing herself as the mistress of the little house, such things her recognized job and her pleasure. If he were not very careful, she would contrive to dig herself in.

She made a complete inspection of the cottage, two small bedrooms and the primitive bathroom above, living-room, kitchen and store-room below, with an outside shed where he could keep his painting kit and also work if he wanted to.

'It's a darling little house,' she said, the wistful note back in her voice, but he would not pander to it, hustling her off towards the vicarage and hoping profoundly that no one had seen her either arrive or leave.

After that, as the rainy, misty weather persisted, she came nearly every day, helping him with the rest of the redecorating which he had undertaken, and playing at 'keeping house' for him. In spite of his protests that he had always done such things for himself, she darned his socks and sewed on his buttons and did his mending.

He was glad of such days as would permit them to work on the boat, since there they could be free of the 'home' atmosphere she was trying to create in the cottage, though he was uncomfortably aware that the pair of them were a source of interest and probably speculation amongst the villagers of Penn Tor, who were always interested in and suspicious of 'foreigners'. Though Freda's grandmother had lived for many years in Sandy Combe, which was a mile and a half from Penn Tor and therefore closely allied with it, she was and always would be, to the true Cornish people, 'a foreigner' and the country on the other side of the Cornish border was known as 'over in England'.

However, Brian was already known to them as having been employed by Mr. Fennal to look after and run *Sprite*, so it did not cause as much comment as it might have done, nor did any news of their association reach the house at the top of the cliff. Freda, kept occupied and made happy by being with Brian, took care to appear as she always had been with him, the jolly companion, the 'little sister', and he became confident that she was settling down into her new life and home and getting over her imagined love-sickness towards him.

He would have felt less comfortable had he known that at Cliff Top she was a different being, listless, uninterested, almost sullen, and that her grandmother worried constantly about her. Unless the girl were roused out of this, she might even develop melancholia or become a psychopath.

She tried to find diversions for her. Such young people as there were within reasonable reach, though there were not many, were invited to the house and Freda paid them polite return visits, but no real friendship developed with them. The long garage, for which Mrs. Fennal had had no use, was cleared and cleaned and turned into a games room, with a table tennis set up there, deck quoits, a darts board and anything else which might have been of interest to the young people, but it was not a success.

'Would you like to invite one of your school friends for part of the Christmas holidays, dear?' Mrs. Fennal asked her one evening.

'No, thank you, Gran,' said Freda without interest, and thought of Una, now happily married with a home of her own in Kenya, and of the girl they had always referred to as 'poor Maisie'. If she were still at school, she supposed she would be known as 'poor Freda'. The thought made her squirm.

She had not kept up a correspondence with any of the girls with whom, on the last night of school, she had sworn eternal friendship, and though letters came for her, sent on from Rose-mead, she did not answer them, nor would she send out Christmas cards when the time came. She threw into the waste-paper basket the cards which came for her, and when Hannah, scandalized, took them out and arrayed them on the mantelpiece in her bedroom, she took them down at once and put them in the fire.

When Christmas came, there were presents for her from both her father and her mother. Richard sent her from New York a writing-case fitted with every possible writing requirement, from sealing-wax with her own specially designed seal to the latest kind of pen which would supply inks of three different colours, whilst Sadie sent her an evening frock of beautiful Italian work-manship in one of her favourite shades of pale apple green.

She wrote dutiful letters of thanks, put the writing-case away in a drawer and hung the frock in the wardrobe but never wore it, even when Mrs. Fennal held a Christmas party for her with dancing in the games room to the music of the new gramophone which was her own gift to her grand-daughter.

'Surely you'll wear your lovely new dress, my dear?' asked Mrs. Fennal when she saw Freda pressing her old, schoolgirlish white silk.

'I'd rather wear this, thank you, Gran,' said Freda, close-lipped, and nothing more was said about it.

How utterly unforgiving the young could be!

Mrs. Fennal was finding it difficult enough to forgive her son and his wife, but life had to go on and old wounds be allowed to heal.

It was a few days after the party, which had been only a superficial success, that Hannah knocked at the door of the sitting-room after Freda had gone to bed and asked to speak to her mistress privately.

'Yes? What is it about, Hannah?' asked Mrs. Fennal crisply. The look on the woman's face seemed to bode no good.

'I don't hardly like to tell you, madam, but I feel it my duty as it's something you ought to know,' began Hannah, and Mrs. Fennal sighed. She knew only too well that when people wore that look and spoke of a 'duty they hardly liked to perform' that she was about to hear something unpleasant and perhaps something that need not have been said.

'Yes, Hannah?'

'It's about Miss Freda, madam, begging your pardon.'

'Indeed?' asked Mrs. Fennal frostily. Old and well-tried friend that Hannah might be, and admitted for many years to her mistress's confidence, it was, she felt, no part of her handmaiden's duty to invite any discussion with her of a member of the family.

Hannah, filled with the righteousness of her cause, swallowed and went manfully on.

'Well, it's like this, madam. Miss Freda goes several days a week over to Penn Tor in Joe Perry's van to see Miss Collen, Miss Ruth that is. Well, madam, she doesn't,' bringing out the last words with a determined effort.

'What do you mean, Hannah?' asked Mrs. Fennal, startled. 'Of course she does. Only the other Sunday, when we went to the church at Penn Tor, the vicar spoke to me and said how kind it was of Miss Freda to go so often to see Miss Ruth and take the books to her. And you have told me yourself that she often asks you for cakes and pasties to take with her.'

'I know, madam, but Miss Freda only goes to the vicarage for a few minutes *and* she doesn't leave the things I give her there either. I had it from my niece, Bertha Drew that was, who's been going in to help Miss Collen, the other Miss Collen, now that their other help has had to give up. Miss Freda never stays longer than five minutes or so with Miss Ruth, and she doesn't take the cakes with her, nor the pasties, nor the bottle of my dandelion wine I gave her to take for Christmas.'

'But—but what does she do with them then?' asked Mrs. Fennal, nonplussed and suffering from loss of dignity in allowing such a conversation to take place but knowing that she could not ignore such a story and put Hannah 'in her place'.

'Well, madam, I don't hardly like to tell you, but it's all over the village that when Miss Freda isn't doing whatever they're doing to that boat, she's up at the cottage, Mr. Preecy's cottage round by Mulberry Farm, with that man Hewet who used to work for Mr. Richard. And there's times when she doesn't come home in the car belonging to Selter's garage like you think she does, but he brings her in his car and she gets down at the corner. I thought you ought to know, madam,' and Hannah drew herself up with the consciousness of a duty performed, crossing her hands in front of her over her spotless white apron.

Mrs. Fennal sat in silence for a few moments, trying to assimilate the unpleasant revelation, wondering if she had to believe it.

She knew that Hannah had always disliked Brian Hewet, resenting the anomalous position he held with Richard Fennal, neither friend nor servant and yet a mixture of both. She knew too that any village is a hotbed of gossip especially ones like Penn Tor and Sandy Combe where the work to be obtained was seasonal and during the intervals gossip was the only alleviation of boredom.

'But there's no smoke without fire,' she reflected, nor would Hannah have wantonly involved Freda in any tale to be carried to her grandmother unless she herself was convinced of its truth.

'Are you quite sure this is not mere malicious gossip, Hannah?' she said at last. 'I did not even know that Hewet was in the neighbourhood.'

'Oh yes, it's him all right, madam. Bertha's boy delivers the morning papers and the name's on the one for the cottage plain for all to see and there wouldn't be two of the same name doing things to Mr. Richard's boat. As for it not being true about Miss Freda going to the vicarage, madam, my niece, Bertha Drew that was, wouldn't have made such a thing up, being at the vicar's and only just confirmed by the bishop himself. She knows

89

for positive that my pasties and things, *nor* my dandelion wine, never reached Miss Ruth, so what I say is, where did they go? Miss Freda always has as much as she wants if she takes her lunch with her and then asks for more for Miss Ruth, and she doesn't like my dandelion wine,' the last an added affront.

'Yes, Hannah. I see what you're suggesting,' said Mrs. Fennal in a worried voice.

There were other things which seriously worried her as well, if she must believe this story.

If it were true that Brian Hewet sometimes drove Freda back from Penn Tor, why did the girl unfailingly collect from her the amount which she had allegedly paid for the hired car? She did not for one moment believe that the young man would take those few shillings from Freda for such a service. What was she doing with the money thus obtained, and why did she want it? Living the quiet life they did, Mrs. Fennal had always considered that the thirty shillings personal allowance from Richard was too much, and there was little evidence that Freda spent more than a small fraction of it. Why then did she want more, *steal* it, in fact, since that was what it amounted to? If she was trying to accumulate money, what was its object?

The thing was so worrying that she almost wished, ostrich-like, that Hannah's niece, 'Bertha Drew that was', had not felt it her duty to tell her aunt, nor Hannah to relay it to her.

'I'll think about it, Hannah,' she said. 'After all, Miss Freda has always been attached to the boat, and if it really gives her pleasure to spend time at Penn Tor painting it, or whatever she is doing, there is not a great deal of harm in it, though she should, of course, have told me.'

'Well, madam, there is something else which I don't hardly like to tell you,' said Hannah, and Mrs. Fennal wished she would feel a little more indulgent to herself if that were so. 'They say that Miss Freda goes in and out of the cottage by the back door and even hangs out Hewet's things on the line, his shirts and things, as if she'd *washed* them,' her tone inexpressibly shocked and affronted.

'Oh, I should not think that, Hannah, at any rate. Miss Freda wouldn't know how to wash a man's shirt! He'd have them washed, or do them himself.'

90

'Nobody does his washing, and when she was hanging them out he was digging the garden,' said Hannah, and Mrs. Fennal realized how far and in what detail the pair were being watched.

'Very well, Hannah,' she said, deciding that it was time to put a stop to these revelations. 'Thank you for telling me. You were quite right to do so, though as you know this young man has been with Mr. Richard for many years and Miss Freda has been in the habit of looking upon him—well—almost as a part of her family rather than a servant. I hope the story will not be repeated and enlarged upon.'

'Not by me it won't, madam, and I've told Bertha she'd better keep her mouth shut and tell Drew the same if she doesn't want to make trouble between me and her.'

'Thank you, Hannah,' said Mrs. Fennal firmly, and the maid accepted the uncompromising dismissal and went away, conscious of a duty performed.

Mrs. Fennal was seriously disturbed and knew that she could not make light of the story.

The association could not be allowed to go on, of course. Freda was much too young to appreciate the harm that could be done by malicious, or even idle, gossip, and the girl was wholly in her charge.

She blamed the man, of course, though she also blamed Richard for having put Hewet in a false position and given him ideas about himself. Though Freda was not yet eighteen, he might even have some notion in his head of enticing her away and eventually getting her to marry him. She would some day be a considerable heiress, and when she was twenty-one would come into a comfortable little legacy left her by Sadie's mother, and in all probability Hewet, who seemed to have been in Richard's confidence about most things, was aware of that. There would also be money to come to Freda when she herself died. That, too, he would surmise.

The thought of Freda marrying anybody at all yet, or even having an affair, was absurd, but Mrs. Fennal was remembering that Sadie had been very little older than Freda was now when she had made her disastrous marriage to Richard, and Freda was growing very much like her mother, in looks anyway.

It must be stopped, but how?

The girl herself was being so difficult, so unapproachable, that any word or hint to her was quite likely to send her headlong to this man and further any schemes he might have. Nor could she expect help from Richard, who was thousands of miles away, and certainly not from the girl's mother, who had abandoned her without a thought for her future.

Finally she sat down to write a letter.

5

'WHAT an amusing situation! Don't tell me that village life is all honey and sweet innocence!'

Meriel Dain looked up from her needlework and smiled at her friend, who had been reading a long letter.

She was staying with her friends, the Harlands, in their London flat. She had found sharing a home with May Gering burdensome and had accepted Louise Harland's invitation to stay with her both to give her a break and also to provide a jumping-off ground for the temporary job she had decided to look for. Louise had been a school friend and Meriel had been a bridesmaid at her wedding the previous year.

'What bit of village scandal have you got hold of?' she asked, ready to be amused.

'Have I ever spoken to you of my godmother, Mrs. Fennal? She lives in some godforsaken hole in Cornwall and I always keep up a dutiful correspondence with her because, being her god-daughter, I have certain small expectations! She's an old darling and I'd hate her to die, but there's no sense in flying in the face of a possible, kindly providence. She's sent me five pounds for my birthday, bless her, and she's also poured out a long tale of

92

woe, though I really don't see what I could do about it. Oh——!'
breaking off on a sudden thought and looking at Meriel specu-
latively.

'Oh what?' asked Meriel, snipping off her cotton.

'You want a job, nothing too arduous or permanent, until your
old fossil comes back. You know you can stay here as long as you
like. We love having you. But if you really mean that you want
to find something to do . . .?'

'I do,' said Meriel. 'It's sweet of you and Bob to want me, but
I'm not going to wear out my welcome, and I don't want to go
back to May. What have you dug up for me? Not something out
of your godmother's letter?'

'Might. Might not. How would you fancy going to Cornwall
as a sort of companion to a girl of seventeen for a month or two?
Good salary and all found?'

Meriel laughed. 'Doesn't sound very exciting,' she said. 'I want
a job, but not in a godforsaken hole in Cornwall playing bear-
leader to a girl of seventeen. It's too long since I've been seventeen
myself. And what's all this about honey and sweet innocence?
Am I supposed to have that, at my time of life?'

'All that was in a manner of speaking. It doesn't sound too bad.
It seems that this girl, Freda, is my godmother's grand-daughter,
if you can work that one out, and she's been thrown over to Mrs.
Fennal by divorcing parents and is living there with her. She
seems to have formed an undesirable association with some man
in the village, and though there's apparently nothing very serious
about it at the moment, my old darling wants to divert her attention by giving her some new interest in the shape of what she calls
a really nice young woman, preferably one who can drive a car,
speak a little French and do nice needlework. It's rather an odd
collection of things, but she offers a really super salary, six
pounds a week, all found and all expenses paid, for a few
months, the period depending on how Freda and the nice young
woman get on.'

'And what makes you think I'm a nice young woman?' asked
Meriel with a chuckle.

'Well, aren't you?' asked her friend, laughing. 'If you're not,
don't tell me. You know, Meriel, it might not be too bad. It
would be something for you to do, not permanent, and look

what she wants. Drive a car, be able to sew and speak a little French. You can do all that.'

'My French is not much more now than the pen of my aunt!'

'Oh well, you could swot it up a bit, and when we were seventeen our French was even less than the pen of my aunt. Do you remember the days we had to talk French at meals? *Passez moi* the salt, and *puis j'avoir* some more pudding?' and the two girls giggled at the reminiscence.

'I really don't think I'd find it much fun,' said Meriel, though she sounded a little thoughtful, 'especially the part about the undesirable association. What is the really nice young woman supposed to do about that?'

'Annex the village swain herself,' suggested Louise. 'You shouldn't find that too difficult. She looks so terribly young,' handing Meriel some snapshots which had been enclosed in the letter. 'I remember that Mrs. Fennal did have a grand-daughter, but I never saw her or the parents. They don't seem to have been much good, do they? Abandoning the child to an elderly woman like that? Freda seems to have taken it rather badly and I can't wonder at that, poor kid.'

Meriel was looking at the photographs. They had been taken in happier days, showing Freda even younger than her present age, a laughing girl in a swimsuit perched on the deck of a small yacht, another in shorts and sweater, a big tabby cat in her arms and two dogs at her feet. She looked very young and carefree. There was a dewy look about her, candid, unaware, oddly appealing when one remembered that she had been cast off by her parents.

'She surely can't be seventeen, or likely to form undesirable attachments?' she asked. 'She's just a child and looks quite sweet. Pretty too.'

'Mrs. Fennal says they were taken some time ago, probably before the home was broken up and the child dumped on her grandmother like an unwanted parcel. Goodness knows what it might do to a girl of that age. I feel desperately sorry for her.'

'Me too,' said Meriel.

'Are you thinking about it? They've probably got quite a nice home, even if it is rather off the earth, and six pounds, all found and all expenses paid, isn't to be sneezed at.'

94

'No,' agreed Meriel thoughtfully.

'She says to write to her first and send a photograph, and if she seems likely to suit, Mrs. Fennal would come up to London to look the joint over.'

'Me being the joint? Tough old mutton rather than tender lamb! Give me the letter and I'll think it over.'

'I shall hate you to leave us, and you can always come back if you don't like it, but it might be an idea, don't you think?' said Louise, giving her the letter. 'It might be fun to try it.'

'I wouldn't say there's much fun in it,' said Meriel dryly, 'but I've never been to Cornwall and if there's a car, and presumably I'd be allowed to drive it, we could get about a bit. Let me think it over.'

The upshot of it was that, a week later, Meriel went to meet Mrs. Fennal in the old-fashioned hotel where she had booked a room for the night, leaving Freda with some misgivings in Hannah's charge.

The two women, one in her seventies and the other in her twenties, liked each other on sight and in a little while Mrs. Fennal spoke quite frankly about the situation.

'I don't say that there is any harm in the association with this young man, Brian Hewet, but of course it must not be allowed to develop and Freda is only seventeen. My son placed the young man in a ridiculous position, treating him as a friend rather than a servant, and Freda grew up in that atmosphere. I know there are no class distinctions nowadays, but my son would certainly not expect his daughter to marry his chauffeur, handyman, or whatever he is.'

'But surely, Mrs. Fennal, there is no suggestion that that might happen? She's such a child,' remembering the look of dewy innocence in the pictured face.

'Well, it has been known, and one cannot think only of marriage, Miss Dain,' said Mrs. Fennal, colouring a little at the bare suggestion that there could be any other kind of association between the sexes, and Meriel nodded.

'Yes, I see,' she said. 'But since you have kindly said that you would like me to come to you, Mrs. Fennal, don't you think I'm rather too old as a companion for Freda? I'm twenty-six, you know.'

95

'Anyone as young as she is would not be likely to have any influence over her.'

'And you think I might have?' asked Meriel with a doubtful smile.

'I think she would take to you. I've explained to you that she is, at the moment—difficult. She resents me, though we've always been very fond of each other in the past. It was a great shock to her, her home breaking up so unexpectedly and her faith in her parents shattered, and I feel that she associates me with them, since of course I cannot discuss my son with her nor show her that I condemn him, as indeed I do. She feels too that she has been forced on me, that I don't really want her, which is certainly not the truth, as I love having her. If she had someone quite fresh, someone with no association whatever with her former life and her parents, someone who is *her* friend, her personal property if I may put it that way, she is quite likely to become attached to you and begin to look at life and the future more sensibly. I think that she needs someone to be fond of. She is naturally an affectionate child, but now that she has turned from me, she spends all her affection on her dogs and her cat, which is why I think she has formed this unfortunate association with this man Hewet.'

'She feels that he is something left out of the home she has lost?'

'I think that is probably so, but, as you see I am sure, she must be weaned away, not only from him but also from all that past which can never be hers again. She has all her life in front of her, but it must be a new life and her own, not other people's.'

'You don't think there is any chance of her parents coming together again?' asked Meriel with some hesitation.

'No, frankly I don't. It was an unsuitable marriage for my son. His wife was a very lovely girl, is a lovely woman still, and I feel now that he fell in love with her looks; and when there is nothing behind them, that sort of thing cannot last. I will speak quite openly to you, Miss Dain, as I have a feeling that you will come to us. If there is a divorce, my son will take the blame, and possibly there is some attached to him, but my own belief is that Sadie, my daughter-in-law, has formed the other attachment which has been the cause of the breaking-up of the marriage.'

96

'Freda doesn't know the actual circumstances, I take it?'

'I'm not sure how much she knows, nor what they told her, but she is very bitter against both of them, at which I am not surprised. As far as I personally am concerned, the whole affair is naturally most distasteful, *most* distasteful. One does not expect, in a decent family, to have to accept a thing like divorce. We do not belong to the sort of people who go in for that sort of thing.'

Meriel forbore giving expression to her secret amusement at an attitude which, in the age to which she belonged, was hopelessly out of date, though at the same time she respected it. The matrimonial troubles of some of her friends and acquaintances always made her feel a certain regret that she had not been born into the age when divorces and broken marriages were almost unheard of, or were at least kept out of sight as something to be ashamed of. Now it seemed an everyday and perfectly ordinary affair about which no one thought twice. She had always felt that if she herself married, it would have to be for ever, and for a moment the thought of Frank brought a cloud into her eyes and made her flinch.

But that was as much in the past now as this of the Fennals must be. It might make it easier for her to understand and to help Freda.

Finally it was arranged that she should go to Sandy Combe the following week and that she should remain for a month to see how the experiment worked out. Before doing so, she was to buy a small car, of her own choice and new if possible, and would drive to Cornwall in it. Mrs. Fennal would make an arrangement with her bank so that the money would be available.

'You're trusting me a lot, Mrs. Fennal,' she said.

'As I propose to trust you with the dearest thing I have in the world—my little grand-daughter,' said the old lady with an almost imperceptible shake in her voice, 'I am not likely to feel that I cannot trust you with a few hundred pounds.'

'I won't betray your trust with either,' said Meriel earnestly.

'I don't think you will, my dear,' said Mrs. Fennal, and rose to show that the interview was over.

It was an exciting moment for Meriel when she went, with Louise, to buy the car, the first she had bought, its choice to be to her own taste and the cost not to be the first consideration. She felt, she said, as if she had been given a rub at Aladdin's Lamp!

She did not indulge her own fancy, which would have been for a fast sports car, but chose a small, sedate saloon. Mrs. Fennal had said that later on, when Freda was old enough for the responsibility, she might have her taught to drive, so Meriel was careful to choose a suitable one. It was, at Mrs. Fennal's suggestion, to be registered in the first place in Meriel's name, so that when she finally set off for the long drive to Cornwall, it was with the satisfying feeling that she was driving her own car, if only nominally.

She was touched by Mrs. Fennal's faith in her and was resolved that it should in no way be betrayed. As for this young man, this Brian Hewet, he should promptly and finally be put in his proper place, which was as far as possible from Freda Fennal.

Though the salesmen had assured her that the car had been efficiently run in, she was taking no chances on that and took two days over the journey, arriving near the end of it in the early afternoon.

A lorry-driver, always the most helpful of people on the road, advised her to stop for petrol at Penn Tor.

'There's a pump at Sandy Combe,' he said, 'but it's a one-eyed place and they often run out. You'll find Selter's along the road. About a mile. Good luck, miss.'

'Thanks, and good luck to you.'

She found the garage, which stood isolated at one side of the winding country road, a stretch of open moorland opposite it, and stopped a little distance from it when she saw that another car was having a fill up.

So this was Penn Tor, what could be seen of it?

She remembered what Mrs. Fennal had said about Penn Tor.

'Of course you'll be absolutely free to go anywhere you like, my dear, but I do suggest that when Freda is with you, you keep away from Penn Tor and the chance of meeting this undesirable young man, who has a cottage there. You need not even shop in Penn Tor, as with the car you can go to the larger towns, and the less the village people have to gossip about, the better.'

She had been prepared to find her new place of abode Louise's 'godforsaken hole' but was pleasantly surprised. It was a February day, but mild and windless, and everything was a soft, pearly grey; light clouds on a pale sky, a thin mist hanging like a veil over the moor so that it merged into the sky with no definition of line, a silent place, a place of peace.

It might not be the right sort of environment for a seventeen-year-old girl with a shattered life to mend, but it seemed to offer something her own torn and bruised heart badly needed. She could be happy here.

A surprising thought came to her. She was already contemplating being happy again, looking forward to going on living! Perhaps it was not so badly broken after all, that heart. Perhaps it was only cracked, or not even that? It had taken a bad knock but was a substantial bit of common pottery, not a delicate porcelain affair which had to be preserved from harm behind glass doors!

She saw the pump attendant taking out the petrol pipe from the car he had been filling, drove her own car up behind it and got out to stretch her legs.

The driver of the other car had his head under the bonnet, but he closed it with a snap when he became aware that the space he was occupying was needed, turned towards Meriel with an apologetic smile and then stood with the smile frozen on his face.

They stared at each other, and then Meriel spoke.

'It can't be true,' she said. 'It just can't be!'

'That's how I feel, that it's one of the things that just don't happen.'

The pump attendant was calling out to her not to move her car as the pipe would reach it, and she nodded automatically and remained staring at the man she knew as Robert Barlin.

He looked disreputable, for he had not even taken off his painting overalls after spending the last hour trying to capture something of the pearly mist of moor and sky.

'What on earth are you doing here, of all places?' he asked.

'I'm on my way to a new job,' she said. 'No need to ask what you're doing here!' with a smiling glance at his paint-smeared denims. He used them to wipe his brushes on.

'Don't just disappear again as you always do,' he said. 'We'll have to move the cars from here when you've had your fill-up, but don't drive off again, will you? I'll park just down the road where there's a sort of natural lay-by. Room for you as well. You're not in a desperate hurry to get anywhere?'

'No, not all that desperate,' she said, for she was earlier than she had expected to be.

When she pulled up again behind his car, he was standing waiting for her. She felt an odd lift of her heart at sight of him, though if she had tried to explain it to herself, she would have said that it was the unexpectedness of finding someone she knew in a perfectly strange setting.

He leaned into her car when she had switched off the engine.

'It's magic,' he said, a twinkling light in his dark eyes. 'What shall we do?'

'At least you don't have to feed me again,' she said. 'I had a late lunch and it's too early for tea. I'd like to stretch my legs. Could we walk for a few minutes?'

'Nothing I'd like better,' he said, and opened the door of the car for her.

She had dressed carefully, and she hoped suitably, for her first meeting with Freda. The tawny brown tweed of her suit was the colour of her eyes, and the yellow blouse not very different from the fair, curly hair. She had a small felt hat in the back of the car which she was going to put on just before she arrived at the house.

'Have you been painting here?' she asked.

'Having an unsatisfactory bash at it,' he said, 'but I've scrubbed it. No good. I did do one thing that's not too bad, though. I haven't got it with me, but like to look at the original?'

He had thought about her so often and so much whilst he had been painting the little stream and the gallant, unbreakable little tree that he wanted to see her in the setting which had seemed so right for her.

'Love to,' she said, 'if it isn't far.'

'I'll take you there, though you'll have to walk a bit.'

She showed him her sturdy, flat-heeled shoes which were comfortable for walking as well as for driving.

'I'm no hot-house flower,' she said, 'and I've come equipped for what I imagined Cornwall would be.'

'We'll have to drive a short distance first,' he said. 'Leave your car and hop into mine. It'll be quite safe.'

'I'll lock the doors,' she said, and did so and got into his car beside him, still not quite able to believe that this was happening.

In a minute or two, they left the car at the entrance to a path across the moors and started to walk.

'Do you realize that I don't even know your name?' he asked. 'It's been worrying me.'

'It's Dain, Meriel Dain,' she said, 'though I don't know why it should have worried you!'

'But of course it has. One doesn't like to have been obliged to think of anyone like you as "the girl I towed". So unromantic! Meriel. Yes, of course, it would have to be something like that. I've tried lots of names for you, but none of them fitted. Meriel. Yes.'

'I've always thought it rather a silly name, a fancy name, but a plain, sensible name like—well, Robert, for instance,' with a mischievous glance of her brown eyes which she did not know were dancing, though he did.

It gave him a small shock to realize that that was the name by which she knew him, as Robert Barlin, but he did not undeceive her. He rather liked to feel that she had a name for him which none of his personal friends used.

'Brown,' he observed.

'Brown? I thought it was Barlin.'

'No, your eyes. I knew I was wrong when I made them blue.'

'You made them blue?' she echoed, bewildered.

He chuckled.

'I'll show you, some day,' he said. 'Actually when we get back to my car. I made a sketch of you from memory, not a very good one. I've always felt that you were reproaching me and now I know why. I gave you blue eyes, with that hair.'

She dropped her eyes from his in some confusion. It put things between them on a very different level to discover that he had thought about her enough actually to make a picture of her. Had she been an artist, she could, she thought, have made a picture of him, now that she saw him again and knew that she had re-membered; the squarish face which, in February, had not lost its sun-tan and look of the open air, the tall body built on lean lines

101

though these were no longer of physical ill-health, the dark grey eyes with hazel flecks in them, the untidy dark hair. Was it always untidy? It gave her a queer little tug inside her, almost of tenderness, to see that mop of hair which looked as though it had been pushed back, impatiently, from his eyes as he worked. He looked today younger than she had remembered him. In the painty overalls, a dab of blue on his chin, he looked like neither the man who had rescued her in Agnes's broken-down car nor the one who had dressed up for the Academy.

But his eyes were the same, and his smile; eager, laughing eyes, friendly smile that somehow inspired confidence; not the kind of man to pick up strange girls, she felt, but hadn't they picked each other up, not once but three times now?

He took her to the place by the stream, turbulent now and looking very cold.

'I've always thought of this as your particular spot,' he said.

'Mine? But why on earth?' she asked.

'I don't know. Have never been able to decide. Because it's capable of being so different at different times.'

'Am I that?' she asked, laughing.

'I don't know, but I rather think you are. Some days cool and clear and serene, and that tree that nothing seems able to break, though there must have been storms to bend it like that. Look at the water now. Ice-cold probably, but before the winter set in I could dabble my hands and face in it and find—a soothing sort of peace. Have you come here to find peace, Meriel?' with a change of look and tone that startled her and made her flush with its significance.

'Perhaps,' she said. 'What makes you think I need to find peace?'

'Something about you the first time I met you.'

She gave a determined little laugh. 'That wasn't looking for peace,' she said. 'It was looking for someone who could make my car go.'

'And you found me, but I couldn't. How far are you going to be from me down here, Meriel?'

She realized for the first time that she was going to be very near.

'At—not very far,' she said, and did not know why she didn't want to tell him. It was too soon. He had the power to disturb her and she did not want to be disturbed.

'It's time I started off again,' she said, and they were silent as they walked back to his car, silent until she was in her own again, but the silence seemed to draw them closer. It was not because they could find nothing to say but the shared knowledge that there was no need.

'How am I going to find you again, Meriel?' he asked at the door of her car.

'I can find you,' she said quickly, too quickly. 'Everybody must know where Robert Barlin lives,' and she let in the clutch and shot forward so that he had to step quickly out of the way.

She was glad to see in the driving-mirror that he made no attempt to follow her as she had half feared that he would. He turned his car round and drove in the other direction. It would have looked very fine if she had arrived at her new job with a man in tow! She was glad she had not told him where he could find her. Apart from the fact that she told herself she wanted no second complication in her life, she did not want any man to be able to enquire for her when her main job here was to separate Freda Fennal from a man.

She concentrated her mind on the thought of the job she had come to do.

Cliff Top, as Mrs. Fennal had described it to her, was unmistakable in its position, the high wall protecting it, the white tower jutting above it, and she opened the wrought-iron gates set in the wall, drove in and shut them carefully behind her again.

Poor little Freda, she thought. The iron gates, the wall, the lonely position on the cliff top with the sea dashing against the rocks far below, gave her a sense of security and protection, but she could imagine that they might seem like a prison to the girl whom they enclosed against her will. She was glad that they would have the car. She could get Freda away from the environment which at present irked her; away too, she hoped, from the mental state which, as described by Mrs. Fennal, had given her a picture of someone unnatural and neurotic.

Freda had learned only that day of the coming of Meriel Dain and she had not received the news with any pleasure.

'She's a charming girl,' Mrs. Fennal had said, ignoring the silent hostility of the girl's face and manner. 'I think it would be nice to put some flowers in her room, don't you? There are just a few of the earliest daffodils in that place under the wall. You can cut them all, as there will be plenty more, and bring them up.'

'Up?' asked Freda, affronted.

All the rooms except those in the tower were on the ground floor. There was no other room on the level of Freda's room but her own, and her bathroom, but there was one on the floor below it, though it had never within her recollection been occupied. She had always regarded the whole tower as her own.

'Yes, I thought it would be nicer for Miss Dain, and for you, to be near each other, so Hannah has made the room ready for her, though you and she will probably like to refurnish it,' said Mrs. Fennal pleasantly.

'Is she going to use my bathroom?' asked Freda with an ominous frown.

'Well, that's as you like, my dear, but I am sure she will not mind using mine.'

'Why not Hannah's?' asked Freda, who did not miss the implication.

'That would be putting her in a false position and suggesting that she is a servant,' said Mrs. Fennal, still determinedly pleasant.

'Isn't she?'

'Of course not, dear. She is coming as a guest for a little while until you see how you get on together. She is a few years older than you, of course, but much nearer to you in age than I am, and I feel sure you will find you have quite a lot in common with her. For one thing, she can drive a car and she is bringing one down with her, a new one. It will be yours, my dear, as soon as you are able to drive it safely.'

Freda's face did register a little pleasure at that.

'Mine?'

'I asked Miss Dain to register it in her own name for convenience, as I left her to choose and buy it, but it can be transferred to you.'

'So it isn't really mine,' commented Freda. 'It's hers.'

'Only nominally and for the time being. It has really been bought for you, a little present.'

'From you or from—them?' asked Freda.

'From me, dear. Now run and get the flowers and when you come up you can tell me how you think the room looks and if there is anything else you think she would like in it until you help her refurnish it.'

Freda's first thought had been that once the car was really hers, and this Miss Dain gone again, she would be free to come and go as she liked, to drive herself to Penn Tor and no longer to be dependent on Joe's van or the hired car, or the reluctance of Brian to bring her back.

She made an effort to overcome her ungraciousness and conjured up a smile.

'Thank you, Gran,' she said awkwardly. 'It's very kind of you.'

Mrs. Fennal's kind eyes were damp as she put an arm about the girl for whom her heart ached unceasingly.

'It's a happiness to me, dear child,' she said. 'My only wish is to see you happy too, and I think and hope that Miss Dain will help you. Her name is Meriel, by the way, and I expect she will like you to call her that. Such a pretty name, and a pretty girl too. I'm quite sure you will like each other.'

'How long is she going to stay?' asked Freda with a stab of fear lest it should be an unbearably long visit, cutting her off from Brian for months and months. She felt sure that she would never be able to see him whilst this Meriel Dain, this unwanted and unwelcome new friend, was there, though she had no idea that that was the main purpose of the 'visit' nor that her grandmother knew anything at all about Brian's presence in Penn Tor.

'Well, that will be something for you both to decide about,' said Mrs. Fennal cheerfully, and went upstairs to look at the guest's room, leaving Freda to pick the flowers for it.

There had been no time to have the room redecorated, but as it had not been used, the pale yellow walls and cream paint were still fresh and clean, and though the furniture was old-fashioned and heavy, it was good and had been polished to a soft, fine glow by Hannah. There was a brown carpet on the floor with cream rugs and plain cream curtains at the windows which, like Freda's, looked out at two sides, on moorland and on sea. It would be nice, thought Mrs. Fennal, for the two girls to drive in the car into Launceston, or even to Tavistock or Bodmin, and choose a new carpet and curtains, perhaps even some more modern furniture, to make the room more attractive for the young girl Meriel still seemed to the older woman to be.

Freda brought the daffodils, arranged in a blue vase, and looked round the room without much interest. She was, in fact, still suffering from a sense of having her privacy invaded, since the tower would no longer be all her own. At any rate, she thought rebelliously, she was not going to be invited to share her bathroom. If Gran liked to share hers, well and good. That was her affair, and it was she who had invited this Meriel Dain down. And if Gran didn't like having anyone cluttering up her bathroom with her towels and washing things, there was always Hannah's bathroom which, with her bedroom, was at the far end of the ground floor beyond the kitchen.

Mrs. Fennal was talking about her idea of the two girls going together to buy new things for the room.

'You could perhaps go tomorrow. Have some lunch in Launceston or wherever you decide to go, and to the pictures in the afternoon and get home before it is too dark. If you decide to buy material for curtains, you could make them the next day, on my sewing machine. You could take it into the games room and make a little sitting-room for yourselves at one end of it. Or if Meriel plays table tennis, you can have the little room next to it which really has nothing but boxes and rubbish in it. If you cleared that out and put a table and some comfortable chairs in it, it would make a nice little room for the two of you. I'm sure you will find all sorts of nice things to do together.'

Freda saw what was going to happen. She was going to have all her time filled up now, never allowed to be alone, always having to be with this girl, finding things she wanted to do and doing them with her. When, if ever, would she be able to see Brian again?

The sulky look settled heavily on her face again and Mrs. Fennal spoke with a sharper note in her voice than she had used so far.

'I hope, Freda, that you're not going to make things difficult

106

and uncomfortable for our guest. It is incumbent on us to make her feel welcome or she will certainly not stay.'

'I didn't ask her,' said Freda sullenly. 'She's your guest, not mine, even though she is being put into my part of the house.'

Mrs. Fennal felt very angry at the girl's attitude.

'I won't ask you to show me any gratitude, Freda,' she said. 'That is something which does not seem to exist for your generation. I do ask and expect common courtesy, however, both to me and to any guests who come to the house either by my invitation or yours. As for this being your part of the house, as you call it, let me remind you that you too are here by my invitation and that it is not for you to try to dictate to me what I shall do with my own house. I am ashamed and disgusted. Unless you can make up your mind to accept the best that I can offer you and do for you, I shall have no option but to ask your father to make other arrangements for you. I will not have my life disrupted by a sullen, ungrateful child such as you are proving to be. There are limits to what I am prepared to do for you and you have today come dangerously near them.'

Freda felt a sense of shock. Nobody had ever spoken to her in that fashion before, but in her heart she knew that she had deserved it. If her grandmother ever carried out her threat of asking for her to be taken away, she would indeed be bereft, for where would she go? Who would have her?

She thought desperately and longingly of Brian. If she were cast off, with nowhere to go, would he not then have her? If only she could go to him, now, this minute, let him see how utterly dependent on him she was, could he go on refusing her?

She had for a moment a truer picture of Brian than the one she usually cherished, his face that was kind and strong, his eyes that could laugh at her, tease her, even be angry with her, but which were never filled with the sort of love she tried to see in them. He didn't love her. Nobody did, and now not even Gran. She was lost in the throes of passionate pity for herself. If only she could die, they would be sorry!

'Well, Freda?' asked Mrs. Fennal's voice inexorably.

'I'm sorry, Gran,' she muttered, though without conviction.

'I hope you mean that and will act on it.'

Belatedly, and from fear of what she might have brought on

107

herself rather than anything else, she looked round the room for something else she could do, hating Meriel for having been the innocent cause of all this.

'I think that chair wants a cushion in it,' she said grudgingly. 'I've got one she can have,' and she went to her own room and brought it down. It was one she did not particularly like, anyway.

Mrs. Fennal guessed this, but wisely did not let it appear. She wanted to have this little scene over and harmony restored before the newcomer arrived and received her first impressions.

'That's a good child,' she said in her usual, kind tone. 'Now why not run and make yourself look nice? Put on one of your prettier dresses and do your hair properly, not tied up in that tail like a little horse. You have such lovely hair and it can be so pretty when you like.'

Freda, not to be cajoled by flattery but just as glad as her grandmother that the scene was over, escaped to her room and did as she was told, changed her dress into one of soft green jersey cloth and did her hair in a way which made her look older, but certainly tidier.

Looking at herself in the mirror, she saw what she hated to see, the ever-increasing likeness to her mother; the likeness which once she had fostered so assiduously. It was one reason why now she let herself look as Sadie would never have allowed herself to appear, in old, unbecoming clothes, her hair scragged back and tied in a pony-tail. To look as she did now, well dressed, well groomed, was to remind her afresh of the mother who had betrayed and deserted her, leaving her 'homeless' as she insisted on regarding herself.

When she married Brian, she would have a home again. She was quite certain that in the end she would accomplish that. People in books were always saying 'If you want a thing enough and concentrate your whole mind on it, you will get it.' Well, heaven knew that she wanted this enough, that it filled all her thoughts, so she would get it.

She was living in two worlds, going through the motions of living with her grandmother at Cliff Top, but really existing in her world of fairy-tale with Brian. She fed her imagination on books which she bought and smuggled into the house to read in

108

secret, books whose mere presence in the house would have horrified her grandmother. They were to be bought for a few pence at the little shop in Sandy Combe which sold everything from notepaper to men's corduroy trousers, novelettes cheap in both conception and production, though most of their innuendoes were mercifully beyond her present understanding.

She identified herself with the always beautiful, misunderstood heroine and Brian with the always handsome hero who, in the end, overcame every obstacle placed in their way by those who deliberately and for their own ends thwarted them, and held her clasped to his breast for ever.

It was not to be wondered at that poor Mrs. Fennal, doing her best to make this girl whom she deeply loved happy and contented, was bewildered by the changes in her attitude and behaviour and felt that she was trying to cope with something fluid which changed its shape often and unexpectedly. She could not know that whereas one day Freda was the delicate, high-born lady Gwendolyn languishing for the Man She Truly Loved but whose presence in the ancestral home was forbidden by her cruel guardian who sought her hand, with her fortune in it, for himself; the next day she might be Florrie, the under-housemaid, loved by the son of the house who had been betrothed at birth to the plain daughter of a neighbouring aristocrat, no one but the said aristocrat knowing that the beautiful serving maid was really the Countess Floribelle, the rightful heiress. Or she might be the dashing, high-spirited Saryea, born of poor, struggling parents (high-born in disguise, of course), who retrieves their fortunes by riding the ultimate outsider to victory in the Derby and ends up by marrying a stable-boy who has Loved Her All The Time and worshipped her in secret and has trained the horse to win the race and his bride.

Sometimes the romances ended unsatisfactorily, and the heroine languished and died artistically, forgiving with her last sad breath all those who, crowding to her bedside and pierced with agonies of remorse too late, mourned the passing of one so young and fair.

She did not, however, like the unhappy endings. Only one really pleased her, and that was the one in which the heroine, unbelievably beautiful, wealthy and sought-after by the highest in the land, went into a convent and became a nun rather than be obliged to marry the Man She Did Not Love.

Looking at herself now in the mirror, her dream was the one she liked best, of herself in white satin and bridal veil, walking up the aisle of St. George's in London, to become the bride of Brian, whose face wore the look which she always refused to admit to herself that it never wore: a look of fatuous, idolizing worship of her.

She never got further than going away with him after the reception in a shower of confetti, the admiring comments and envious glances of all the other girls who hadn't married Brian following them. It was not that she did not know what happened afterwards, when the honeymoon really started, but she preferred not to think of it. It was a mystery for which even her imagination waited, but it would be quite all right when it came because it would be Brian.

Brian had just put his arm about her in the departing car and whispered to her, 'Now you are mine for ever, beautiful and adored one,' when she heard the sound of a car stopping outside and went out on her balcony to look down at the girl who, she had now convinced herself, had been brought to Cliff Top as her gaoler.

Meriel got out of the car with a look of pleased interest at the house and a smile for Mrs. Fennal, who had come out to welcome her.

Hannah's voice called up the stairs.

'You'd better come down, Miss Freda. The young lady's here.'

Freda went slowly down the stairs and into the hall, where the two spaniels were already giving the new arrival a rapturous welcome. Richard Fennal had always maintained that if a burglar broke into the house at dead of night, the dogs would be only too delighted to see him to break the monotony of being shut up alone and would say to him, 'Do come in and help yourself, old man,' and obligingly show him where the silver was.

He maligned them, for they were good house dogs and would have recognized on sight anyone who had no right to be there, but obviously they thought that Meriel Dain had every right.

Freda, well mannered from years of training when strangers

110

had to be received, came forward to take Meriel's hand and smiled perfunctorily.

'I'm so absolutely charmed by my first sight of Cliff Top,' said Meriel. 'Is it all right to call you Freda? Miss Fennal sounds so formal. I'm Meriel.'

She had intentionally struck the right note in at once accepting Freda as being of her own generation rather than as a child and Freda relaxed a little, though all she managed to say was a muttered, 'Of course.'

'Freda, take Meriel up to her room, dear, and show her where everything is,' said Mrs. Fennal. 'They'll bring your luggage up, my dear.'

'I shall have to unlock the boot,' said Meriel. 'Coming, Freda? I'll show you how it works. You'll find the lock a bit tricky.'

So it really *was* to be regarded as her car? Freda restrained herself from sending a look of gratitude to her grandmother. She had already said 'thank you' for it and it remained to be seen whether they really did intend it to be her car in fact and not just nominally.

'I do hope you like it,' said Meriel, as the two went out to the car. 'Is the colour all right? When Mrs. Fennal told me that your hair is such a lovely colour, I fell for the green one, though I could have got grey. You wouldn't rather have had the grey?'

Freda's glance took in the good design of the little car, its sturdy, compact look with no fussy details. The lime green was just what she would have chosen herself.

'I think it's lovely,' she said with a shy, reluctant smile.

'That's a relief! You'll find it so easy to drive, too. Very light on the steering but holding the road well.'

'I can't drive,' muttered Freda, unwilling to be cajoled.

'You soon will, if they'll let me teach you. You'll drive well. You have good hands,' which Meriel knew was really nothing to do with it, but it served.

Freda looked at her hands and whipped them quickly out of sight. She had begun recently to bite her nails. They looked quite as horrid as Mrs. Fennal told her they did. If she was going to have to display them on the steering-wheel of the car, she had better manage somehow to stop biting them.

111

'I've brought an application form so that you can get a provisional driving licence,' went on Meriel, unlocking the boot and lifting out her cases, 'and those beastly L-plates too. We'll soon get rid of those!'

'Shan't I be able to go out alone in the car until then?' asked Freda. She might have known there would be a snag in it somewhere!

'Afraid not, but I hope you won't want to, not just yet anyway. I do so want us to be friends, Freda,' but she saw at once that she had said the wrong thing. The girl's face had shut up like a closed book. What was there between the covers, and would she ever be able to find out?

'I'll take you to your room,' said Freda, wooden-faced. 'It's in my tower,' and Meriel heard the faint emphasis on the 'my'.

She exclaimed with pleasure at the sight of the room.

'You could use my bathroom, which is on my own floor above,' said Freda grudgingly, 'but there's another one on the floor below,' and Meriel was not slow to take the hint.

'Then I may as well use that,' she said cheerfully. 'It's only one flight down instead of one flight up, so what's the odds? And there's a basin in here for night ablutions, which is an unheard-of luxury for me! I've never had a fitted basin in my bedroom before!'

'Do you want to wash now or anything?' asked Freda, still distant and unsmiling.

'Just my hands, I think. Isn't it odd how dirty one's hands get, just doing nothing?' though her conscience pricked her a little as she spoke, remembering that she had got her hands dirty by pulling at the bracken as she walked across the moor with Robert Barlin.

'I'm on the floor above if you want to come up when you've finished,' said Freda without enthusiasm. After all, since she would not long be able to prevent this unwanted visitor from invading her room, she might as well get it over right away.

'Thank you. I'll do that,' said Meriel pleasantly, and Freda stalked away and left her.

Meriel sighed. It was not going to be easy. The girl's antagonism was barely veiled and it was obvious that she resented her coming.

112

Still, she had taken on the job and it was not in her not to do to the best of her ability anything she had undertaken.

Poor child, she thought, having her first love affair, if it could be called that, and if it had actually reached that stage. She wondered idly what he was like, this 'undesirable association'. Mrs. Fennal had told her that he had at one time been employed by Freda's father and that this had given him ideas 'above his station'. Meriel had no particular use for 'stations' in that sense, but, seeing Cliff Top and the way which it was obviously run, rather on the standards of past days than by those of the post-two-world-wars present, seeing Hannah in her black-and-white uniform and old William, who had touched his forelock, it was understandable that Mrs. Fennal hadbeen shocked by the knowledge that her grand-daughter was hobnobbing with a late employee of her father (in a 'menial' capacity, Mrs. Fennal had given her to understand). Meriel did not think so much herself of the man. It wasn't quite playing the game to carry on a secret association with his former employer's daughter, taking advantage of a girl of seventeen who might some day be quite a rich woman and was barely out of the schoolroom, with no knowledge of the world and of men.

Well, if she was careful, she could probably prevent them from meeting again, which was what Mrs. Fennal had hoped she would do. She had been expressly asked to avoid Penn Tor, at any rate when Freda was with her, though Meriel felt a sort of prick inside her as she realized that that, for her, probably meant that she would not see Robert Barlin again. Still, she was to be left free herself apart from her guardianship of Freda's comings and goings, and she *might* one day find that she had to go to Penn Tor for something, without Freda of course, and at any rate, according to what Mrs. Fennal had been able to find out, this Brian Hewet was in the neighbourhood only temporarily and might disappear for good at any time and Penn Tor no longer be out of bounds.

Meantime Freda's life must be filled up in some other way, and Meriel fully realized that it would have been a dull and empty thing with no one but two old women for companionship. She was to do needlework and improve her French, Mrs. Fennal had said. Not much fun there for a seventeen-year-old girl! She did

113

not make friends easily nor seem to want them, her grandmother had said, and Meriel herself was choosey about her friends and could understand anyone's reluctance to have ready-made friends foisted on one merely through propinquity.

What other interests might she find in Freda or for her, to wean her away from this Brian Hewet? Mrs. Fennal had mentioned having given her a gramophone for Christmas, which suggested that the girl liked music, but what sort? Meriel hoped wryly that she would not find her charge addicted to rock-'n'-roll, but she was prepared to put up with even that, and she had herself been persuaded to rock-'n'-roll on occasion by the Harlands, who liked it and held wild parties in their flat, to the loud protests of the tenants of the floor below.

Well, if Freda wanted to rock-'n'-roll, then rock-'n'-roll she should. At least there was no one under the games room, of which Mrs Fennal had told her!

What else did she like? Books? Meriel hoped so. She herself had a wide taste ranging from the classics to whodunnits and she could take a good romance in her stride.

Since Mrs. Fennal had said that tea would not be ready for half an hour and she still had ten minutes in hand and did not want to appear too eager to invade the room which Freda had made quite clear was 'hers', she opened one of her cases and took out the few well-read and well-loved books which she had brought with her and started to put them on the bookshelf which was part of the thoughtful arrangements for her comfort.

She fingered *Jane Eyre* affectionately. If Freda had not read it (and it had passed out of the ken of most modern young girls), she might enjoy it. She could not know that Freda had already identified herself with poor Jane and come triumphantly into the arms of her Mr. Rochester (Brian Hewet, of course) at last.

When it was time for her to go down to tea, she went up first to tap at the door of the only room which could be Freda's.

'May I come in?' she asked, and Freda opened the door to admit her grudgingly, showing her the bedroom, the blue-and-white bathroom which again she referred to as 'her bathroom', and the balcony which looked out on a scene that was now shrouded in mist.

'Ugh,' said Meriel with a shiver, when she had been taken out

114

on it, 'I shouldn't want to spend much time out here in this weather!'

'I like it,' said Freda. 'I always like being up here, in all weathers, in my own tower. It's always been mine,' and her tone and face gave definite indication to the guest that there was to be no encroachment on these premises even if she were obliged to accept the guest's presence on the floor below.

'It's lovely to have your own place, like this, isn't it?' asked Meriel, as they prepared to go downstairs. 'I always think one needs some spot to call one's own, where one can be really alone and think one's private thoughts. I'm not one of the people who can't bear to be alone. It always suggests to me that such people have nothing in their minds at all but must depend on other people to supply their thoughts.'

Freda did not reply. She was glad that any rate she was not going to be companioned and spied upon *all* the time.

6

It was difficult to decide how Meriel Dain's guardianship of Freda was working out. Though Meriel felt that by nature the girl was frank and open, Freda was now so reserved and secretive that she felt she knew her no better after a fortnight than she had done on the first day. The name of Brian Hewet was never mentioned and neither of them went in the direction of Penn Tor though they used the little car a great deal.

That, at least, was providing a new interest for Freda. She was keen to learn to drive and quick to respond to Meriel's careful tuition. She showed good road sense and was not unduly nervous.

'When can I take it out alone?' she asked at the end of the fortnight.

'Not just yet,' said Meriel. 'You will have to get your full licence first and get rid of the L-plates.'

'Well—just as far as Penn Tor? We've never been down that way, and it's quite the easiest road round about.'

'Wait a week or two longer and we'll apply for you to have your test the first time there's an examiner in the offing,' said Meriel.

But that afternoon, when they were out in the car, Freda at the wheel, she electrified Meriel by taking the turning which led to Penn Tor instead of the usual one in the other direction.

'I don't think we ought to go this way,' she said, knowing that she could do nothing about it except turn off the ignition and probably provoke a discussion which she would not be able to justify, and she had to sit there and let Freda take them to Penn Tor, past the garage where she had met Robert Barlin, past the turning into the path over the moors where they had walked together.

She found herself looking for the red sports car, wondering what she was to do about it if they saw it, knowing that Freda, though she watched the road and took it carefully, was also looking for someone, this Brian Hewet, of course.

They were both disappointed; and Meriel, relieved, suggested when they reached the end of the village street that they should now turn and go back.

'I've forgotten something,' said Freda. 'I really ought to pop in to see Ruth Collen. She's one of the vicar's daughters and she's completely bedridden and I always used to come down to see her nearly every day and I haven't been all the time you've been here. She'll be wondering what's happened to me. Couldn't you— would you—just drive about somewhere, look at the shops or something, whilst I—I go in and see her? We're quite close to the vicarage.'

'I'll come with you,' said Meriel.

'Oh, no, she wouldn't like that!' said Freda quickly. 'You see, she's very shy of strangers seeing her, never likes anyone she doesn't know to go. She's quite a dear really, and so brave, but her illness makes her like that. It would upset her, make her much worse, if I took you in.'

Meriel was at a loss as to how to combat this. She was afraid

116

to let the girl out of her sight whilst they were in Penn Tor, but they were almost outside the vicarage gates, the house unmistakable with its name outside it, and at that moment a middle-aged woman came out, a shopping basket on her arm.

Freda called out to her.

'Miss Collen!' and started to get out of the car, and the woman turned and came towards it with a pleased smile.

'Freda! We were wondering what had happened to you. Ruth has missed your visits so much,' she said.

'I know. I haven't been able to come. I've been so busy learning to drive the car. It's mine. Isn't it lovely? And this is Miss Dain, who's staying with us. I was just coming in to see Ruth, Miss Collen.'

She was, thought Meriel, completely changed; bright-eyed, alert, a normal, happy-looking girl, and all because she was going to visit a bedridden friend, an errand of mercy!

'Oh, Freda, how kind of you,' said Miss Collen. 'As a matter of fact, you couldn't have come at a better time as she's alone. She always says she doesn't mind, but we never like to leave her alone if we can help it, but I've simply got to do my shopping and Father's taking a funeral, poor old Mrs. Parsons, though really it's the best thing, poor soul, and he will have to go back to the house afterwards.'

'Why not take Miss Dain to the shops, or get her to take you?' suggested Freda, now on the path near the vicarage gates. 'You won't mind driving Miss Collen down and bringing her back, Meriel, will you? I'll stay with Ruth, and you can pick me up again when Miss Collen's finished,' and with a gay wave of the hand she had opened the gates and started to go towards the house.

There was not much that Meriel could do about it and, after all, if she actually left Freda at the vicarage and called for her there when she brought Miss Collen back, what harm could there possibly be?

It transpired that the principal item of Miss Collen's shopping was a visit to the village dressmaker's to have a dress fitted, and though Meriel offered to wait for her, she refused the offer.

'I shall probably be at least an hour,' she said, 'but I didn't tell Freda in case she thought that in those circumstances you might

117

not drive me down. Of course I'm delighted to have the ride in the car, which is quite a treat for me, but I did so want Freda to go in and be with Ruth. If you wouldn't mind very much, Miss Day' (Meriel did not correct her, since it was not important) 'don't call right away to take Freda away. She's so good with Ruth and I know how happy it will make her to have anyone young and bright with her again. If you could—well, there are lots of interesting things to look at, the shops and the quay . . .' vaguely.

Meriel doubted her interest in either the little village shops or the deserted quay, which they had already passed, but she left the voluble Miss Collen at the dressmaker's door and drove off without any real intention of going back to the road to Sandy Combe, and even less of leaving the car where she had left it before and walking across the moor to the spot which Robert had told her he always associated with her.

And when she reached it, there he was, sitting at his easel and so absorbed in his work that he did not at first even know she was there.

Her heart was behaving in a ridiculous fashion, and she knew that Robert Barlin could mean something to her if she let him. What a fool she was to invite a return of that old commotion within her that had already brought her so much unhappiness!

But as if a sixth sense had warned him that she was there, he had turned and seen her and had thrown down palette and brushes, overturned his stool and come striding towards her.

'Meriel! You have a knack of walking out of my dreams,' he cried. 'Or haven't you? Are you still in them so that I'm going to wake up and find that you're not here at all?' and he took her hands, both of them, and looked down into her face from his tall height, surprise, delight, satisfaction in the eyes that eagerly sought her own.

'No, you're real,' he said as her hands, in spite of herself, stayed in his and she did not try to draw away from him or look anywhere else but into his eyes. 'You're really here. This is me and this is you! Have you dropped out of the skies, to get here?'

She laughed.

'Not quite like that. I—I had something to do in Penn Tor, and a bit of time to fill in, so I thought—I might as well get some petrol,' she said, ending up rather lamely.

'With the car facing the other way?' he asked mischievously, for he could see it from where they stood. 'Never mind what brought you here. It may have been petrol, but I prefer to think it was because you've been here before, with me, and thought that by chance I might be here again. Please say that. Don't let's pretend to each other—darling,' the final word coming out daringly, laughter in his eyes which was mingled with something she would not let herself define.

'No,' she said, 'no!' answering, as both knew, not his words but his look, his touch, that endearment which still seemed to hang in the air between them.

She thought, wildly: 'I'm not going to be such an idiot. Not again. Not ever again. Haven't I had enough?'

'I wonder what you're saying "no" to? Not to what I said about not pretending to each other. Why should there be any pretence about being glad to see each other again? If you're not glad, if you hadn't been thinking of me, why did you come here at all, to this particular place?'

His hands were still holding hers and when she tried desperately to draw them away, he held them the more tightly.

She could not lie to him, say that it was not the thought of him which had brought her here. He would not have believed it anyway.

'Please, Robert, let me go,' she said in a frightened whisper.

'Why? Give me just one good reason,' he said, and still held her.

'We—we don't know each other,' she said.

'What difference does that make? We know the one thing that matters, the big thing. All the other things will come later, the little things like what you have for breakfast and all that.'

The look in his eyes, half serious, half laughing, wholly tender, was like a hand stretched out to find her heart, to take it and draw it from her body. To twist and tear to shreds again?

'No,' she said in a frightened whisper. 'No! Not again. Not any more.'

119

'Why do you say "again" like that, and with that look in your eyes? Is there someone else? Was there? You're not married already?'

'Oh no. No,' she said in the same tone of shrinking fear.

She knew that with every moment she was slipping further and further from her own control, along the road she had sworn never to tread again, never to suffer a second time the heartache, the disillusionment, the bitterness which only a woman, loving and betrayed, can know.

'Then what? There was someone else, but there isn't now? If he were still in your life, you wouldn't have said "again". Tell me, darling.'

The laughter had gone from his eyes now, but not the tenderness. His voice was gentle but as inexorable as the hands which would not let hers go. She could not escape. She knew in a panic that the will to escape was leaving her, that in a moment she would not even try any more.

'I loved him,' she said. 'I believed him and trusted him. I can't go through all that again.'

'You won't have to. You can believe me and trust me, Meriel, and love me. I shall never let you down. You're the first girl I've ever said things like this to, or wanted to. I've been waiting for you and knew that somewhere you were waiting for me, and that we should find each other. Now we have. Don't be afraid any more, darling. Don't you know that there's no reason to be? That I'll take care of you always, all our lives?'

And all her defences went down before that look in his eyes from which she could not tear her own, before the tone in his voice, before the words he was saying in which her heart believed even whilst her mind and her memory still told her that it was madness, that she knew nothing about him, that it was only her senses that were being ensnared and chained by him.

She gave a little inarticulate cry and came into the arms that went about her and closed her eyes as his mouth came down on her own, hard, firm, compelling. She could not go on fighting. The enemy was within the gates. It was her own heart.

'And now?' he asked, when at last he took his lips from hers, held his head back a little so that he could look at her, his arms still close about her.

120

'Are you—are you saying that you want to marry me, Robert?' she asked quiveringly.

He smiled at the unfamiliar name by which she still knew him. That was another thing she would have to know about him, but not yet. Calling him by that name seemed to set them in a secret world which belonged only to them.

'What else?' he asked. 'Will you, Meriel?'

She moved in his arms and this time, though reluctantly, he let her go. He saw that she was still afraid and there must be no fear in whatever lay before them.

'I don't know,' she said. 'I don't know. I wish this hadn't happened. Not now. Not yet.'

'Because of this other man? Is he anything at all to you now?'

'No. Not in that way. I don't care for him any more. I couldn't. But—it's too soon. It hurt too much. I was so shattered by it. I'm not a whole person again yet.'

'Will you let me help you to pick up the pieces and put them together again? I can, you know. I'll wait. I won't rush you into anything. I want all of you, not just to have you in my arms and kiss you and make love to you. Of course I want that. But yourself, Meriel, your trust in me. That's what really counts. Life's too long a journey for two people to make up their minds to start on it together without perfect faith and trust. Will you give us a chance to make sure?'

'Oh, I want to, I want to! I do love you, Robert, but——'

He kissed her again, gently this time, closing her lips on the words she could not speak.

'I'll let that be enough for now, my darling,' he said. 'I won't kiss you again, I won't even touch you, until you're sure, as sure as I am, and you're not afraid any more. It's really yourself you're afraid of, not me, isn't it?'

She nodded. She could not speak.

'My little sweet, to have been so hurt! To think that any man could put that look into your eyes! I never shall. Some day, perhaps soon, you'll believe that. When you do, you'll never be afraid again.'

She knew that she must go, not just because of Freda nor because, by being here at all, she was neglecting the duty she had undertaken, but because with every moment she was losing herself the more blindly and might never find herself again. This must not be, she told herself in desperation. This must not happen.

But she knew that it already had happened.

'I must go,' she said, and turned and fled from him, running, stumbling across the rough grass, back the way she had come, away from him but still with him as even then she knew she would always be.

He let her go and did not attempt to follow her. He, too, knew that she would come back. The thread had been spun between them, fine as the mist that was about them but strong as steel.

He did not know how to find her. Why had he let her go like that again? But as he bent down to pick up and start to pack his scattered belongings, he was not afraid that he had lost her. That thread would hold and bring her back to him.

She got into the car, turned it and drove back towards the village. Now that the thought of Freda had returned, she felt anxious and conscience-stricken, and thankful when, nearing the vicarage, she saw the girl walking along the road, her head bent, her whole attitude one of dejection.

If she had indeed hoped to find this man Hewet, she had obviously been disappointed. She felt a stab of relief. She did not deserve to be so lucky.

She pulled up the car and leant over to open the other door without leaving the driving seat. She was not taking a second chance.

'Did you see your friend?' she asked with a welcoming smile.

'No. I mean, yes. Yes, of course. She's always there. She can't walk, you know,' and Freda got into the car and slumped down in the seat and made no suggestion that she should drive.

Meriel thought of the road back to Sandy Cove. What if Robert were on it? She had not seen his car, but if he had it, he would have to come this way and the last thing in the world she wanted just now was that she should see him again.

'Is there any other way of getting back home?' she asked. 'We've been on the top road before. It would make a change to go another way, and—I've remembered that we want some more cotton for that dress we're making.'

122

'Yes. We can go through the village and round by the quay and get back on the road further on, at the fork,' said Freda, her tone brightening a little as she thought there might be a chance of seeing Brian at the quay after all.

She had been bitterly disappointed at not finding him. Since he had not been at the quay when they saw it from the road above, she had felt so sure that he would be in the cottage. But he might possibly have been on the quay, though it had looked deserted. There were a good many boats there, some, like *Sprite*, hauled up. One of them might have hidden him from sight for the moment.

She had spent her usual few minutes with Ruth Collen, irritated by the invalid's glad welcome and wish to detain her.

'It's such a long time since you've been, Freda. Do sit down and tell me all your news. Pull up that comfortable chair. It's so lovely to see you again, and apart from wanting to see you, as I always do, I seem to have got wrong with my knitting and you know how hopeless Mary is with a pattern! Where did I go wrong? You're always so clever about it.'

Freda could not refuse. It was her own pattern and she had started Ruth on it. She took up the jersey and tried to concentrate on it, though her mind was on Brian, on the shortness of the time she had, on the fear that she would hear Meriel coming back with the car before she had had time to slip out of the back door of the vicarage as she had done so many times and across the garden and through the gap in the hedge which would take her into the lane. From there it was only a matter of a few yards to the place where she could scramble over the fence into the garden of the cottage. It took only a few minutes, as she knew well, but today those few minutes were so precious.

Frantically, she found the mistake and put the knitting right and knew that it was unkind when she cut across the invalid girl's soft voice to say that she must go.

'I'll come again,' she promised, 'but I've really got to go now.'

'But you've only just come! Can't you stay till Mary comes back? Have tea with us?' pleaded Ruth.

'I will next time,' said Freda.

'Soon?'

'Yes, quite soon,' she said, and ran from the room.

It had never taken so long, she thought, to get to the cottage, but she reached it at last, threw open the back door which was never locked, and ran inside.

'Brian!' she called breathlessly. 'It's me. Freda,' but there was no answer. He was not there.

It was a cruel disappointment. She had been so sure she would find him there. She could not bear to leave at once. She would listen for the car so that she could dash out and get to the road before it stopped at the vicarage and enabled Meriel to call there.

She looked about her and automatically began to tidy up. Brian never left things in a mess, but some things were out of their accustomed place, books left on the table, a pipe on the mantelpiece, the fire behind the spark-proof guard needing attention.

She replaced the books and the pipe, made up the fire and went out to the woodshed for more logs and banked them up beside the hearth. She filled the kettle and set it on the oil-cooker without lighting the burner since she did not know how long he would be. She set the tray for tea, and, hoping against hope, put two cups on it. There might just be time for her to have it with him, and it looked companionable anyway.

But she had to realize at last that there would not be time, that he would not even be back before she had to go, and she went into the living-room, found paper and pencil and wrote him a note.

Darling Brian, she wrote, scrubbing the tears from her eyes, *I've been waiting for you. It's such ages since I've seen you but I'll tell you why later. Please write to me. Don't telephone me in case someone else answers. I wish you had the telephone here but I'll come again soon. I'll manage somehow. It's awful not seeing you. I love you.*

Your loving and lonely
Freda.

Then she heard the car and ran to the road.

When Brian read the note, he crumpled it up and put it into the fire with a gesture of irritation. What a silly child she was! How was he to get rid of all this unwanted affection without cutting her out entirely and telling her plainly that he did not want to see

124

her again? He had promised her father that he would 'keep an eye on her', but he had never imagined that it could mean getting involved in such an idiotic position.

He was sincerely fond of the child, as he always had been, but after all, that was all she was, a child in spite of her belief that she was grown-up and her affectation of grown-up ways. He could not take seriously these ridiculous protestations that she 'loved' him; there was something unhealthy about it. She should be with people of her own age, growing up with them, playing games or whatever one did at seventeen, not indulging in these ridiculous ideas of marrying a man years older, and who had no such ideas at all himself.

Marrying Freda! What on earth would the Fennals think if they could have read her absurd note, or knew the sort of thing the child said to him? Why couldn't her grandmother look after her properly, find her something to do and someone to do it with?

Perhaps some day soon he could talk to Meriel about her, tell her the whole ridiculous story, ask her what he could do about it. The best thing that could happen, for Freda, was for him to be openly engaged to Meriel so that the silly child would realize that she could not go on indulging herself in all these fancies.

He threw aside the thought of Freda and let himself think of Meriel instead; Meriel, his girl, *his*.

There was no doubt in his mind. She had trembled in his arms, but she had kissed him. He could still feel her lips beneath his own, soft, willing, the lips of a woman in love. She had been afraid, but she would not always be. He thought, murderously, of the other man she had loved, the man who had hurt her so badly and set that look in her eyes, that shrinking fear in her heart, fear of being hurt again, of letting herself love again. What a swine the man had been! What a fool to have had Meriel and lost her!

But there was joy there too, for in losing her, he had given her to Brian—Robert Barlin!

He thought tenderly of the way she said that name. Perhaps he would take it as his own. As Robert Barlin he had done the only worth-while thing he had yet accomplished. By that name he was already known by the kind of people who really counted with him. He could paint. He knew that he could paint, and that the one picture which had brought him that first recognition would not be his last or his best. The world had gone crazy over materials things, crazy for power, crazy with greed and the fear which it brought with it. Science and the terrible potentialities of what it had discovered and created, the atom bombs, machines hurled into space and given a place in the God-made universe, to what terrible end no one could know—such things men worshipped and feared but their progress could not be stopped, even if it meant eventual annihilation.

But, in spite of it all, there still remained in the hearts of men beauty and peace, things which would live and could not be destroyed even if the world destroyed itself.

Surely the human soul would remain, somewhere, in some shape or form? Love would remain, and faith and trust.

He went outside and, in the darkness, walked up the straggling street and climbed the familiar path to the top of the cliff. Penn Tor lay in its shelter, the village tucked into a hollow in its side, the sea below with the little natural harbour which had brought the village into being.

It was a clear, cold night and the crescent moon lit the water so that it sparkled with tiny, phosphorescent points of light. Nothing moved but those points of light. Nothing seemed to be alive or even to exist but the sea which he loved and which was surely eternal.

It brought him peace, as it always could, peace and the feeling that this must go on, that it was ageless, changeless, infinite. What power had mere man to destroy what God had created? He could destroy what he had created himself, the palaces and the factories, the cities where men lived herded together and lived their feverish little lives, the gold and the oil they worshipped, and that made all their little wheels go round.

But they could not destroy *themselves* in the end. They could not destroy him and the power which God had put into him, the soul which no man could make. The part is not greater than the whole, nor does God cease to exist because men deny Him.

When Brian went in, he was at peace.

He could not know the full extent to which a young, innocent and naturally affectionate girl could delude herself in her own mind, when so cruelly torn from all the things on which that affection had been spent.

Of all those things, only Brian remained. She had passed the stage at which her dogs and cat would have been enough. She needed to centre her love on a human being and, beginning to become a woman, she turned to a man. She was feeding her imagination on the sort of books she read in secret, hiding them in a locked drawer and guarding the key. With them in her mind, she was dramatizing herself and her position and constantly seeking ways in which she might escape from it.

Whilst she had been able to get from her grandmother the money for the hire of the car from Penn Tor when Brian drove her back, she had been saving it, adding it to the thirty shillings a week pocket money which she could rarely be prevailed upon to spend. There was a vague idea in her mind that it would in the end enable her to leave Cliff Top and the kindly woman who had become, in her thoughts, the keeper of her prison. She did not know yet what she was going to do when she left her grandmother's home, but if she had the fare to London and enough to keep her for a few weeks, she felt sure that she would be able to find some sort of job which would keep her until, able then to show Brian that she was really grown up and responsible, he would see that it was not a fantastic idea for them to marry and live together. Whilst she was obliged to live as she did now, he would go on thinking of her as a child.

Now that Meriel was here, and the convenient visits to Penn Tor to see Ruth Collen had stopped, she had lost that small source of income, and when Meriel had gone and she was able to go in the car by herself it would be reasonable for her grandmother to expect her, out of her own money, to provide herself with petrol, or at least some of it.

Somehow, before that happened, she must contrive to add to the little store of money which was also in the locked drawer. Mrs. Fennal was not extravagant, but she lived well and spent money liberally, gave quite largely to the church and to certain charities in which she was interested, and Freda watched it going out jealously. Who really needed it more than she did? Wasn't she an 'orphan'? Wasn't she a 'distressed person'? Wasn't she homeless, just as much as they were?

The first time she actually stole money, she felt guilty and ashamed and would have put it back had she been able to see a way in which she could do it undetected. It was, in its way, a particularly mean little theft.

Hannah was out one day, and Mrs. Fennal taking her afternoon nap; and Meriel had gone to Maryworthy, the little town on the other side of Sandy Combe, to do some shopping for herself, Freda having chosen to stay behind.

When she heard a knock at the back door, she went to answer it and found a woman there who had occasionally helped in the house and who had an epileptic son who was a great trouble and expense to her.

Having been told that Hannah was out and Mrs. Fennal resting, she poured out her troubles to Freda, saying that her son had at last been taken into hospital at Bodmin and that she wanted to go and see him but had not the money for the fare. She had come to ask Mrs Fennal to lend her two pounds, which she promised faithfully to pay back as soon as she could. Freda knew that her grandmother, sorry for the woman, had given her money before and that, whatever the woman promised as to its repayment, she was never able to return it nor would Mrs. Fennal have asked for it.

'I'll ask my grandmother,' said Freda when she had listened to the long, involved tale, 'but she may be asleep.'

She hoped that she would be. It annoyed her to think that in all probability the money would be forthcoming. She had become miserly about money even when it was not her own.

But at her soft tap at the bedroom door, Mrs. Fennal called to her to come in.

'It's Mrs. Larch, Gran. She wants to borrow two pounds to go and see her son in Bodmin,' she said, and repeated the substance of the story.

'Poor soul,' sighed Mrs. Fennal. 'I won't lend it to her, of course, I'll give it to her, but don't tell her that. Tell her I expect her to repay it. You know the little drawer in my bureau, dear, the one inside the flap part. I put bits of loose money in there— what I have over at the end of the week when I have paid the bills and so on. I never know quite what is there, but there's certainly more than two pounds. Better give her three, dear. If she thinks she owes as much as that, she won't come back for more just yet. Here, take my keys. This is the one. Mind you make her understand that it is a loan. It's so bad for people to *ask* for charity. You can give me the keys back when I have finished my rest.'

Freda took the three pound notes from the drawer, fingering them as she went slowly back to where Mrs. Larch waited, and at the last moment, before she had the conscious thought of intention, she slipped one of them into the pocket of her cardigan and gave Mrs. Larch the other two.

The woman's eyes swam with tears.

'Oh, Miss Freda, I'm that grateful,' she said. 'Tell your grandma that if I can't pay it back soon, I'll come and work for nothing till it's paid,' and she went off, still mumbling her thanks and mopping her eyes.

After she had done it, Freda was terrified at having yielded to such a temptation. She stood a long time with the keys in her hand, trying to believe that she was going to put the pound note back in the drawer. If ever Mrs. Larch referred to the loan again, which she was not likely to do, Freda could always say that she had mistaken what her grandmother had said about giving the three pounds.

But Mrs. Larch would not mention it. She would not, in fact, come anywhere near Cliff Top for a long time, conscious of the unpaid debt and many others which had preceded it.

The pound note, folded small, lay in Freda's pocket all day, and she was terribly conscious of it, but when she went to bed she transferred it to the locked drawer.

She had been so right in thinking that Mrs. Larch would not come to Cliff Top for a very long time. She was run over and killed by a car as she left the hospital after seeing her son.

The relief to Freda in knowing that her theft would never be discovered was wiped out by the tragic way in which that relief had come. She vowed that she would never steal from anyone again.

But she did.

One day when her grandmother, most unusually, left the keys about, she yielded to the temptation to take money from the drawer, only a few shillings, but it was a start. After that, obsessed with the idea of saving enough to get away from Sandy Combe, she contrived to take small amounts in varying ways. She added a few pence here and there to the supposed cost of things she bought for the house when she and Meriel were out shopping together.

'Butter up again?' asked Meriel. 'We won't go there any more for it. It's cheaper in the other shops.'

Or: 'Fancy all that for a cabbage! Next week we shall be able to cut our own from the garden.'

Once Meriel wanted a zipp fastener to replace a broken one and asked Freda to get it whilst she went into another shop. Freda knew that there was one in her grandmother's work-basket which had never been used and was like the one Meriel wanted. When they got home, she managed to find it, put it into a paper bag which had come from the same shop, gave it to Meriel and accepted the money for it.

It had become too easy and the amount in the locked drawer was steadily increasing. She refused to pay for petrol, but had it put down to her grandmother's account at the Sandy Combe garage.

'Gran can't give me a car and expect me to pay for petrol,' she said, when Meriel protested.

'But you can afford to pay for it sometimes. What do you do with your money?' asked Meriel, half angry, half laughing. She often paid for the petrol herself.

'Whatever I do with it, I'm not wasting it on petrol,' said Freda calmly, and Meriel knew she was not going to get anywhere by pursuing the matter.

She felt that she was not, in fact, getting anywhere at all with the girl whose friendship and confidence she had hoped so greatly to win. Freda was reserved to the point of secretiveness and Meriel knew that she had no more idea of what went on in her mind than she had done when she came to Cliff Top a month ago. No mention had ever been made of the man, Brian Hewet, and Meriel felt she could be pretty sure that they were not meeting, as she gave them no second opportunity after the risk she had taken, and for which she never ceased to reproach herself, on that one day they had gone to Penn Tor.

What she could not know was that Freda, daily growing more bitter at her inability to see Brian, and waiting for the letter which never came, had only one thought in her mind, which was to escape from the place which she had persuaded herself was a prison, the three women in it her gaolers and therefore her enemies, bent on keeping her there for life, or at any rate until Brian had gone away and it would be impossible for ever afterwards to find him. She even began to suspect that they knew of her love for him, though she had guarded her secret so carefully. For what other reason could they be keeping her away from Penn Tor and any chance of seeing him, as she realized they were keeping her? Meriel's reasons for not going in that direction when they went out were so various and often so thin that there could be no other reason. Even when, in desperation, she insisted that she must go to see Ruth Collen again, Meriel not only went to Penn Tor with her, after a private consultation with Mrs. Fennal, but went into the vicarage with her, stayed in Ruth's room all the time, and left with her. Whatever she might have said about the invalid girl's objection to seeing strangers, it was not borne out by Ruth's reception of her, for it was warmly welcoming and she begged Meriel to come again.

If she were going to get away before Brian left the district (and she had no idea of the duration of his arrangement with Mr. Preecy), she must do it soon.

She counted again, as she had counted many times, the amount of money she had saved, but it filled her with apprehension. She had set as the least amount that would serve her purpose at fifty pounds, and however many times she counted the money in her drawer, it did not come to more than thirty-two pounds and a few odd shillings.

In amassing this, having started with the collection from her grandmother of the fares for the hired cars she had not used, and progressing through the pound she had not given Mrs. Larch and the small defalcations in the household shopping, she had lost all sense of wrong-doing by theft. The bitter repetition in her mind was that, as they had robbed her of everything she had, she was justified in robbing them of anything she could get. The shock her parents had given her, and the complete change in her circumstances and expected future, had warped and twisted her mind at a critical stage in her life. The standards which her parents had set her, of truth and honesty and honour, had been torn down for her by their own failure to observe them and she threw into the scale against them any wrong-doing of her own. She was, she told herself deliberately, what they had made her.

It would take her months to reach her goal of fifty pounds, for now, even though Mrs. Fennal had made no demur about the petrol bills, she was being obliged to spend some of her money on the things which she and Meriel did together. Meriel was teaching her to make her own clothes, a thing which in other circumstances she would have enjoyed, but her grandmother thought it only right that she should herself pay for the materials she used, saying that it would give her a sense of values and teach her to spend money wisely. They were not expensive materials, chiefly gay cottons for the summer, but she chose cheaper ones than either Mrs. Fennal or Meriel approved. Even so, she could not now save all her thirty shillings a week. There were other things too. Though the meat for the dogs came out of the general housekeeping money, Mrs. Fennal said that as they were Freda's dogs, she should be willing to contribute towards their keep and buy their biscuits, not a heavy item but one which had to be paid week by week, and not even with her feverish object in view could she let those devoted friends suffer. She did not know what she was going to do about her pets when she left Cliff Top, as she could not take them with her, but she consoled herself with the thought that they would be well taken care of even if she were not there, and as soon as she and Brian were married, she could have them.

Desperate for the completion of the fifty pounds, she seized one day on a daring scheme which suddenly presented itself to her mind.

When her weekly registered letter arrived from the bank and had been placed by Hannah as usual beside her plate at luncheon, Mrs. Fennal mentioned it with an anxious frown.

'Where do you keep your money, Freda?' she asked. 'I am not very happy about it coming to the house in cash every Friday like this, in case there are people who know. Don't you think you ought to open a banking account and have a monthly cheque sent to you? You must have quite a little store of money somewhere now, and there have been a number of small robberies round about lately. I myself saw a strange man, a rather suspicious-looking character, lurking about on the cliff path yesterday and looking up at the house. Do you keep the money in your room?'

'Yes,' said Freda defensively, and it was at that moment that the idea was born.

If the money were stolen, or if her grandmother thought it had been stolen, she would almost certainly offer to replace it. She was like that, the girl had to admit grudgingly. She would not let her lose all her money, though afterwards she would not allow her to keep it in the house.

But 'afterwards' would not then matter.

'Shall I go and get it, Gran?' she asked, her heart beating almost to suffocation, though she managed to appear perfectly calm.

'Yes, dear, I think you should. I'll put it in as safe a place as I can find, perhaps in that little strong-box in my room where I keep my papers. Then tomorrow you and Meriel can go to the bank and open an account there for you.'

Freda ran up to her room, leaving Mrs. Fennal and Meriel at the table with Hannah carrying in the lunch.

The money was in a paper bag. She unlocked the drawer and took it out, left the drawer unlocked without any thought of its other contents, looked round feverishly for some place in which to hide it and then quickly and neatly, with her nail scissors, cut the stitches along the edge of her mattress for a few inches, pushed the paper bag with the money in it into the slit and pulled the edges together again. There was no time now to sew it up, but as she always made her own bed, and it was, of course, made for the day, it was not likely to be discovered. Tonight she would sew it up.

She opened the drawers of her dressing-table and her wardrobe doors and left them open and created such confusion as she would have made in a quick and frantic search, saw that one of the windows leading to the balcony was ajar, as it usually was whatever the weather, and ran downstairs again, her heart jumping uncomfortably, her hands hot and shaking, her legs trembling.

133

She had no need to pretend anything about that. The fear that was almost choking her made such effects real.

She flung open the door of the dining-room, knocking a dish out of Hannah's hand as she did so.

'It's gone!' she announced. 'My money's gone! Somebody has stolen it!'

There were confused cries, questions, alarm, and they all trooped up to the tower room, Freda by now in quite genuine tears, for the strain on her nerves had been tremendous.

She showed them where she had kept the money and the drawer was ransacked again. Fortunately, she remembered now, she had removed some time ago the paper-backed novelettes which she had originally kept there and had managed to destroy them by stealing downstairs at night and putting them into the kitchen boiler, a few at a time until they were all gone. They had served their purpose and since the coming of Meriel she had had less time to indulge in surreptitious reading. She was always afraid that Meriel, though she never came into the room without knocking, might find her with them.

They turned out the room, searching everywhere in case, as Mrs. Fennal suggested, she had put the money somewhere else and had forgotten it. As if she would! Her heart was in her mouth more than once when one of them came near the bed, and once Hannah actually suggested that the packet might be under the mattress! Freda helped her to lift it and search under it, keeping her own hand carefully over the slit in the seam, and at last they all had to come to the conclusion that the money was not there and must have been stolen.

'I shall have to inform the police, of course,' said Mrs. Fennal, much worried, 'though it always seems to be so difficult for them to trace actual money, not like jewellery which can be recognized if it is found. I must try to get a clear picture of that man I saw on the cliff path. If your windows were open, it *would* have been possible for an agile man, used to such things, to climb up to the balcony. I think you had better go down to Penn Tor this afternoon, Meriel, and tell the police about it. You need not go, Freda, my dear. It would be so upsetting for you to have to go to the police station, and they will come up here to ask you any questions.'

134

Freda decided that she would not ask to go. She would have to move very carefully now and have time to decide what she was going to say to the police before she had to face them.

'Thank you, Gran,' she said tremulously. 'I don't think I'd like to go. I'd rather stay here quietly with you. I—I feel so upset at losing my money.'

'Well, let us go down and have our interrupted lunch and we can talk about that,' said Mrs. Fennal with the utmost kindness, putting her arm about the girl. 'You stay here, Hannah, and put the room straight again, will you?'

'I can do that, Gran,' said Freda quickly, but Mrs. Fennal led her firmly away.

'No, darling, Hannah will do it,' she said. 'You'll feel all the better for a meal, and I think it would do you good to have a small glass of port, for once.'

'I'll stay and help Hannah,' offered Meriel, thinking that the two would be better on their own for a short while. She longed above all to see a closer relationship between these two, the one so anxious and loving, the other so antagonistic. She did not miss the scared look the girl gave her nor her reluctance to be led away from the room, but she misinterpreted it.

When they were alone, Freda finding it very difficult to swallow her food, Mrs. Fennal spoke kindly, and said the very thing which her grand-daughter had hoped she would say and which was the prime cause of all this.

'I know you're very much upset about this, my dear,' she said, and of course we must never risk such a thing again, but I don't want you to lose your money like this. The police may be able to get it back, but if they can't, I can afford to lose it better than you can and I'm going to give it back to you. How much was it?'

Freda swallowed hard. She had anticipated this moment, but now that it had come, she was torn between two desires, the first and better of them to tell her grandmother the truth, the second, and winning one, to take as much advantage as she could of the situation. If she got another thirty-two pounds, she would have more than the fifty she wanted; on the other hand, if she asked for more than the thirty-two, she was sure she would get it, and the fifty planned for had been in her mind the bare minimum.

135

'F—fifty pounds, Gran,' she said, choking on the figure.

Mrs. Fennal looked astonished.

'Fifty pounds, my dear?' she echoed. 'That is a great deal of money, much more than I should have thought you could save out of your allowance.'

It would, in fact, have been impossible for her to save it in the time, and Freda blundered on, her face blanching, her eyes avoiding her grandmother's.

'My—my father sent me some,' she said. 'Quite—quite a lot.'

Mrs. Fennal was silent. She knew that this was not true. Only a few days before she had had a letter from her son in which he had spoken of the allowance he made to his daughter through the bank.

I should have liked to send Freda a little money in addition to the thirty shillings a week, he had written, *but as you made such a point of my not giving her more, and I promised you that I would not do so, I have not sent her anything and will not do so without your consent.*

Mrs. Fennal believed him. He trusted her judgment implicitly where Freda was concerned, now that he had made her responsible for her, and he knew that she had been adamant that the girl should not be given too much money until she had proved herself wise in dealing with what, in Mrs. Fennal's opinion, was already too much. Richard had not sent her money and would not do so.

She was greatly perturbed, not only as to where the girl had obtained the money but also because she was lying to her. There had been several occasions since she had undertaken the charge of Freda when she had more than suspected that she did not always tell the truth, but she had never let the girl know of such suspicions, fearing to open still further the cleft between them. But she had worried about it a great deal. As a child, Freda had always been transparently honest and truthful, not even trying to shield herself from the consequences of any little act of wrong-doing but owning up to it honestly. The fact that she was no longer truthful was yet another evidence, to her mind, of the

136

harm which had been done to the child by the defection of the two she had loved best in the world.

What could she say now, however? She could not go on letting these things pass, but she must have time to make up her mind how best to deal with this one.

'I will write you a cheque tomorrow, my dear,' she said, 'and you can go to the bank and open an account with it and Meriel will show you how to use it and to write your own cheques when you need to draw any of it out. The dogs seem to be getting restless, so why not take them out for their run now if you have finished your lunch?'

Freda rose from her chair thankfully and called the dogs to her.

'Thank you, Gran. About the money,' she said jerkily, and went quickly from the room.

She would have liked to run upstairs to make sure that all was well in her bedroom and that the paper bag had not been found, but as she went into the hall, the dogs leaping joyfully about her, she saw Meriel and Hannah on the stairs and went out of the house instead.

7

MRS. FENNAL knew as soon as Meriel came into the room that there was more trouble in store for her.

'Can I talk to you, Mrs. Fennal?' she asked, her face pale and strained.

'Have your lunch first, my dear,' said Mrs. Fennal, but Meriel shook her head.

'I can't,' she said. 'I couldn't eat it. I'll have something at tea time. May we go into the other room? I see that Freda has gone out with the dogs.'

'Come into my bedroom, dear. We shall not be disturbed in there. I'm afraid something very unpleasant has happened.'

Meriel told it as quietly and evenly as she could.

First of all, in remaking the bed, they had found the money. Meriel handed the paper bag to Mrs. Fennal, who took it out and counted it automatically.

Thirty-two pounds, not fifty, and not only was the top of the bag turned over, but it was held by a paper-clip, and the amount noted on the outside in Freda's unmistakable figures.

She laid it down and waited, knowing that there was something else.

'We found this too,' said Meriel. 'It was in the writing-case in the drawer in which the money was supposed to have been kept. I have not read it all, but when I saw the beginning of it, I felt that you ought to see it.'

Her hand was shaking as she gave Mrs. Fennal the sheets of notepaper covered with Freda's handwriting.

My darling, beloved Brian, the letter ran,

How can I bear it until we are together again, your arms around me and your burning kisses on my lips. Do you remember what you said to me the other night when I crept out of the house and you were waiting for me in the garden as you have done so many times? You said that my eyes are like stars in a velvet sky, drowning your soul in their sweet delight.

Oh, Brian, my beloved, my only love, when will you come to me again and take me in your arms and whisper that you love me? I only live for the day when you can come and take me away with you for ever, out of this dreadful prison where I am incarser—incercar—

The writing finished there. The spelling of the word had evidently been too much for the writer, and she had either given up the attempt or postponed it until she had access to the dictionary which was kept downstairs.

Mrs. Fennal read it to the end, in horror, disgust and a terrible fear.

It did not occur to her that Freda had drawn wholly on her unhealthily fed imagination, nor that she had never intended to send the letter at all. She had written such letters before, tearing them into minute pieces afterwards or burning them. By sheer ill-chance, having been interrupted by the sound of Meriel's voice asking if she might come in, she had pushed the letter into the writing-case and into the drawer and forgotten that she had done so.

'I was not prying,' said Meriel in a choked voice. 'I was still looking for the money and wondered if we had looked in the writing-case. This was on the top. I don't know now whether it is right to bring it to you, but . . .'

She turned away. She could not go on. She was as shocked and distressed as was Mrs. Fennal.

'It was quite right. If this sort of thing has been going on, of course I must know. But how—when—oh, Meriel, this simply crushes me! What am I to do? What can I do? What can anyone do if—if—anything really *wrong* has happened to her?' her agonized meaning unmistakable.

'I can't really believe that,' said Meriel, deeply compassionate for Mrs. Fennal, terribly angry with Freda and with this man Hewet who had been carrying on in this unspeakable fashion with a young girl, had put such ideas into her head and given her such knowledge. 'Not with a girl brought up as Freda has been. It may be just—silliness. There can't be real experience, nothing really *bad*.'

'Perhaps you'd better read the letter,' said Mrs. Fennal, and passed it to her.

Meriel read it and, in spite of her perturbation, she had to smile.

'Such absurd expressions,' she said. 'He must be a very silly man, as silly as Freda herself, probably trying to impress her and pandering to her romantic ideas. Stars in a velvet sky, indeed! I don't think any man who is really serious about an affair would talk like that. I rather gathered from you when we spoke of him that he is not a man of her standing and education. He probably read things like that somewhere and said them, as I suggested, to impress her.'

'He is not of her social standing, of course, but I would not say that he is uneducated. Freda's father always made a great fuss of him and I believe he helped with his education, so he is not exactly without it.'

Meriel was looking at the letter again.

'She had a bit of trouble over "incarceration",' she said. 'Perhaps that was why it ended so abruptly, and at least, it was never sent.'

'All that about this being a prison, and wanting the man to take her away—it's all so hurtful, Meriel, so terribly wounding! I have tried so hard to make her happy, getting you to come here, and giving her the car and everything, and today, just now——'

She broke off and sat back in her chair, closing her eyes, a look of exhaustion, of sudden old age, coming into her face. Freda had been prepared not only to take from her the actual amount she pretended she had lost, but to rob her, actually rob her, of even more.

Why? Why did she want so much money?

The inference of that, and of the letter, seemed obvious. She wanted it in order to get away, to have money for this man who presumably had none, or at any rate very little.

'It must be put a stop to,' she said at last, when Meriel had remained silent, looking at her in deep compassion, aware that there was nothing she could say which would help her. 'At all costs, it must be ended, the whole association, the possibility of their meeting again. If necessary, I shall have to ask you to take her away. Whilst she stays here, even if we could force him to leave the neighbourhood, he could always find her.'

Meriel frowned uncertainly.

'I think that should be the last and rather desperate resort,' she said. 'She has been dug up by the roots once and lost her home and her own people, and that is probably the real cause for all this. If she is dug up again——'

'Yes. Yes, that is so,' agreed Mrs. Fennal wearily, passing her hand across her brow.

She felt tired and old and ill. Meriel longed to be able to do something to relieve her and the thought of Robert Barlin came into her mind, blowing through it like a fresh breeze amidst sultry heat. She longed to see him, to confide in him, to tell him all about this and ask him what she could do. He was of her own generation. He would be disturbed, even shocked, but he would not be numbed by it as anyone of Mrs. Fennal's generation and ideas was numbed. He knew these things happened even with girls of Freda's type and upbringing. Also he was a man, and if anyone had to see Brian Hewet, talk to him, put the fear of God into him and clear him out of Freda's reach, it was surely a man like Robert?

But first perhaps she herself ought to see this man, get some idea what sort he was and where he was most likely to be vulnerable. She shrank from it, but it might be her duty.

'Would you—would you like me to see this man? See if there is any way in which he could be induced to disappear and let Freda alone?' she asked hesitatingly.

Mrs. Fennal's brow cleared a little.

'Would you, Meriel?' she asked. 'Would you really do that? It seems such a dreadful thing to ask you to do, but I simply do not know how to act for the best. Of course Freda's father is the right person to do it, but he is not available, and her mother, even if she could be reached, would be worse than useless. She is a light woman,' she continued harshly. 'I shall never believe that my son is the cause of this breakdown in their marriage, though he is ready to take the blame. It seems that Freda is like her mother.'

'It may not be anything like as serious as we fear,' said Meriel gently.

'I hope not. Indeed I hope not, but it is quite obvious from this appalling letter that the man has been making some sort of love to her and she to him. Quite disgusting, of course, even if Freda had not been a mere child. However, if you really will go and see him and try to do something, I shall be most grateful. Take the car, of course, and get away before Freda comes back. I understand that the man has been employed in some capacity on the boat, in which case you may find him at the quay, or somewhere about there.'

Meriel lost no time in getting out the car and driving towards Penn Tor.

First this man Hewet and then, if she had any luck at all—Robert.

The most direct way led past Selter's garage and the path that went across the moor, and when she came to the point at which this joined the road, she saw with a leap of her heart that the red

141

sports car was parked there, but empty. He was probably painting somewhere not far away and she longed to stop the car and go to him, but felt that she must keep to her decision to see Brian Hewet first.

She drove down to the quay, left the car for a few minutes, and went to where several boats lay at anchor, amongst them two whose names she could read, *Sprite* and *Sally May*. *Sprite* looked very spruce, *Sally May* smaller and not quite as elegant and smart, but both looked as though they had had care and attention.

No one appeared to be on them, though both were fastened to the quay and not anchored a little distance off as the majority were.

When she enquired of a fisherman busy with his nets as to where she was likely to find Mr. Hewet, he looked at the two boats and then around the little harbour and shook his head. Mr. Hewet had been down there that very morning, he said, bringing the two boats in and letting their engines run for a time, but he seemed to have gone now.

'Can you tell me where he lives?' she asked, and when the cottage was pointed out to her, she thanked him and drove to it and knocked at the door.

There was obviously no one in. She walked round and looked through the windows, but there was no sign of life and she sighed, partly in disappointment but also, she had to admit to herself, with some relief. There was now nothing to stop her from going to find Robert. She would have to tell him the story without being able to say what kind of man Brian Hewet was.

She had experienced a revival of the feeling of guilt when she saw how near the cottage was to the vicarage and the risk she had taken that day in letting Freda out of her sight in that very place, but it could not be helped now. If Freda had been able to seize the opportunity of seeing Brian Hewet on that occasion, it was only one of the many times they must have contrived to meet. It made her lip curl in disdain to think of him lurking about outside Cliff Top after dark, waiting for Freda to go down to join him for a love scene with the rest of the household asleep, with no idea what was going on. He must be a very nasty piece of work indeed.

But all thought of Brian Hewet went out of her mind when,

gaining the upper road again, she saw that the red car was still there.

She parked her own close to it and picked her way down the muddy path and found him where, perhaps unreasonably, she had been sure she would find him, in *their* spot, hers as he had told her he thought of it.

He saw her before she reached him and came striding towards her and caught her in his arms.

'My darling! My little love! Heaven bless you for coming! It's been so long since I've seen you that I had almost made up my mind to defy all your commands and go and look for you. Would you have minded so much if I had? Have you missed me as much as I've been missing you?'

She could say nothing, do nothing, think of nothing in that first moment but that she was in his arms, in their security, in the feeling that she was no longer alone, fighting a battle against heavy odds.

She returned his kisses, linking her arms about his neck, though to do so she had to let him lift her right off her feet and hold her there, happy and triumphant.

'Now say you don't love me!' he commanded. 'Now say that it's too soon and that you're afraid and that I'm trying to sweep you off your feet. I have, haven't I? Your feet aren't touching the ground, and as my head's in the clouds, we're both a long way up. As far up as heaven, my darling?' tilting back her head to look into her eyes.

She nodded. Why pretend anything else but that she was wildly and for ever in love with him? For ever this time. There could be no other thought.

'Yes, in heaven,' she said softly.

He kissed her again and then set her down, lightly, gently.

'You'll never disappear again? You're with me for keeps?' he asked.

She laughed.

'You're not asking me to spend the rest of my life on a muddy path on the open moor with a storm blowing up, are you?' she asked.

He looked up at the sky.

'Confound it. You're right,' he said. 'I believe there is a storm blowing up, but it won't break yet. I can give it at least half an hour, and as for the muddy path and the open moor—don't let's get back to other people yet. What about that?' indicating a fallen tree-trunk just off the path. Let's sit down and tell each other the story of our lives.'

She sat on it with him and remembered what she must tell him, the help and advice she must ask.

'Robert, I'm worried,' she said. 'That's really the reason why I came to find you. One of the reasons anyway,' smiling as she saw that he was about to question that.

'About me?' he asked. 'My life's a fairly open book. A page or two that ought to be stuck together here and there, I'm afraid, but you can unstick them and know the worst.'

'No, not about you. It's about a girl, quite a young girl. Freda Fennal.'

It was going to be more difficult than she had thought. There was a nastiness about it which would have to be revealed, something that would be as foreign to him as to her, and she kept her head turned from him whilst she made up her mind how to begin.

She missed his start of surprise, though she heard a little of it when he repeated the name.

'Freda Fennal?'

'Perhaps you know her, or at any rate who she is,' she said. 'She lives with her grandmother at Sandy Combe, a house called Cliff Top,' and then she went on with the story, or some of it, which was, for her, also the story of Brian Hewet.

He listened, amazed and shocked, to her pitiless denunciation of him, describing the effect he was having on the impressionable mind of a very young girl; even in the end telling him, stammering a little over the ridiculous phrases and trying unsuccessfully to laugh at them, of the letter which Freda had written to him.

He had put his arm about her as soon as they sat down, and though he was filled with incredulous horror at what she was saying, he still held her and she turned suddenly and hid her face against him.

'I've hated telling you all this,' she said. 'It's so—so utterly beastly. Hold me, darling. Hold me very tightly. It's so wonderful to be with you—with someone like you. . . .'

144

And then, quite suddenly and without warning, they heard Freda's voice beside them, shrill, strident with anger.

'Brian—and you, Meriel, you! Both of you—like this—behind my back! It's horrible! Beastly! I hate you. I never want to see or speak to either of you again!' and she turned and ran like a hare down the path almost before either of them could comprehend what had happened or believe that she had been there at all.

. . . . . .

Mrs. Fennal had made up her mind whilst Freda was out with the dogs that she must tell her what had been discovered, both about the hidden money and the letter. It was the worst thing she had ever been called upon to do, but she felt that there was no other way of bringing her to her senses and safeguarding both her physical and her moral welfare.

She called her into her bedroom when she heard her come in, and Freda, answering the summons cheerfully now that she felt she had cause for satisfaction in the way she thought she had handled the affair of the money, immediately saw the paper bag on the dressing-table and almost collapsed from shock. She had been making plans for her escape whilst she was out. She could not go until her grandmother's cheque had been put into the bank so that she could draw on it, and she knew, nervously, that if she went away before the police had made their investigation, suspicion would fall on her.

The exact details of how she was to leave the house with a suitcase remained to be worked out, but she was confident that she would find a way. The sight of the bag containing the money therefore petrified her.

Mrs Fennal watched her face and nodded.

'Yes, Freda,' she said sternly, 'I know. There is this too,' handing her the unfinished letter to Brian. 'I am disgusted with you. You have shown yourself to be a thief and a liar and a cheap little slut.'

She did not mince her words nor try to soften them. The time for that had gone, she felt, and she told Freda exactly what she thought of her, that she could not decide what was to be done with her until her father had been consulted, but that in the meantime her liberty, day and night, would be curtailed by herself or Meriel or Hannah, nor would she be allowed to handle her own money until some arrangement had been made about it.

'You will not, of course, receive the cheque you tried to trick me into giving you, nor will you be allowed to have any further contact with this man. I have sent Meriel down to Penn Tor to find him and tell him that this disgusting affair has been discovered and that the law can be evoked on account of your age if he does not immediately leave the district and give his word, for what it is worth, not to try to contact you again.'

The speech, and the manner in which she had felt obliged to make it, had cost her a tremendous effort. She was deathly white and shaking from head to foot but held herself erect, facing the girl with cold eyes and set lips.

When Freda could speak, the words burst from her in a torrent of fury. She was completely beside herself with anger, disappointment, fear.

'You've no right to take my money and you've no right to keep me locked up like a prisoner. I knew you'd got Meriel here to spy on me. You all spy on me and I shall see Brian if I want to. He's my friend. He's the only real friend I've got and the only one who loves me. I hate you! I hate you all! Oh——'

She broke off as Mrs. Fennal, who had been standing by the bed, gave a moan and suddenly collapsed upon it, clutching at the foot-board as she fell and lying half on the bed, half on the floor.

Freda herself might have staged a faint at so apposite a moment, but she knew that this was not her grandmother's way and that the sudden collapse was genuine and she ran to the door and called Hannah. She was terrified in case her grandmother had died.

The maid came hurrying in, gave a quick glance at her mistress, and took the situation in hand. Mrs. Fennal had had similar attacks before, and she knew what to do.

'I suppose this is your doing, giving her all this trouble,' she said to the girl angrily. 'Help me to get her on the bed and then go and put on the kettle for hot-water bottles. Get me the little bottle out of the bathroom cupboard first, the one with the blue label, and hurry!'

Freda, not as badly frightened now that Hannah had taken

146

charge and Mrs. Fennal had shown that she was alive by moving and moaning faintly, ran to obey.

But when she had put the kettle on in the kitchen, she felt that she could not go back into the room.

Her own memory was returning, and with it the agonizing thought of Meriel finding Brian, telling him the whole story, about the money, about the letter which she had never meant to send and at which he would either laugh or be angry. In any case, if Meriel got to him, it would all be ended and she would never see him again.

She listened at her grandmother's door, heard Hannah's voice speaking soothingly as she cared for the mistress she adored, and then ran out of the house. She saw that the car had gone and knew that Meriel must have taken it. Somehow she must get to Penn Tor. Her one thought was to reach Brian.

She started to run along the road, without hat or coat, and when she had gone a few yards, she heard a lorry pull up beside her.

'You're in a hurry, aren't you?' asked the driver. 'Where's the fire? Want a lift?'

She did not know him but did not care.

'Will you? Just to Penn Tor?' she gasped, and climbed up beside him.

'Somebody's ill,' she said on the spur of the moment. 'I'm going for the doctor.'

'No telephone?' he asked, driving on. 'These benighted places. Give me the willies to live in 'em,' and he went on talking though Freda did not listen. Her eyes were watching the road, hoping for some sign that they might be able to overtake Meriel, and suddenly she saw the two cars parked off the road.

'I'll get down here,' she said quickly. 'I—there's someone I know. I—they'll help me,' and he drew up.

She sprang out before the lorry was at a standstill.

'Thanks a lot,' she said automatically, and hurried across the road whilst the driver, with a shrug, went on.

She ran along the path, looking about her in a frenzy, and saw them just as Brian drew Meriel more closely to him and kissed the top of the head that lay on his breast.

Meriel was for the first moment unable to take in what had happened.

Then she realized it in a blinding flash, pulled herself out of Brian's arms and stood before him, white and shaking.

'You? *You* are Brian Hewet?' she cried, appalled, with a sick feeling of incredulity though she knew in her heart that it was true.

Freda had seen him, had faced him. Freda knew who he was, and that he was Brian Hewet, not Robert at all.

He was as shocked as she, more by the sight of her face, the look in her eyes, than by the revelation which had been bound to come and which he himself would have made a moment later if Freda had not done so.

'Yes,' he said. 'I am. I took my mother's name for my pictures. I should have told you, of course. I was just going to. Meriel, don't look at me like that—as if you—as if you hated me. Surely you can't believe . . .'

He had made a movement to lay his hand on her arm. She snatched it away.

'Believe? Believe what?' she asked harshly. 'Anything at all about you, Brian Hewet? But never mind that now. We don't matter. It's that poor child. I must go after her. She might do anything—anything. Don't you realize that she's insane about you?' and she started to run in the direction Freda had taken. They could see her flying figure as she made for the road.

'I'm coming with you,' he said curtly, but she took no notice of him, running madly after Freda. If she ran into the road like that, in her present state, she might be killed.

And then one of those maddening, inconsequent things happened.

One of her shoes, tied too loosely, stuck in the thick mud and when she pulled her foot impatiently, the shoe came off, the impetus of her mad rush making her stumble and fall.

Brian put out a hand to help her up, but she thrust it angrily aside and scrambled to her feet, picking up the shoe.

'Go on!' she cried. 'Go after her. Stop her before she gets to the road!' But he refused.

'I'm not leaving you,' he said stubbornly. 'Here. Give it to me,'

148

as she was trying, from her standing position, to put her shoe on again.

'I can do it,' she snapped.

'You can't. Give it to me and hold on to me. I'm not a snake. I shan't bite you,' and he took the shoe from her, giving her no option but to steady herself by his shoulder whilst he unfastened the lace, put the shoe on her foot and tied it up again.

But the mishap had given Freda enough time to reach the road, to throw open the door of the car and scramble into the driving seat. Careful as a rule not to do so, for once Meriel had left the ignition key in and the car, still warm, started at once and careered at breakneck speed down the road that led to Penn Tor.

'She'll kill herself! She can't drive properly yet,' gasped Meriel. 'Your car. Quick. We must stop her.'

'Oh, damnation!' said Brian, getting into his car whilst she sprang into it beside him. 'She's empty. Ran out of petrol right here and I didn't bother. Meant to go along to the garage and get a canful to take me there,' and he pressed the starter unavailingly. The engine refused to fire.

'Of course that would happen!' cried Meriel, distraught.

'I'll have to get some,' said Brian. 'Will you stay here? I'll run.'

'I haven't much choice,' she said bitterly, 'but hurry!'

Her own car had already disappeared round a bend in the road. Beyond it lay the steep slope down to the quay. There might be a car there by now, people, anything. She was frantic with anxiety and though it was only a few minutes before Brian came back carrying the can of petrol, it seemed hours.

He slopped it into the tank, threw the can by the side of the road and got back into the car, but it was an old one and the feed was poor and a few more minutes were wasted before he could get it to start.

When they reached the top of the slope and could look down at the quay, there was no sign of Freda or the car.

Actually, though they could not know it, in her frenzied haste she had mistaken her way, in spite of knowing it so well, and instead of threading through the jumble of boathouses, small workshops and fishermen's cottages, she found herself up one of the yards, which was a dead end. It was too narrow to allow an

149

inexperienced driver to turn the car, and she was wrestling frantically with the gears whilst Brian drove along by the proper route and missed seeing her. She was shut off by the buildings.

'It's possible that she's gone to my cottage,' he said. 'We'd better make sure first,' but when they reached it, there was still no sign of the car and he turned back to the road to Sandy Combe.

'I don't think she could have gone back there,' said Meriel helplessly, 'but where else could she have gone? She might have gone in the other direction altogether. Where does it go, the other way?'

'Nowhere,' he said grimly. 'She must have gone this way. Meriel, you've got to speak to me. You've got to say something.'

'Oh, for heaven's sake, not now! What does it matter? We've got to find her before she kills herself in that car. Don't you understand? She can't drive properly. She can't manage it. If there was anything in the way, she wouldn't know what to do.'

'Well, nothing's happened to her so far or we should have seen her,' he said grimly, 'so she must be able to manage better than you think.'

He was still driving as he spoke, his eyes and his driver's mind automatically on the road whilst Meriel's searched for some sign of the disaster which she felt was bound to happen with Freda in charge of the car and in the state she had been in.

'I know you're anxious,' he said, 'and so am I, but you needn't treat me as if I were a leper, or as if all this is my fault.'

'Then whose fault is it?' she snapped. 'You a grown man and she just a silly child who imagines herself to be in love with you. Whose fault is that but yours? Leading her on and making love to her behind her grandmother's back!'

'I didn't do anything of the sort,' he retorted.

'Do you expect me to believe that, or anything you say, Brian Hewet or *Robert Barlin* or whoever you are?' said Meriel in angry scorn, in bitterness at her own belief in him. That she, of all people, could have been taken in by a man again, fancied herself in love with one, and with this one of all men!

'I've told you how I came to use that name. I can explain——'

'Explain nothing. There's no need, now that I know you for who you are, what you are. Keep your mind on your driving if you don't want us to end in a ditch as well. I suppose you're going to Cliff Top? Mrs. Fennal will be charmed to see you!'

'Of course I'm going to Cliff Top,' he said doggedly, 'and as far as Mrs. Fennal is concerned, I have nothing to blame myself about. I never encouraged the silly child.'

'Then how did this happen? It's obvious from her letter that you have been seeing her, and seeing her in secret.'

'That letter? You know I never had it.'

'But others like it,' she retorted, and he remembered uncomfortably letters and notes that he *had* received from Freda, blaming himself that he had not done anything more to stop them though he had been tied by his promise to Richard Fennal to see her from time to time.

But how explain all this, here and now, to the girl he loved with all his heart and seemed about to lose, if he could not clear himself?

'You're determined not to give me the benefit of any doubt, aren't you?' he asked, anger at the injustice of it mingling with the anguish of the position between them.

'What possible doubt is there? Silly as it is, and as she is, not even she could have made it all up, and obviously there has been something between you. Just how much, I wonder, and to what extent have you ruined her life?'

The inference was obvious and it infuriated him.

'You'd better take back that abominable suggestion,' he said angrily.

'I take nothing back. Drive on. You're slowing down,' and he said no more. What indeed could he say?

When they reached the house, there was still no sign of the car or of Freda and Meriel learned, to her alarm, that Mrs. Fennal was too ill to see them, to see Brian at least.

'Shall I go in, Hannah?' asked Meriel anxiously, as the three of them stood in the hall, Hannah having cast one hostile, withering glance at Brian and then ignored him.

'I shouldn't, Miss Meriel,' she said. 'I've given her one of the pills the doctor left for her the last time she had one of these attacks, and she's sleeping how.'

'Will she be all right? Hadn't you better get the doctor?'

'I will if she isn't better in an hour or so, but she's been like this before when something's happened to upset her and I know what to do for her. I shan't be out of call for a minute, of course,' jealous as she always was of anyone else doing anything for her beloved mistress.

'I know she'll be all right with you, Hannah,' said Meriel. 'But what about Miss Freda? Where could she have gone?' in desperate anxiety.

'I don't know, Miss Meriel. I didn't even know she was out of the house till I called her and she didn't answer, but I knew you had the car so she couldn't have gone far.'

'That's just it, Hannah. I did have the car, but she found it and took it and now she's out in it alone somewhere and she might have gone anywhere! Do you think you would have heard it if she passed the house?'

'I don't think so. I've been too busy looking after the mistress,' said Hannah, too much concerned about her to think too much about Freda.

Brian spoke for the first time.

'I think we'd better telephone the police,' he said, and Meriel nodded and left him to do it whilst she ran up to Freda's room to see if by any chance she had left a message or any clue to what she intended to do, but found nothing.

Girl and car seemed to have vanished into thin air. How could they have missed her? How could she, with her lack of experience, have got as far away as she appeared to have done?

When she went down again, Hannah had gone back to Mrs. Fennal and Brian told her that he had telephoned both the Penn Tor and the Maryworthy police to ask them to locate the car if they could. Meantime there seemed nothing to do but wait at Cliff Top so that they could be contacted if there were any news.

It was almost dark by now, and the threatened storm had begun to blow up, with wind and lashing rain. From where they stood, in the sitting-room, they could see the white breakers dashing against the rocks below. It was going to be a wild night, and Freda was out in it somewhere, alone.

'I don't expect she's even got any money with her,' said Meriel, frantic with anxiety, especially now that Mrs. Fennal was ill and the full responsibility had devolved upon her, and upon this man who had caused all the havoc.

Determinedly he came to her and put his hands on her shoulders and held her by them in spite of her instant repulse of him.

'We can't go on like this or leave it here, Meriel,' he said, and she was beginning to recognize the determination of the mouth that could be so tender, and the obstinate jut of his chin. There was a look of steel in his eyes.

'Take your hands off me,' she said. 'I don't want you to touch me. I don't want ever to see you again or hear your name, whatever your name is!'

'It's Robert to you, Meriel.'

'It's nothing to me.'

'You're being very unfair.'

'And what have you been?' she countered furiously.

She was sore in heart and in mind because she had allowed herself to love again, and to love someone who had not even existed. Beneath it all, making her unable to think clearly of herself and her position, was the anxiety for Freda, the terrible imaginings of what might have happened to her. She needed help and now that 'Robert' had failed her, she had nowhere to turn for it.

'I've never been unfair to you nor lied to you about anything but my name,' he said, 'and that was not a lie. Many people know me as Robert Barlin. If I can ever paint again after this, it will be under that name. In no other way have I ever deceived you.'

'What about Freda and the way you've behaved towards her?'

'How could I have known that you were interested in her? If I had known, I should have told you about her at the beginning, been thankful to be able to tell you because I badly needed your help.'

'And what would you have told me about her?' she asked, her lip curling in disdain. 'Did you need help to carry on an affair with a girl of seventeen who was besotted with you? As for deceit, even if you did not know you were deceiving me, is that any excuse for deceiving her grandmother? Meeting her without her knowledge? Coming here——'

'I never came here. That was a lie.'

'But you did meet in secret. Where? At your cottage?' remembering how near it was to the vicarage, how easy it must

153

have been for them to meet there whilst Freda was ostensibly visiting Ruth Collen.

'She did come there, yes,' he said, 'but not with my consent nor by any arrangement of mine.'

'If you didn't want her to come, you could easily have stopped her by telling Mrs. Fennal.'

'Mrs. Fennal dislikes and distrusts me.'

'I don't wonder!' said Meriel bitterly and he flinched.

He had not set her free, but she stood straight and stiff in his hold, disdaining the indignity of a struggle to free herself.

'You're bitter and unyielding, aren't you? Mrs. Fennal's attitude to me made it very difficult. For one thing, I felt that Freda was going through a bad time, was lonely and felt that the world was against her. If I had cast her off, or broken my word to her not to tell Mrs. Fennal that she was coming to see her, it would only have made things worse for her. Also I had promised her father to look after her——'

'And that was the way you did it? And this ghastly thing we're in now is the result.'

The sound of the telephone bell interrupted them, and he went quickly to answer it, Meriel following him and standing by.

'Oh, my God!' he said, when he had listened for a moment. 'Have you warned the coastguard station? I'll come down at once. Ask someone to fill up the fuel tank of *Sally May* and get her engine running,' and he put up the receiver and turned a haggard face to Meriel.

'What is it?' she asked.

'She's gone out in *Sprite*. In this,' he said, glancing out of the window. 'We must have missed her somehow. The police say they found the car abandoned in a yard there and that some men saw *Sprite* go out. They thought I was in her.'

'What are you going to do?'

'Go after her in the other boat.'

'Will you be able to find her?'

'God knows. I'd better take something with me. Brandy. Hot coffee or something if you've got it, but be quick.'

She ran to the kitchen. There was always coffee made, and whilst it was heating, she snatched up her shopping basket, put what she could find into it, bread, cheese, some of Hannah's

154

famous pasties, a bottle half full of brandy, and then filled two flasks with the coffee.

Brian was waiting for it, the car's engine already running, and Meriel was pulling on her mackintosh as she ran, a thick jersey over her arm.

'What are you doing?' he asked, as she went round the car and started to open the door.

'I'm coming with you,' she said, and got in, piling the basket and the jersey into the space behind the seats.

'What for? You can't do anything. I've told you that I'm going out in the other boat.'

'I'm still coming with you.'

'Don't be an idiot. You don't know anything about boats and you hate being on the sea and you're always ill. You told me so.'

'I'm still coming with you,' she repeated. 'Get on, for heaven's sake, and don't argue. Of course I must go with you, and if I'm no good on boats and I'm sick, at least I shall be there if you find her. She'll need someone. I've got food and a jersey for her.'

He started off even if he intended to go on arguing with her, and he felt a little flicker of something like joy at the thought that she was still with him, though he told himself that he could not for a moment entertain any thought of her going out with him in *Sally May*. It would be a desperate adventure, even for him, and he had no idea how he was going to find *Sprite*, on the open sea and in a storm at night. But it was the only thing he could do, and since he felt that he was in some way responsible for the mad thing Freda had done, he could not merely leave the finding of her, and her possible rescue, to other people whilst he stood helplessly by.

'I've got to call at the cottage for a pea-jacket,' he said, for he was still in his painting denims over jersey and slacks.

She nodded and they sat in hostile silence until he pulled up at the gate.

'You'd better stay in the cottage now that you've come so far. You may not be able to get back. The police said the car was damaged.'

'I've told you that I'm going with you. Get whatever it is you want and be quick about it. Get something warm,' she added on an impulse which she at once regretted.

Why should she care whether he was warm or cold?

When he came out again, he added a thick cardigan to the other things in the car. He was now warmly enough dressed himself, but if she insisted on going with him and he could not prevent her without wasting more time in argument, she would need more than the thin mackintosh.

There was a little knot of people on the quay when they reached it and Brian jumped out and went to them. They were gathered near *Sally May*. One of the fishermen was on her and the engine was running.

'Shall I come with you, Mr. Hewet?' he asked doubtfully as Brian jumped aboard.

'No!' cried a woman in the crowd, and Brian echoed it without hesitation. *Sally May* was smaller than *Sprite*, and in the ordinary way easily handled by one man, especially an expert like himself, and if he were going to risk his own life for Freda, as he knew he was doing, he would not draw another man, husband, father or son, into the same danger.

Meriel handed the basket and the clothing to him and climbed down into the boat herself.

He looked at her in dismay but realized that there was little he could do about it, short of picking her up and putting her forcibly back on the quay.

'It's madness to come,' he said.

'Then I'm mad,' she said. 'Don't fuss or argue. It's a waste of time. If there's anything for me to do, just tell me and I'll be as intelligent as I can about doing it.'

'If you're sick, don't expect me to help you,' he said ungraciously, though in spite of the added anxiety she would be to him and the danger, he felt again that thrill at having her with him.

'Most people are sick without help,' she said, and at any other time they would both have laughed.

He knew at once that he would need all his strength, his resource and his knowledge of boats and the sea to control the tiny cruiser, which consisted only of the open cockpit with one small cabin which held an oil-cooker in addition to two bunks and a detachable table between them. There was the smallest possible toilet accommodation, a locker for gear and nothing else. She was not as well found as *Sprite* and he did not know her vagaries so well, but he had been over her thoroughly on her owner's behalf and knew that she was seaworthy, though how she would stand up to a heavy sea he had yet to find out.

The only thing that worried him was that her engine was not as reliable as *Sprite*'s. He had, in fact, advised Mr. Preecy to get a new one, to which he had agreed and it was on order, though that did not help much now.

As soon as she found that they had left the quay and that there could be no more argument about whether she was coming or not, Meriel went into the cabin and hung up the spare clothing, already wishing that she had brought a warmer garment for herself than the thin mackintosh.

She had never been in a small boat before. She had been in very few boats at all, as a matter of fact. She had crossed to France in a Channel steamer several times, had hated it and been seasick the whole time. She resolved, rather waveringly, that she was not going to be sick now, tightened her belt and hoped for the best.

Brian bent down to look into the cabin and speak to her.

'Are you all right?' he asked.

'Yes.'

'Like to get some air before we get into the rough water? You'll find some sou'westers down there somewhere. Put one on and give me one, will you?'

Rough water! she thought, and wondered what this was, for already the light little craft was pitching and tossing as she rode the waves.

She found the sou'westers and went out to him, too proud to let him guess that already she was beginning to wish she had not come.

She fixed her thoughts determinedly on Freda instead of on herself.

'Can she handle a boat?' she asked.

'Better than you feel she can a car,' he said, 'but no girl can handle even a boat like *Sprite* alone in what we're going to get if we don't sight her soon.'

'You mean it's going to get worse?' she asked in a small voice.

'Worse? We haven't started yet. See that light over there?

157

That's at the end of the reef of rocks which makes the protection for the harbour. If we can sight her before then . . .' and he stopped.

'Do you think we might? How do you know which way to go?'

'With the tide and the currents and the wind to contend with, she'll drift a bit. My only fear is that her fuel won't last. There's not much in her. I tuned her up this morning to take her to-morrow into the next bay as they want the Penn Tor moorings. I was going to fill her up before I went. If I hadn't got her ready, dammit, Freda wouldn't have been able to take her out. I can't think what possessed her, silly young idiot.'

Meriel forbore to tell him that it was he who had possessed her, though what she had hoped to gain by going out in *Sprite*, other than in a spirit of defiance and bravado, she could not imagine. Her one idea, wounded and bruised as she had been by discovering Brian's perfidy, must have been to get away, anyhow and anywhere, and when the car would no longer serve her pur-pose, she must have seen the boat and rushed to it headlong as her only means of escape.

Poor Freda. Poor child. No one knew better than Meriel the utter devastation which can follow the discovery of the treachery and betrayal of first love. She herself had not wanted to live after Frank Lean had failed her.

She looked at Brian. His face was set and resolute and showed no fear. His strong hands held the wheel firmly. His eyes were piercing the darkness. He looked like a man sure of himself, a man on whom any woman could believe herself able to rely.

But how had she and Freda found him? Certainly not that.

She gave a gulp and went back into the cabin.

A little while later she heard him give a shout and went into the cockpit.

'I can see her,' he said.

'Freda?'

'Well, *Sprite*, so presumably Freda,' and he tried to point her out, and after some time she was able to descry something which looked infinitesimally small and scarcely distinguishable from the 'white horses' on which the boat tossed like a cockle-shell.

8

'SHE looks out of control,' said Brian anxiously. 'Either the fuel's given out or Freda can't hold her. I hope to God she's far enough beyond the point to drift to the other side or she'll break up against the rocks.'

'What's on the other side?' asked Meriel fearfully.

'Another small bay. There's no quay there, only a hard built out amongst the rocks. If she's driven in, as she may be, she'll break up, but if Freda can get clear of her in time she might be able to get ashore. She's a very strong swimmer and she knows the bay and where to find shallow water.'

'Swim? In this?' asked Meriel, appalled.

'It won't be as bad on the other side of the point, but still pretty bad,' he said, clenching his teeth and turning the wheel.

'What are you going to do?' she asked.

'Keep *Sally May* off the reef at all costs,' he said, 'but I've got to make for the point. You'd better go below. You'll be drenched,' for the rain had come on more heavily again, and now, as he turned into the giant waves, they dashed over the bows before the little craft dipped with a sickening lurch down on the other side.

Meriel shuddered, too sick with fear to be normally seasick. It seemed impossible that the boat could go on righting herself, that she could rise again each time after those fearful nosedives into the dark gulf beyond, but Brian stood there, calm, confident, and as she obeyed him and went into the cabin, she tried to hold before her that vision of him.

He lost sight of *Sprite* and could only hope that she had been tossed round to the other side of the point and not driven on to the rocks. All his skill and attention were needed to keep *Sally May* on her course and prevent her from sharing the same fate, if *Sprite* had indeed met her doom and inevitably taken Freda with her. Near the shore she might be able to swim, or at least to keep herself afloat. Out there not even the strongest swimmer could have lived.

He was not happy about the behaviour of the one engine of *Sally May*. It had been asked to do more than that type of engine was designed for, even when new, and though it had stood up to it manfully, the coughs and temporary pauses before it went on again told their own tale. If it held out until they had rounded the point, he could with any luck steer the boat into the quieter waters of the bay and eventually they would drift inshore as he hoped and prayed *Sprite* was doing.

Already they were abreast of the light which marked the submerged end of the reef. He turned further out to sea so as to be well clear of it when he tried to round it, and then, with a final apologetic gurgle, the engine stopped.

He shouted down to Meriel to come up and she came at once.

'Engine's failed,' he said. 'I'll have to get a sea anchor out, so that we can keep her head to the sea while I find out what has gone wrong.'

Meriel helped him to fling the canvas sea anchor overboard, her fingers struggling with the wet rope; and he showed her how to keep the boat pointing into the wind, while he disappeared through the hatch covering the engine and lowered himself down, his body cramped, his head and shoulders above the deck level.

She held on with all her strength, glad of something to do even if the doing of it seemed to be about to pull her arms out of their sockets, and presently he heaved himself up to relieve her. The engine was still dead.

'Have I done all right?' she asked anxiously.

'You've done fine,' he said, and for the first time since they had sprung apart to see Freda staring at them, they smiled at each other, an uncertain, fugitive smile, but at least the shadow of one.

'We're well past the point,' he told her. 'I can't get the engine going yet, but I'll hold her till we've turned into the current again, and then I'll have another go. Hi! There's *Sprite*! Thank God she's still afloat. Can you see her? Drifting inshore? With any luck at all, and if Freda's still all right, not hurt or too exhausted, she should be able to make it. Can you take over again now? Just hang on as before, but shout if we're getting too near the point.'

She was cold and her teeth were chattering. Her feet felt like slabs of ice, her shoes oozing with the water that dripped off a mackintosh wet with rain and sea water and her stockings clinging damply to her legs. Hands and arms ached intolerably from her battle with the wheel, whilst she was bruised with the buffeting of the waves which constantly knocked her from side to side in the little cockpit.

But she hung on grimly, half unconscious with the numbing pain and the cold until a sudden lurch of the boat tore the wheel from her grasp, and immediately the little craft leaped and heeled over as if it had gone mad. She realized they were much nearer to the rocky promontory of the reef than they had been a few minutes ago, and struggling desperately to bring the bows round again, she shouted to her companion above the turmoil of wind and sea and did not realize until afterwards what she had called him.

'Robert! Come quickly! We're going the wrong way!'

He came at once, crawling up to the deck level and shutting down the hatch with a gesture of finality. He had discovered what was wrong with the engine and it was something which he could not rectify whilst they were at sea. His face was set and grim, but it relaxed a little when he came to her, giving a quick glance round.

'What did you do?' he asked. 'Put your arm out to say you were turning to the left and lose the wheel?' taking it from her in his strong, grimed hands, but his tone held no reproof. It was kind, a little teasing. After her struggle there alone, it was wonderful comfort to have him in charge and with her again.

'I did try to hang on,' she said, her teeth chattering.

'You couldn't help it, he said, 'and it doesn't matter. We're still all right, but the tide's turning and driving us back. You're terrbily cold, aren't you? Go down and put on Freda's jersey.'

'No, I must keep that dry for her if . . . if . . .'

She could not go on. Ahead of them, the distance widening as their helpless boat was thrown back by the turning tide, they could still see *Sprite*, near the shore now but turning, twisting, dipping, bobbing up again in the queer, luminous light from the frothing breakers and the still not totally black night.

His lips tightened as he followed her glance. Then he turned his attention back to her.

'Then put mine on,' he said. 'I brought it for you. I'm warm enough in this, and dry. Do you think it would be possible for us to drink a drop of coffee or whatever you brought? Just a little in each cup.'

She put the big, thick jersey under her mackintosh, then realized that the water had gone through that, and she took it off again, threw it in a wet heap on the cabin floor and felt the grateful warmth of his jersey hugging her frozen body. It came down to her knees and she had to roll up the sleeves and thought, for one surprisingly light-hearted moment, what a figure of fun she must look, but she no longer cared if only she could be warm again. The thought that he had brought it for her sent a little thrill of added warmth through her.

She carried the two cups half filled with coffee into which she had put a little of the brandy out to the cockpit, arriving with at least most of the hot liquid still in the cups, and they drank it gratefully.

'Could you eat something?' she asked, for it was a long time since lunch time and she remembered that she had not eaten even that. 'I've got some pasties.'

'I will if you will,' he said, and she brought them and sat on the deck of the cockpit, hunched up beside him, whilst he stood at the wheel, both munching the savoury pasties.

'Hannah never imagined in what circumstances these would be eaten when she made them,' said Meriel.

'She'd have put a spot of arsenic in if she'd known which was going to be mine,' he said, and a little silence hung between them as they both realized that their ordinary life, the one which was suspended for a time but would claim them again if they came out of this alive, was touching their minds again but with the strain eased by the very fact that it could be mentioned.

'Can you still see *Sprite*?' asked Meriel, after that silence which had been full of thoughts for both of them.

'Only just. I'm afraid she'll break up when she gets to the rocks. Bound to. Then it's up to Freda.'

162

Meriel gave a little, inarticulate, choking cry and he took one hand off the wheel for a moment, laid it on her shoulder with a comforting touch, and took it away again.

'Nothing we or anyone can do now, dear,' he said quietly.

'Can she possibly do it? Get ashore, I mean?'

'She's got a chance if she keeps her head and jumps clear at the right time and place, and she knows this coast and the bay. We often had picnics there in the old days and swam even in a fairly rough sea. There's a kind of little lagoon. If she can get into that, she'll get through. The arms act as breakwaters. I can't see well enough now, but it looked to me as if the boat must be going in that direction. She's like a fish in the water and very strong. When we had a really long swim, she knew how to rest at intervals and conserve her strength.'

Meriel knew that he was talking to hearten and comfort her, and that he was probably as anxious as she was for the girl's safety, but she realized that it did not hurt as much as she would have thought to hear him talking about Freda. They were so much alone now, the two of them, and there might be nothing else for them but these few hours, possibly not even hours. She was letting herself remember that she had loved him. She could not think now of all that miserable business of Freda. They were all of them too near the possibility of death.

When she got to her feet again, she gave a little cry of alarm, for the shore was now scarcely visible and even if *Sprite* had been there, they could not have seen her. The land was no more than a heavier smudge against the dark sky.

'We're further away!' she said.

'Yes. I shan't be able to get the engine going, so we've got to drift, and the tide is taking us out.'

'Out? Where to?' she asked fearfully.

'Well—let me see. The coast of Wales, Ireland, possibly America,' he said, and she looked at his face and saw that he was smiling cheerfully and teasing her with his reply.

'You mean we're just drifting out to sea?'

'Yes, but that's better than drifting on to Penn Tor point or anywhere else on the rocks. Unless something rams us (and there's not much sea traffic about here and the fishing boats won't be out), we shan't come to much harm. Even if her engine's failed,

163

Sally May has proved herself, and when the daylight comes, we can hoist a signal and we may be spotted. The coastguards will be looking out for us now though we're probably too small to see yet. Somebody will have seen *Sprite* anyway by now and get some sort of help to Freda. Are you very frightened, darling?' gently.

Her eyes filled with foolish tears which had their origin in too many things to be defined. She dashed them away with the back of her hand and smiled at him, her face only a pale blur now in the darkness.

'Not very. Not with you,' she said, and his hand came to touch her again with its comforting reassurance. She touched it with her own before he had to withdraw it to keep the boat on the course he was trying to set without compass, without even the stars to guide him. The sky was pitch black though the rain had almost stopped.

One of the miracles to Meriel was that she had not been sick, though the mere gentle rise and fall of the Channel steamers had been enough to send her miserably below.

As if he could divine her thoughts, he mentioned it.

'How have you managed not to carry out your threat of being seasick?' he asked. 'Or haven't you?'

'I don't know. Perhaps because you told me you wouldn't help me if I were. I've been too busy, too. When I've been across to France, I haven't had to steer the boat or work in the kitchen.'

'Galley, woman, galley! Kitchen indeed! By the way, did you manage to get a light down there?'

'No, I fumbled and lit matches. Is there one?'

'Of course there is? They're in gimbals.'

'What on earth are gimbals?'

'Things that keep the lamps steady when the boat's rolling. Why not try to light one and roll yourself in a blanket and have a sleep?'

'A sleep? In this?' she jeered.

'You will if you're tired enough, as you must be. You've been a good crew. I'm sorry I haven't been as good a chief engineer, but there we are.'

'Are we going to be all right, Robert?' her voice quiet and steady.

164

'I think so. I hope so. Will you do as I say, darling, and try to sleep?'

'I can't, and leave you up here.'

'I may be able to come down presently. The sea's going down a bit. At least until the tide turns again we shan't be driven on the rocks and our lights are burning all right.'

'I'd rather stay here with you.'

'Please go down, dear. I shall be happier if I know you are warmer and more comfortable,' and at last, with a half-shy smile at him, she did so.

Though she was warm, tucked up in half of the good supply of blankets, the other half folded up on the second bunk, she could not sleep, and presently she heard him come into the cabin, moving softly.

'Asleep?' he asked in a whisper.

'No.'

'I came to forage for more coffee and something else to eat. Have we got any more of Hannah's pasties?'

'Yes, two more, and lots of coffee,' and she made a movement as if to get out of the bunk, but he pushed her gently back.

'No. Lie still. I'll get them. Perhaps we'd better save the pasties for breakfast. What else have we got? There are probably some tins of stuff somewhere,' opening the cupboard over the oil-cooker.

'Yes. Baked beans and sardines and I don't fancy those together, do you?'

'No, nor separately. Didn't you say there was some bread and cheese?'

'Yes, in the basket. And some butter.'

'I'll make some sandwiches out of that,' and he cut them, thick slabs, and brought her some, and some coffee, and sat on the edge of her bunk whilst they ate.

With the wind still howling and the sea still tossing them about as if they were a small toy in the hands of a giant child, she felt strangely at peace. In the fitful light of the swinging lamp, his face looked strong and calm with something in it as impregnable and enduring as the rocks from which he had saved them.

'You look so undisturbed,' she said, 'as if you're not a bit afraid of anything that might happen.'

165

'I'm not, except for you.'

'I don't think I'm afraid any more.'

'You've been wonderful.'

'I've been with you,' she said in a low voice.

He made no reply nor movement and she could not tell if he had even heard, but he had.

How much of that did she mean, and how much would she mean when, if ever, they got ashore again? He longed to hold her, to pour out all his love for her, but dare not. There was still so much that would have to be said, so much to make her understand and believe, so much to be wiped away between them, and unless it could be wiped away for ever, there could be nothing true or lasting. Only the perfect restoration of her faith in him, their mutual forgiveness for bitter words said, could form a basis for any shared future, and this was not the time or place. He could not take advantage of their position, of her tired body and overwrought nerves, of the fear which she had denied but which he knew she could not escape.

And suddenly, without warning, they felt a terrific jar as a huge wave, the last of its size as it happened, caught the boat and swung her round, sweeping over her, pounding the deck close above their heads, whilst something seemed to have been wrenched away as if the boat were being torn to pieces.

He was flung off the edge of the bunk and she saved herself only by clutching frantically at it. The plates with their unfinished sandwiches and the rest of the coffee crashed off the table and he pushed them aside as he scrambled to his feet and out on deck, Meriel following him.

'Are we wrecked?' she asked chokingly.

'Dunno. Don't think so. We're still afloat anyway. Stay there. Hang on to something and stay there whilst I investigate,' he shouted to her and tremblingly she did so, standing at the entrance to the cabin and holding to both sides of it whilst he crawled about the boat which was still shuddering from the shock of the great wave, sliding down into its trough but still riding.

She prayed voicelessly.

'Oh, God, don't let anything happen to him. Don't let him die. Save him,' and as she said the words over and over in her mind,

166

she knew that her terror was for him, not for herself at the possibility of being left alone. She could not think of herself at all, only of him, Robert, whom she loved.

When he crawled back to her from the little upper forward deck beyond the cockpit and above the cabin where, slipping and sliding, it had seemed impossible to her that he had not been flung into the sea, his face wore a grimly resigned smile.

'Rudder's gone,' he said. 'Anchor's gone. Whole lot seems to have been torn away, but we're still afloat, and as far as I can see, likely to remain so. For some time anyway. Thing is that there's nothing to steer her with now, nothing to hold her with if we drift inshore a bit presently, nothing to do but hope for the best and wait for it. Sorry, dear. I landed you into this.'

She could smile now that he was safely back with her.

'You didn't. You did your best to keep me from coming with you.'

'I should have chucked you back on the quay.'

'Like a dead fish? I'm neither a fish nor dead.'

'And you're not going to be. Dead, I mean.'

'I'd rather have died just now, if you had.'

He came to her then and put his arms about her and held her against him. He could no longer deny himself, and she came closely to him and laid her head, curly and wet, on his breast. His fingers ran through her hair and then he lifted her face up by it and kissed her, long, hard, desperate kisses, as if he could never let her go again.

When they drew away from each other, though still holding closely, he looked into her eyes which did not flinch from the question which seemed to search her very soul.

'I love you,' she said. 'I always shall.'

'I think you mean it.'

'I do. Oh, Robert, I do! Believe me!'

'As you believe me?'

'Always. Always,' and he kissed her again and there seemed nothing left to say. It had all been said in that look.

'What are we going to do now?' she asked, trying to shake herself back into reality. 'Is there anything?'

'Only to work out something in case we really are wrecked,' he said. 'Can you swim?'

167

'Not a stroke. I've always been nervous of the water.'

He grinned.

'Hasn't looked like it so far,' he said.

'I haven't been right in it so far. Only in patches. A yard or two at a time, or a foot or two,' looking down at her soaked shoes ruefully. They had cost her more than she could afford and they would never be any good again after this.

Then she checked herself as she had to keep on doing.

'Again? After this? Would there be anything at all after this?

'Now listen carefully,' he said. 'I don't think we're going to capsize. I think we shall weather it. But with no means of controlling the boat at all, nobody can say what might happen, and if we do capsize, or get thrown into the water any other way, catch hold of anything you can, or turn on your back and float till I can get to you if we're separated, but if you possibly can, keep near the boat, which is not likely actually to sink even if she's upside down. You understand? That's the first and most important thing for any well-conducted shipwrecked people to remember. *Keep as near the boat as you can,* the idea being that anyone looking for us can see the boat better than they could see us and also we can find each other better. So, if you can, keep near the boat. I'll keep with you if I possibly can. You know that. There are no lifebelts. The boat was not really ready to put out. There are to be new lifebelts but they haven't come so we haven't got them. There's no raft or anything on a boat of this size, but I've had a look round and I've found a cork bathmat. Keep it with you wherever you go on the boat and if you do have to go over, hang on to it. It'll keep you up for the time being.'

Though he was being deadly serious, she burst out laughing.

'Adrift in the Atlantic on a bathmat!' she said. 'What a good headline for the papers! Are we in the Atlantic, by the way?'

'We're in the Bristol Channel at the moment, I should say,' he said, loving her courage.

As if that giant wave had been the final act of the storm, a sudden hush had succeeded it. The sea was, by comparison, almost calm, and Brian saw what he had feared most. The fog, kept at bay by the wind and rain, was creeping upon them. It hung low over the sea, shrouding the little boat like the folds of a heavy grey blanket, but a blanket which brought chill instead of warmth.

Meriel shivered as it touched her face like a clammy hand. With the sudden calm of the sea, the silence was weird and eerie. Their world had narrowed down to this tiny, floating speck in a grey infinity of space.

He put an arm about her.

'Come, darling. Let's go down to the cabin. It won't be warm but at least it won't be as cold as out here.'

He wrapped her up in the blankets again, bent down to kiss her lightly and then went towards the door.

'Where are you going?' she asked, fearing that he might be putting himself into danger with more of that ghastly scrambling about on the upper deck.

'First watch,' he said with a smile, though he did not turn to look at her.

'What for?'

'In case anything looms up out of the fog and either rams us or could take us on board. If I saw anything, I could pretend to be a fog-horn and beep-beep at them.'

'You—you won't run into danger, Robert?' she asked, her voice shaking.

He hesitated for a moment and then came back to her and sat on the edge of her bunk as he had done before, but not too near her.

'My sweet, the danger's here,' he said lightly, though with an undercurrent of seriousness. 'We both know it, don't we? And you're in my care. You trust me.'

'Is that why you won't stay down here?' she asked in a whisper.

She would never have believed it possible that she could feel like this, think such thoughts as were racing hotly through her mind. If he took her in his arms now, kissed her as he had done a little while ago, she knew that she would be ready to give herself wholly to him, she who had guarded herself so fiercely in the past from any attempt on the part of a man, even of Frank, to take liberties with her! In an age when such things were apparently of little importance, physical love taken and given lightly, not even kept secret from other people's knowledge in many cases, she had kept herself inviolate, both by instinct and by early

169

training, until she should give herself wholly in marriage to the man she loved. Frank had teased her about it, calling her old-fashioned and a prude, had even been angry at her refusal of the small intimacies which he took to be his right once they were engaged. More than once they had quarrelled and almost parted because of it. He told her that she was frigid, an iceberg and not a woman at all, but she had prevailed.

Now she knew how wrong he had been to call her frigid. Her whole being was warm and alive, longing for Robert's touch, to be held in his arms as no man had ever held her, to withhold nothing from him. It thrilled her and shamed her. She had always faced life and herself with honesty and courage. She saw herself now as the sort of girl she had always despised as that tide of desire and longing swept over her, bearing away all the defences behind which in the past she had felt herself to be so secure, so invincibly protected.

But he did not touch her as he sat there in the little cabin with its one feeble light, steady now and showing her his strong face, his dark eyes, his mouth that could be so hard and relentless, so tender on her own.

'Yes,' he said quietly, 'that's why, Meriel. I love you and I want you desperately and for all our lives, but not like this, when you trust me and are so defenceless.'

She struggled with all her courage against the wild urge within her to tear down his defences as her own had been torn down.

She gave a shaky little laugh.

'Are you saving me from "a fate worse than death"?' she asked, and he smiled and nodded.

'That's just what I'm doing,' he said and he rose, tucked in a stray end of the blanket and went towards the door again.

'You can't stay up there all night,' she said. 'Can I take second watch?'

'All right. I'll call you,' he said. 'You can have the dog-watch. It's the worst one,' and with another smile he left her.

She was so tired that she fell asleep almost at once, and woke with a start, but fully conscious, to find him standing beside her, looking at her with a frown of indecision. He hated to wake her but knew that he would have to get some sleep if he were to be fit for whatever still lay in front of them when daylight came, or the fog lifted.

'Is it time?' she asked, sitting up and rubbing the sleep from her eyes.

His heart seemed to twist with tenderness. She looked so young, her face flushed from sleep, her hair in a child's disordered curls, and he took a step away from her.

'I hated waking you,' he said.

'Nonsense. You've got to get some sleep,' she said, beginning to climb out of the nest of blankets.

'Put on the warmest things we've got. It's bitterly cold out there and still foggy. I wish you'd got something else to put on your feet,' picking up the brown brogues, still damp but beginning to stiffen as they dried. 'Mine wouldn't be much good to you, Cinderella.'

'I'll be all right,' she said cheerfully, and again his heart twisted.

'You're a wonderful shipmate,' he said, and left her abruptly.

She took a blanket with her and wrapped it round her when she went into the cockpit, insisting that he should go down and get some sleep; but it was bitterly cold. Perhaps somewhere the dawn was breaking, but here there was little sign of it, though now and then she could see the drift and swirl of the fog.

She had nothing to do but think. It was automatic to look and to listen for anything that might break through that icy mist, but it was as if she was alone in a world where there were not even shadows. Was that what death was like? This utter loneliness and silence for ever?

She shivered and drew the blanket more closely about her.

It was life that she wanted, not death; life with Robert, love and its fulfilment with him.

It was difficult to believe that so short a time ago they had been bitter enemies; that she had told him, and meant it, that she hoped she would never see him again. She thought of Freda, but tried not to remember that the girl might not even be alive any longer. Whatever had transpired between those two, it was not as she had been so ready to believe. Indeed she marvelled now that she had believed it for a second. It did not seem possible that a girl's fevered imagination could have made it all up and he had admitted freely that they had been meeting in secret, but it had

171

not been in the way Freda had made it appear. She felt completely certain of that, needed none of the explanation which he could and would give her. She had not even wanted to talk about it when they had had all the time there was for talking. Her mind was at peace, asking no questions, needing no answers.

It began to permeate her consciousness at last that she could now see, though vaguely, the bows of the boat, 'the sharp end' as she had called it to his derision. Trickles of water had started to run down the glass screen in front of her, and he had told her that if it started to rain again, it was a sign that the fog was lifting. From some long way off she heard the faint sound of a fog-horn piercing the silence with its mournful note. He had told her that she must wake him if she saw or heard anything, and she went reluctantly to do so.

She touched his shoulder gently, and he started up at once, blinked and then smiled at her.

'You had an evening dress on,' he said.

'I don't know where I got it from,' she said laughingly.

'I liked it. It was sort of blue and fluffy, miles of net or something.'

'Not at all my line. I must have looked hideous in it.'

'No, you looked beautiful. And you still do.'

She laughed again.

'Wrapped in a blanket like an Indian squaw, with a dirty face and my hair like a bird's nest? It was warmer, anyway, than your miles of net! I'd have been pretty cold up there in that.'

He was getting up from the bunk, hers that had been warm from her body, pulling down his jersey, putting on the pea-jacket, running his fingers ineffectually through the wild mop of his dark hair, feeling with a grimace his dark, unshaven chin.

He remembered thankfully that amongst the jumble of oddments which someone, Mr. Preecy probably, had left in one of the lockers, he had seen a safety-razor. It was probably rusty and would be agonizing to use, but if there were a blade in it at all, he would manage somehow.

'My poor darling, are you terribly cold?' he asked.

'Well, I'm not exactly in a glow of warmth,' she said, and he kissed her, but this time there was no danger for them in the kiss. They had come through that.

172

'You know, it would be rather nice if you could bring yourself to call me darling or something like that, just for once,' he observed in a conversational tone.

'My darling,' she said, and though she tried to say it lightly, her voice was not quite steady, and he smiled and let her go.

'That'll do for the present,' he said. 'By the way, what did you really wake me for?'

'Oh, Robert, I forgot! I heard a fog-horn somewhere, and it's raining.'

'Is it, by Jove? I'll come up,' and she went with him.

It was raining quite fast now, and though the fog still hung over the sea, they had some yards of visibility and the fog-horn sounded more clearly, though from a long way off.

They might still be drifting about for a long time, and as they were short of fresh water, they collected all the receptacles they could find, buckets, saucepans, anything that would hold the precious water, and set them where they could catch it. Then they huddled side by side on the wooden bench in the cockpit, his arm about her, her head on his shoulder.

There was nothing to do but wait and watch and in spite of their precarious position, they were content.

'Do you want to talk?' he asked, after they had sat there in happy silence for some time.

'What about?'

'Anything. You, me, the world.'

'Does it exist?' she asked dreamily.

'No, but we do. Tell me about yourself, everything you've done and wanted to do; where you've been all my life whilst I've been waiting for you—as I have been. You know that?'

'Yes.'

'You haven't always been so sure, have you?' and he put a hand under her chin and tilted up her face so that he could look into her eyes. 'Why didn't you trust me?'

She felt a shiver of fear, of passionate regret and contempt for herself, run through her. She could find nothing to say, but she let him look into her eyes. Surely he would find in them all that he needed to know?

His face was grave, his eyes a little sad.

'You could have done, you know. You should have done. Why

173

were you so ready to think ill of me? If you loved me as I love you, you couldn't have done. Without explanation, without reason, with apparently everything against me, you should still have believed in me. Why didn't you, Meriel? Do you now?'

'I think I always did—in my heart. But—I'd been so hurt before.'

His arm came more closely about her and he let her hide her face against him again.

'I know,' he said. 'If I had remembered that, perhaps I should not have felt so bitter, or that your love lacked the essential quality it must have if two people are to go all the way together. Is that how you want it? The way together, *all* the way?'

'More than anything in the world,' she said, her voice muffled against him. 'More than anything, my darling.'

He was silent, holding her, knowing that there was no need for more words, and not then, nor at any other time, did he ever tell her the full story of Freda, the pitiful story which must remain her own secret and only partially his.

Suddenly, in anticlimax, there came a booming and a clatter of ships' bells, of shouts echoing through the lifting fog, and their arms fell from each other and they scrambled to their feet to see, dangerously near them, a little cargo-boat which, small though it was, looked enormous beside their tiny craft.

'Hulloo there!' someone was calling through cupped hands. 'Want help?'

'I'll say we do!' Brian yelled back. 'We've no engine.'

'Keep as clear as you can. We'll put a boat off for you.'

Meriel caught at Brian's hand. He gripped it and looked at her and smiled. She knew his thoughts. They were both of them almost sorry that it was over.

'Never mind,' he said. 'We've got tomorrow—now.'

9

FREDA had done exactly what Brian had hoped she would do.

During the time of her peril, when the fuel had given out and *Sprite* was adrift, at the mercy of the sea and the treacherous rocks on to which she knew she could be driven by the power of the currents, she had faced herself at last, all the fantasy and glamour of her imagination shorn away. She knew herself to be young, helpless, ignorant of the real world; a child more than the woman she had tried to be.

She was desperately afraid. She wanted her parents, her grandmother, home and security around her. They had never been more precious. She scarcely even thought of Brian, and not at all of Meriel Dain. If only she could get back to the people who loved her, safe in her home, and it was of Cliff Top she thought now. Rosemead and her life there had become shadowy and unreal. It was for her tower room she longed, and the kindness and love that had surrounded her there. She scarcely knew now why she had run away, nor what she had intended by her flight. If only she could get back, everything would be different; she herself would be different.

She thought, with a throb of despair, of the last sight she had had of her grandmother, lying in her bed where she and Hannah had put her, lying with eyes closed and surely death in her face?

It was anguish for her to think that she might even now be dead, that if ever she got back, it might be too late.

For a long time she sobbed helplessly. Then, the primitive instinct for self-preservation returning, all her mind concentrated on the little bay where, in spite of the rocky shore, there might be a hope of reaching safety.

She did not know that already she had been spotted at the coastguard station and that help was on its way.

She had remembered the little lagoon and had hoped to make it, but realized that she could not do so. It was still too far for her to be able to swim to the shore in such a sea, but with such light as there was, she calculated her chances of being able to reach the mouth of the lagoon before *Sprite*, beloved, gallant little boat, was broken up and lost for ever.

And at the precise moment, just as Brian had foreseen she would do if she had been able to keep her senses about her, she jumped.

She did not hear the shouts from the boat which had put out for her, did not know that she was not alone in the lashing waves which submerged her when she jumped. Coming to the surface, bruised and battered and gasping for breath, she struck out desperately, refusing to admit what was almost certainly the truth, that she could not hope to reach the lagoon, that, strong swimmer as she was, her strength would not hold out against the fury of the sea seeking its prey.

And then, almost running her down as she came out of a mountainous wave, the boat was miraculously there, high above her one moment and then disappearing as the wave passed, and she saw the lifebelt come hurtling through the air on its rope. She caught at it, missed it, and it was flung again, and this time she reached for it desperately, felt one of its cords beneath her hand and clung to it whilst her head was drawn under again.

But she had not let go, and in the moment's breathing space she had before another wave caught her, she found and held the belt itself and dragged it beneath her body and held it with both her tortured arms.

It was only minutes but it seemed hours before other hands were drawing her through the water, willing arms stretched down to her, her almost lifeless body, relaxing limply now, hauled up into the boat which the coastguards had sent out for her.

She had no clear idea at all of what happened then, only that she was safe, that there was now no longer any battle to be fought, a losing battle as she now knew it had been.

At the coastguard station she was given something hot to drink and warm clothing to replace her own sodden garments and carried out to a car when she protested weakly, but insistently, that she wanted to be taken 'home'.

Nobody told her that Brian had gone out after her, that a watch, so far ineffectual, was being kept for the little *Sally May*, nor did she even think of him. All she wanted was to be 'home', to know that her grandmother was all right, that she was alive, that all this misery of sorrow and regret and shame could be poured out to her. She even longed to see Hannah again, that stern-faced, uncompromising woman who had always been her hardest critic, whom she had tried to think of as her enemy, but who, in the condition she was in now, appeared as a haven of refuge. Hannah would look after her. Her eyes might reproach her and her harsh voice, but her hands would be kind.

It was Hannah who, advised by telephone of her coming, stood at the door to welcome her, who put her own strong arm about her to replace that of one of the men who had brought her, Hannah who was saying to her, 'Come in, my lamb, and let Hannah see to you,' Hannah who dismissed the man with a word of thanks and an assurance that 'the mistress' would see to it that he did not go unrewarded.

Then they were alone, in the white hall with its gleaming old oak and its polished brass, in the dear, familiar smell of floor polish and *pot pourri* and lavender.

'How is she? Gran?' asked Freda in a small, wavering voice as she leaned against Hannah's supporting arm.

Even the smell of Hannah's starched apron and carbolic soap was dear to her.

'She's better, thank God,' said Hannah. 'She knows you're safe and sends you her love and she'll want to see you presently but just now it's bed and a hot-water bottle and a good, hot drink for you. Come along. Lean on me. That's the way. One step at a time, and the top one's the last.'

'Oh, Hannah—*dear* Hannah,' whispered Freda weakly, the tears rolling down her cheeks.

'That's all right, my lamb. Hannah knows,' said the comforting voice, no longer harsh, no longer condemning, offering only love.

Hannah helped her out of the miscellaneous garments provided by the coastguard's wife, got her into her own warmed nightgown and put her between the lavender-scented sheets with a hot-water bottle at her feet.

She swallowed, at Hannah's insistence, the hot milk laced generously with brandy. All she wanted now was to go to sleep,

177

and the woman whose heart of gold had been allowed to show through, for once, its hard outer covering stayed with her until she was asleep. Then she tiptoed downstairs to her mistress to tell her that all was well.

'No need to lock the door on her now,' she said with a return of the old grimness. 'She won't want to get out again. Her wings are pretty well battered.'

'Did she say that she was glad to be home?' asked Mrs. Fennal, still in bed but recovered now.

Hannah nodded.

'Yes, she said just that. That she was glad to be home.'

'Did she call it that? Home?'

'She did, and what else would she call it, I should like to know. And the first thing she asked about was you, madam.'

Mrs. Fennal smiled contentedly and lay back on her pillows. Freda had come home.

'Did you send the cable?' she asked.

'Yes. Just what you said.'

'Perhaps there was no need, after all, but—it's gone, anyway. Thank you, Hannah. I don't need anything. Be within call if Miss Freda wakes, will you?'

'I will, though from the look of her she won't do that for hours.'

Sadie Fennal shivered in spite of the luxurious fur coat, in spite of the fact that the reception room at the airport where she was waiting for her flight to be announced was comfortably warmed.

This feeling of intense cold had nothing to do with the atmosphere, and she had no fear of flying. It came from something inside her, a feeling of being quite alone for the first time in her life, though she was not there alone. She had always been sure of herself, sure of what lay ahead, her purpose clear, her way to it direct and straight whatever obstacles lay in her path. She never doubted her ability to surmount them or push them aside.

But now her purpose was vague and blurred, and she could not see her way anywhere.

178

Paul Erskine, tall, good-looking, arrogant, looked at her without smiling.

'I suppose you know what you're doing, Sadie?' he asked, his voice cold and disapproving.

She did not look at him. Her hands were twisting the gold-mounted bag they held, one of his many expensive gifts to her.

'Only that I'm going to my child, Paul,' she said.

'And what else? To meet Fennal again?'

'I don't know if they will have sent for him or only for me. I don't even know why Mrs. Fennal cabled me, unless it is that she doesn't know how to find Richard. He was always the one Freda wanted most. I doubt if she would have asked for me if her father had been available. Perhaps she didn't ask for me.'

'Then why go? You gave her up when you came out here. You've always said that it was the smaller sacrifice.'

'I thought so then, but—perhaps I don't any more. Don't you see, Paul, that I've got to go? She's ill. That was all the cable said, that she was ill and that Mrs. Fennal thought I ought to come. She may be dying. Mrs. Fennal would not have sent for me if it had not been desperate. She never liked me or approved of me, but she's the sort of woman who would always do the correct thing. That's probably the only reason why she sent for me.'

'And the only reason why you're going? To do the correct thing?' he asked, a note of scorn in his voice which she knew to be justifiable. She had certainly not done the correct thing when she left her husband and her child to come out here and make it possible for her eventually to marry another man.

She lifted her head to look at him.

'No,' she said. 'It's not because it's the correct thing. When have I ever done that? It's because Freda is my child and I *want* to go to her.'

'And Fennal? You want to go to him too?'

'I'm not thinking about him. Nor about myself.'

'Nor about me, presumably. You might as well face it, Sadie. I meant what I said, that if you go now, you go for good. I won't share a woman, any woman, with anyone else.'

Her face hardened.

She was still lovely, still with her beauty cherished and cared

179

for, but there was an indefinable difference in her. There were tiny lines about her eyes which had not been there before, a shadow in them, a faint drooping of her lovely mouth. She did not know, but he did. He had known it for some time, ever since he flew out to Italy to spend a snatched holdiay with her. He had seen it at once, the first faint signs that all was not well with her, that there was dissatisfaction behind her restless gaiety, behind her acceptance of his love, behind the vagueness with which she now talked of their future together.

And then the telegram had come and she had not thought twice about going, about leaving him here with some days of the holiday yet unspent.

'Have you ever been willing to share anything at all with anyone, Paul?' she asked with that direct look. 'I don't think it's because of Freda that we have reached this stage, not just because of her. You don't think so either, do you?'

'I've never varied or changed my mind. I want you. I still do.'

She looked away from him. This was not being easy, but nothing in her association with Paul Erskine had ever been easy.

'I hope you won't go on doing so,' she said in a low voice, 'because it isn't any use, Paul. If I weren't going now, or to Freda, I should still have gone. I've been realizing that, and trying not to, for a long time now. I've come to see things differently, not just you and me, but life in general. We're not very young any more, Paul. I'm thirty-eight and you're more than that. We've had half of our lives, the best half, the time when we were young and—some things mattered more. They're out of proportion when one is young.'

'And that best half of your life, as you call it—is that what you want all over again?'

'I don't know, but I couldn't have it even if I did. It's gone and you can never get anything back.'

'Not Fennal? You're not hoping to get him back?' asked the cold, cutting voice.

She made a little hopeless gesture, one almost of anger.

'I've told you. I don't hope to get him back. I couldn't even if I wanted to. Richard is not like that. For him when a thing is finished, it's finished. He would never want me back. He knows what we've been to each other, the terms we're on.'

180

'You told him?' he asked quickly, frowning.

'Yes, before I left him. Perhaps I wanted him to know that he was not losing anything of any great value,' her lip curling.

'You're of value to me, Sadie. You thought so once. It meant enough to you for you to be ready to give up what now seems, rather belatedly, to have been of value to you.'

'Freda. Yes. I didn't realize it at the time. I thought I could be happy without her even though I knew that—that there would never be any more children for me. You made it quite plain that you would never want them.'

'I'd give you even that, if it would make any difference now, if you would stay here with me and not go to her.'

That stabbed her, for she knew what it had cost him, would cost him if she accepted his bargain. He had told her from the first, before they ever became lovers, that he did not want her to have children, and she had accepted it, believed that he and he alone could fill her life and her heart, that though she loved Freda, what he would give her in happiness would make up for that loss. Now she knew that it would not, could never do, even if he fulfilled his promise and she, after all these years, had other children. She did not really want them. She wanted Freda.

She looked out of the window at the activity on the tarmac, at the waiting planes, at the luggage being wheeled to them, at the people waving their good-byes as they went up the steps. Very soon now she would hear the summons calling her to her own flight and once she had obeyed it, once she was on the plane for England, it would be too late. She would no longer have any choice. When she had left Paul Erskine behind, she would have left him for ever.

And with what in exhange?

She had never thought of being back with Richard; did not think of it now even though Paul had obliged her to. Why should he ever want her back? That was all over and done with. She could never go back, not after Paul and what they had been to each other.

Without Paul, there would be no one. She was going to Freda, but if she lived (she shut her mind quickly on that thought), she had no reason at all to suppose that she would want her. Her infrequent letters, always carefully written, carefully grammatical, had never given any indication that she was not entirely happy, that she missed her mother or even thought about her when she was not writing those careful letters.

So why should she suppose that even Freda would want her?

Paul's voice broke in on her painful thoughts.

'Well, Sadie? Not much time left.'

'I know,' she said in a low voice, not looking at him.

'Why is it so difficult? Surely you must know whether you really want to go? Whether you really want to leave me?'

She looked at him then. Her eyes were very sad but clear. For the first time for many weeks she saw that purpose that had eluded her restless searching for it.

'I must, Paul,' she said. 'We both know that even without this, it had to come.'

'That you would have left me in any case?'

'Yes.'

He walked away from her and stood with his back to her.

It was a blow which he had not thought would fall on him. He had never married, had never cared deeply for any woman until Sadie had come into his life, and there might never be another. But he knew, by that one word, by the look in her eyes, that she would go and that she would never come back.

Nor would he ask her to do so. It was as she had said. He would never share anything with anyone; least of all would he share the woman he loved, and even if she came back to him, even if they could be married, he would always share her in his own mind with Richard, the man with whom she had spent that 'best half' of her life, all the part of it that mattered.

The summons came to her to go out to the plane and he turned to her again and bent to pick up the small bag she was taking with her, but she took it from him. ——

'Don't come out with me,' she said. 'Just let me go,' and she walked steadily away from him and he did as she asked.

He let her go.

She went up the steps into the plane, sat down and automatically fastened her seat-belt, smiled mechanically at the air-hostess who came to offer help, did not look out of the window as the plane ran along the airstrip, paused whilst the engines had their final test, took off with the gathered momentum and was soon high above the Italian coast.

She did not know what she would find at the end of her journey, nor what she expected to find. Mrs. Fennal's cable had been terse and to the point.

Freda ill. Think you should come. Fennal.

It might even have been Richard who had sent it, but she did not think so. However he felt about her, he would not have signed it like that.

She had had to take a plane to London, the first available. For the first time in her life there would be no one to meet her, no one to deal with luggage and tickets, to put her into the right train, to load her with flowers, with chocolates, with reading matter, with all the little fuss of attention which a pretty woman takes as her right.

But somehow she managed it, coped with her passport and the various forms which made her feel as if she were a criminal with no right even to return to her own country, certainly no welcome in the suspicious minds of the officials; got herself to the London station, waited for the train and got into the right one, did not move from her seat during the long journey into Cornwall until she had to change for the little branch line that would take her to Penn Tor.

And there she found Richard.

She stared at him, the colour rushing to her face, her eyes filling with sudden tears, though she blinked them away.

'I didn't expect to see you,' she said weakly.

'I was in London,' he said. 'I rang up. I didn't know about Freda, and I came down at once.'

'How—how is she?'

'Up and doing,' he said cheerfully.

'I—I thought—the telegram . . .'

'When they found out that there was nothing the matter with her, it was too late to stop you,' he said. 'I couldn't get to London to meet you, but I've got a car here. Any more luggage?'

'No, only that,' indicating the suitcase which he had already taken from her.

183

So it had all been for nothing? She need not have come at all, need not have gone through all that with Paul. . . .

Her mind paused. She was even glad that that had happened. She might not be wanted here, might not be wanted anywhere, but there was no longer Paul. That had had to happen.

'I'll tell you all about it as we go along,' he said, and took her to the car, a hired one, put her luggage into it and opened the door for her to get into the seat next to the driver's.

'You're driving yourself?' she asked.

'Yes. I thought we might like to be alone for the first few minutes,' he said, and drove carefully out of the station.

She looked at his hands on the wheel, strong hands, kind hands, hands that had touched her so often and so lovingly, hands that would never touch her again. They had not even shaken hands when they met on the platform, though that would have been stupid. He had avoided it by stooping to take her case.

A little strangled sob rose unexpectedly in her throat. She stifled it, wondered if he had heard it, but if he had done, he did not betray it.

He told her something of what had happened to Freda, though not all.

'Silly child took out *Sprite* on her own, got caught in a storm, had to abandon ship and got rescued by the coastguards. My mother was worried, thought she'd got pneumonia at least, thought she was going to die and that one of us ought to be there. As she didn't know I was in England, and didn't think I could have got there in time, she sent for you, but in no time the kid was sitting up and taking notice, as right as rain.'

'Does she know I'm coming?' asked Sadie in a low voice.

'Oh yes. She's very bucked about it. Wanted to come with me to meet you but I said better not. There's quite a cold wind blowing. Are you all right? Warm enough? I expect this strikes cold after Italy.'

'I'm quite warm,' she said.

'Quite an effective heater in this car. British manufacturers are at last waking up to the fact that it is not always as hot as the tropics in England!'

He was talking to her, she thought, as if she were just a friend he had been sent to meet, or even a casual stranger making an

184

arranged call. He didn't seem to care that it was she, Sadie, sitting beside him. It didn't matter to him any more. She didn't matter.

He talked to her, brightly and cheerfully, of things in which she could have no possible interest, she thought bitterly. He pointed out unimportant landmarks which she knew as well as he, spoke of Cliff Top and the alterations which were planned for the garden, mentioned Meriel Dain.

'You'll like her,' he said. 'She's young, though not as young as Freda. My mother asked her down as some sort of companion for her though I don't think she's staying long. A pretty girl, very bright and amusing and fond of Freda. It's rather a pity she can't stay for good.'

Sadie felt a swift stab of something. What was it? It couldn't be jealousy, not of this unknown girl whom Richard seemed to admire so much.

Meriel was in the hall to meet them.

'Poor Mrs. Fennal,' she said, when Richard introduced them. 'Are you frozen? Mrs. Fennal and Freda are in the sitting-room by the fire. I didn't want either of them to come out to the door. The central heating is not doing its best today. Would you have a look at it, Mr. Fennal? It defies Hannah and me.'

She was easy, natural, perfectly at home here and already on good terms with Richard though he had arrived only that day, and Richard did not make friends easily.

Sadie opened the sitting-room door, leaving Richard and Meriel to deal with the luggage, and Freda ran straight into her arms.

'Oh, Mummy—Mummy,' she cried, and Sadie held her closely, her eyes too misty to see the other figure which rose from the chair and went quietly out, leaving them alone.

'Darling, I've missed you so terribly,' said Sadie. 'I've wanted you so badly.'

'Me too, Mummy. Oh, me too!' and she hugged and kissed her mother as if she never wanted to stop.

With the optimism of youth, seeing obstacles knocked down before they had actually even been touched, she felt that all was right with her world again. Her two best beloved beings were with her again, and together, and everything that had happened to her lately no longer mattered. How could anything go wrong again now that they were both here, Mummy so lovely and sweet, and Daddy such a—such a *darling*?

They talked of all sorts of things, sitting close together on the couch, her mother's arm about her. They talked about her escapade with *Sprite* and the lamented loss of the boat, and Sadie, thinking of what might so easily have happened, tightened her arm about her and made her promise that she would never take a boat out again unless she had someone capable and experienced with her. It was not difficult to give that promise!

In that connection, they even spoke of Brian, and Freda found that that was not too difficult either. With her parents there, and the home atmosphere which they had brought with them, he seemed to have slipped back into the old place, just the familiar friend of her childhood, and her mother called him Hewet and she didn't even mind.

Of one thing only was she desperately afraid, and that was that her grandmother might tell them about the money. How was she ever to face them again if they knew that?

Mrs. Fennal had no intention of doing so. She knew that Freda was no more a thief and a cheat than she was a natural liar, and that some solution must and would be found to the problem of Freda's environment which would restore her to her real self, though she could not think as yet what that solution would be.

Once Richard opened the door and looked in, but seeing the pair so closely together, so absorbed and happy, he closed it softly again and left them.

It was Hannah who disturbed them at length, Hannah who, with Meriel, brought in the enormous Cornish tea which, with all normal mealtimes made impossible by the exigencies of the day, would do duty for both tea and supper.

Sadie surveyed the table loaded with slices of ham and home-pressed tongue, with eggs under little cosies, with the famous pasties, with buns and scones and butter and jam and a great bowl of Cornish cream, and she gasped.

'Heavens!' she cried. 'Is part of that meant for me? I'm longing to go the rounds of the lot, but what about my poor figure?'

Freda laughed.

'Your figure's lovely. Isn't it, Daddy?'

186

Richard surveyed the slim form with critical interest. 'As if I were something put up for sale,' Sadie thought indignantly. 'As if he'd never seen me before. As if I didn't belong to him.'

'Yes, very nice,' he said smoothly, and turned his eyes away again.

'Madam asks you to excuse her, Mrs. Richard,' said Hannah primly. 'She has had one of her bad turns and has gone to bed, but she hopes that you and Mr. Richard will go in and say good night to her presently.'

'Of course, Hannah,' said Sadie, in the pleasant but always reserved tone she seemed to keep entirely for Hannah. She knew that her mother-in-law's maid had never approved of her, and as she must have known what had happened to her and Richard, she must now disapprove of her even more strongly.

'You'll pour out, won't you, Mrs. Fennal?' asked Meriel.

Sadie hesitated, unwilling to appear as if she considered herself the temporary mistress of the house which held both herself and Richard.

'Oh—won't you, Miss Dain?' she asked. 'It is Dain, isn't it?'

'It is, but I'm Meriel here,' said the girl with a smile and took her place behind the big silver teapot and the delicate, valuable china which Mrs. Fennal liked to use rather than keep in a glass case.

'I've always loved this china,' said Sadie.

'Gran says that it will be mine some day, but yours first, of course,' said Freda happily, and no one could find any reply to that.

With the meal finished, Meriel took Freda firmly away.

'I promised your grandmother that I'd hustle you off to bed the very minute you'd had whatever meal we're calling this,' she said.

Freda looked from Sadie to Richard lovingly.

'Will you come up and say good night?' she asked. 'You haven't seen my lovely tower room yet, Mummy, and what do you think? I've got my *own* bathroom and nobody else uses it, not even Meriel!'

'It would be more than my life's worth to do so,' laughed Meriel.

Freda linked her arm in hers.

187

'I wouldn't really mind if *you* did,' she said, and they went out together.

Freda held no grudge against anyone. Now that she had her beloved two back again, if Brian and Meriel wanted each other she didn't mind any more. It was queer to feel like that about Brian, queer but—nice.

'They seem very fond of each other,' said Sadie, when she and Richard were alone, since she had to say something.

'Yes, I think they are. Nobody could help being fond of Meriel,' and again she felt that painful stab.

Then she remembered that, as far as she knew, he had never met Meriel until that day, and, hard on the heels of that thought, came the reminder that Richard had fallen in love with her, Sadie, the first minute they met.

Hannah came in to clear away the remains of the meal, made up the fire and left them again.

'Richard,' began Sadie desperately, so that he should not at once start talking about themselves, if indeed he meant to, 'is there something I don't know but ought to know? About Freda? I had a sort of idea. About this sudden idea of taking out the boat, for one thing. Why did she?'

'A crazy idea,' he said. 'In fact, she's been a bit crazy lately. She imagined that she had a sort of crush on Brian and I suppose she had some notion of showing herself off as a grown-up person, able to do the same things that he can.'

It was the best job he could make, on the spur of the moment, of the story he had had from his mother who, having had a long talk with Meriel, had reluctantly absolved Brian from blame.

'A crush on Brian? Brian Hewet?' asked Sadie incredulously. 'Why, she's only a child!'

'She's nearly eighteen, and you married me before you were nineteen,' he reminded her.

'But I was grown-up at fifteen! Have we got to do anything about it?' unconsciously linking herself with him in anything that touched Freda.

'I don't think so. I think he's already done the best thing he could do. I'm pretty sure that he's in love with Meriel Dain.'

'Did he tell you so? Have you seen him then?'

'He was here when I arrived this afternoon and I saw them

188

together, not for long but long enough. I heard him tell her that he would come back this evening, but he told her, not me.'

'Do you think that would be all right? For them, I mean?'

He wondered at little at the intensity of her interest, but he nodded.

'Perfectly, I should say. They're of an age, and she's a delightful girl and you know how I've always felt about Brian,' he said, and she felt a throb of relief. How stupid she'd been!

'But what on earth gave Freda such an insane idea?' she asked. 'After knowing him all her life and never having shown anything of that sort before—I can't understand it at all.'

'Can't you, Sadie?' he asked in his quiet voice. 'I think I can. She's a loving little thing. She likes to twine, and when we took away all her supports and left her stranded, she turned to the only one she felt she had left, and it happened to be Brian. I think we can count ourselves, and Freda, fortunate that it *was* Brian.'

'And now, if he is in love with Meriel Dain, how is she going to take that?'

'I don't know. It leaves her with nothing again, doesn't it?'

He heard her draw a sharp breath and saw her grip her hands together in her lap. Looking at them, he saw that she wore only one ring, their wedding ring.

'Yes, I suppose it does,' she said unhappily.

'You still wear it,' he said. 'Does it mean anything to you?' and she saw that he was looking at the wedding ring.

'Would you rather I didn't, Richard?' she asked in a low voice, her eyes averted from his. 'I haven't any right to.'

'You're still my wife. Why have you never done anything about that, Sadie? Could it be that you wanted to go on wearing my ring?'

She nodded her head slowly. She could not speak. All that she had been thinking, suffering, in the past few hours came swirling about her. She felt lost and hopeless and terribly alone. Soon this little flash of happiness, the old feeling of belonging again, would be gone, and there would be nothing left.

'As far as I am concerned,' said Richard very quietly, 'it can stay there always.'

She looked up at that, with hope and fear and that lost look which she did not know was there.

'You mean—what do you mean, Richard?'

'That you're still my wife, my dear, and that I'm still your husband and your lover and always have been. There has never been anybody else. I think you know that.'

She laid her hands on the arm of her chair and bent her head down on them.

'I've been such a fool, such an unutterable fool,' she said, her voice muffled, despairing.

'Have you come back to me, my dear?' he asked, looking at her, at the lovely head bowed down at last, as the spirit within her was bowed down.

But he must know, he must be sure. There must be no second mistake, for Freda's sake, for all their sakes.

'You can't possibly want me, Richard. Not after—after everything,' she said, her face still hidden from him.

'I do want you, Sadie, but only if you want it too,' he said gently.

'Oh, Richard, you make me feel so ashamed, so—so humble,' she said, and he knew that she was crying, Sadie who never cried.

It hurt him unbearably. He had loved her gaiety and her pride.

'I don't want you to be,' he said. 'I know I didn't come up to your expectations, not even from the first, when we were young and happy. But I loved you in my own way, in the only way I knew, and with all my heart. I still love you, though perhaps it could never be in your way.'

She lifted her face, the tears running down it unchecked, and put out her hands blindly for his.

'I'd rather it were your way,' she said chokily. 'It's the only way that really matters, the only way that lasts.'

He held her hands and stroked them. He felt awkward and embarrassed. He had always hated 'scenes' though Sadie had revelled in them and made them dramatic. He was a peace-loving person.

'That's all right then,' he said. 'Shall we go up and tell Freda?'

'We've got to see your mother,' she said shrinkingly.

'Freda first. Then we shall know what to say to Mother,' and he made a movement to let her hands go, but she clung to them.

'Richard—not back to Rosemead,' she said unsteadily. 'Let's —start again somewhere.'

190

He nodded.

'Yes, I think so too,' he said, and he opened the door for her. 'Do you want to go to your room first? I'm not sure which it is, but we'll ask Hannah.'

'Won't—won't yours do, Richard?' she asked, and he stood for a moment in the open doorway and looked into her eyes and at last he smiled.

It was the first time he had done that since they had started to talk.

'It will do for me,' he said.

'And for me too,' she whispered, and she slipped her hand into his again, and, like that, hand in hand, they went up the stairs to Freda.